Salvation
and
Other Disasters

Other Books by Josip Novakovich

Apricots from Chernobyl
Fiction Writer's Workshop
Yolk

Salvation
and
Other Disasters

short stories by

JOSIP NOVAKOVICH

GRAYWOLF PRESS

Saint Paul

Publication of this volume is made possible in part by a grant provided by the
Minnesota State Arts Board through an appropriation by the Minnesota State
Legislature, and by a grant from the National Endowment for the Arts. Significant support has also been provided by Dayton's, Mervyn's, and Target stores
through the Dayton Hudson Foundation, the Andrew W. Mellon Foundation,
the McKnight Foundation, the General Mills Foundation, the St. Paul Companies, and other generous contributions from foundations, corporations, and individuals. To these organizations and individuals we offer our heartfelt thanks.

Special funding for this title was provided by the Jerome Foundation.

Published by Graywolf Press
2402 University Avenue, Suite 203
Saint Paul, Minnesota 55114
All rights reserved.

www.graywolfpress.org

Published in the United States of America.
ISBN 1-55597-271-3

2 4 6 8 9 7 5 3 1
First Graywolf Printing, 1998

Library of Congress Catalog Card Number 97-80084

Cover art: Ivan Generalic, "Smrt Ivana Viriusa"

Cover design: Ann Elliot Artz

Acknowledgments

Grateful acknowledgment is given to the editors of the magazines below in which the stories were first published.

AGNI: A Free Fall
Antaeus: Bread
Boston Review: Fritz: A Fable
Boulevard: Real Estate, Rye Harvest (Pushcart Prize XII: Best of the Small Press 1997/98)
DoubleTake: Out of the Woods
The Kenyon Review: Bruno
Mānoa: Crimson (O. Henry Awards 98)
Michigan Quarterly Review: The Devil's Celluloid Tail
New Letters: The End
North Dakota Quarterly: On Becoming a Prophet
Ploughshares: Rye Harvest
Quarterly West: A Woman Walks through the Crowd
Sound of Writing (NPR), DoubleTake: Ice
Story: Sheepskin
The Sun: The Enemy (O. Henry Awards 97—Honorable Mention)
The Threepenny Review: A Whale's Throat

I thank Anne Czarniecki for helping me compile and edit this book, Fiona McCrae for publishing it, and my wife Jeanette for reading and commenting on the stories in progress. I am also grateful to the Howard Taft Fund at the University of Cincinnati, the Whiting Foundation, the National Endowment for the Arts, the Ingram Merrill Foundation, U-Cross, Yaddo, Ragdale, the Vogelstein Foundation, the Fine Arts Work Center in Provinceton, Villa Montalvo, and Centrum for giving me the time to write this book.

contents

To my daughter Eva, who loves stories

Salvation
and
Other Disasters

Sheepskin

⚜⚜

Since I can't tell this to anybody, I'm writing it, not just to sort it out for myself, but for someone nosy who'll rummage through my papers one day. In a way I want to be caught but I won't call this story a confession. I should pretend that it's somebody else's story, that it is fiction. I wish I could set it in a different country—outside Croatia and outside the former Yugoslavia—and that it was about somebody else, a former self, a formerly uninformed me. I don't mean that I want a complete break with my past—nothing as dramatic as suicide, although, of course, I've entertained thoughts of it, but the thoughts have not entertained me. I have survived knives and bombs: I should be able to survive thoughts and memories.

I'll start with a scene on a train in western Slavonia. Though it was hot, I closed the window. Not that I am superstitious against drafts as many of our people are. Dandelion seeds floated in, like dry snowflakes, and all sorts of pollens and other emissaries of the wild fields filled the air with smells of chamomile, menthol, and other teas. It would have been pleasant if I hadn't had a cold that made me sneeze and squint. The countryside seemed mostly abandoned.

I had never seen vegetation so free and jubilant. The war had loosened the earth, shaken the farmers off its back. Strewn mines kept them from venturing into the fields, but did not bother the flowers. The color intensity of grasses and beeches in the background gave me a dizziness I could not attribute to my cold. I saw a fox leap out of orange bushes of tea. Of course, it was not tea, but many of these wildflowers would be teas if broken by human hands and dried in the sun, mellifluous teas, curing asthma, improving memory, and filling you with tenderness. If we had stuck to drinking tea, maybe the war would have never happened.

I leaned against the wooden side of the train, but gave up, since the magnum I had strapped on my side pressed into my arm painfully. I would have probably fallen asleep, intoxicated with the fields and the musty oil, which doused the wood beneath the tracks. As a child I had loved the oily smell of rails; it had transformed for me the iron clanking of the gaps in the tracks into a transcontinental guitar with two hammered strings and thousands of sorrowful frets that fell into diminished distances. I'd have dozed off if every time I leaned against the vibrating wall of the train the gun hadn't pinched a nerve and shaken me awake. And just when I was beginning to slumber, the door screeched.

A gaunt man entered. I was startled, recognizing my old tormentor from the Vukovar hospital. He took off his hat and revealed unruly cowlicked hair, grayer than I remembered it. His thick eyebrows, which almost met above his nose, were black. I wondered whether he colored them.

The man did not look toward me, although he stiffened. I was sure he was aware of me. I had dreamed of this moment many times, imagining that if given the opportunity the first thing I'd do would be to jump at the man, grab his throat, and strangle him with the sheer power of rage. My heart leaped, but I didn't. I gazed at him from the corner of my eye. He looked a little thinner and taller than I remembered. I did not know his name, but in my mind I had always called him Milos. I ceased to believe we coexisted in the same world—imagined that he was in Serbia, off the map as far as I was concerned.

I looked out the window, and the sunlit fields glowed even more, with the dark undersides, shadows, enhancing the light in the foreground. The train was pulling into Djulevci. The Catholic church gaped open, its tower missing, its front wall and gate in rubble, the pews crushed, overturned, and the side wall had several big howitzer holes; only here and there pale mortar remained, reflecting the sun so violently that my eyes hurt. At the train station there was a pile of oak logs, probably a decade old, but still not rotten. And past the train station stood the Serb Orthodox church, pockmarked. It probably wouldn't be standing if there hadn't been guards around it, night and day. The Croatian government wanted to demonstrate to the world—although journalists never bothered to come to this village—how much better Croats were than Serbs, but that was a show. The Croat policemen sat on chairs, one wiggled a semi-automatic rifle, and the other tossed a crushed can of Coke over his shoulder.

There was a time when I would have thrown grenades into the church, owing to my traveling companion and other Serb soldiers who had surrounded and choked the city of Vukovar for months. Fearing that I would starve to death, I had minced my sheepskin jacket and made a soup out of it. The day before the soldiers invaded the city, I'd seen a cat struck in the neck with shrapnel. I picked her up and skinned her. I overgrilled her because I was squeamish to eat a cat, and once I had eaten most of her, I grew feverish. I wasn't sure whether the cat had gotten some disease from rats—I would not have been surprised if I had caught the plague this way—or whether it was sheer guilt and disgust with myself, that I had eaten a cat, that made me ill. My body, unused to food, just could not take it; I was delirious in the hospital, but there was no doubt what I saw was not a dream: soldiers laughing, crashing wine bottles on the chairs, dragging old men in torn pajamas out of their hospital beds. A man with black eyebrows and a gray cowlick that shot out trembling strands of hair above his forehead came to my side and spat at me. He pulled the sheet off my bed and stabbed my thigh with a broken wine bottle. I coiled and shrieked, and he uncoiled me, pulling my arms, and another pulled my legs, while the third one pissed over my wound and said, "This is the best disinfectant around, absolutely the best. *Na zdravlye!*"

"There, pig, you'll thank me one day, you'll see," said Milos, and stabbed my leg again.

Other soldiers came and dragged a wailing old woman down the stairs.

"How about this guy?" one of the soldiers asked about me.

"No, he's bleeding too much," said Milos. "I don't want to get contaminated by his shitty blood."

A tall French journalist came in and took pictures of me, and muttered in English.

"What are you staring at?" I asked. "There are worse sights around."

"Yes, but they are not alive," he said. He carried me out, while my blood soaked his clothes. He pushed me into his jeep, and we drove out and passed several checkpoints without any inspection. He took me to the Vinkovci hospital, which was often bombed. Two nurses pulled glass from my leg, tied rubber above and below the wound, stitched me up, wrapped the wound—all without painkillers. I wished I could swoon from the pain. I ground my teeth so hard that a molar cracked.

Thanks a lot for the pleasure, I thought now and looked at my silent companion on the train. At Virovitica, we'd have to change trains. Mine was going to Zagreb, and I did not know whether he was going there, or east, to Osijek.

He got out of the compartment first, and I did not want to be obvious about following him. Many peasants with loud white chickens in their pleated baskets filled the corridor between us.

When I jumped off the train into the gravel, his head covered with a hat slid behind a wall. His shadow moved jerkily on the gray cement of the platform, but I could not see the shadow's owner. Milos must have been behind the corner. Maybe he was aware of being followed.

I thought he could be waiting for me in ambush. People walked and stepped on his shadow, but they could not trample it, because as they stepped on it, it climbed on them, and I was no longer sure whether it was Milos's shadow, or whether they were casting shadows over each other. Not that it mattered one way or another, but I suppose that's part of my professional photographer's distortion and disorientation that I look at light and shadow wherever I turn, and I frame what I see in rectangular snatches; I keep squaring the world, in my head, to some early and primitive cosmology of a flat earth, where nothing comes around.

I rushed past the corner. There was a kiosk stocked with cigarettes and many magazines featuring pictures of naked blondes. I stopped and pretended to be reading the train schedule posted at the station entrance so I could observe Milos's reflection on the glass over the departures schedule. He rolled the magazine he had bought into a flute, and entered a restaurant. I followed. There was an outdoor section under a tin roof, with large wooden tables and benches. A TV set was blaring out a sequence of Croatian President Tudjman kissing the flag at the Knin fort, after his forces captured Knin. The President lifted his clenched fist to the sky. What kind of kiss was it, from thin bloodless lips sinking through the concave mouth of a politician? I detest flags. Anyhow, I was not in a loving mood right then, toward anybody. In Vukovar we thought that Tudjman had abandoned us. Maybe he was partly responsible for my wantonly following a stranger down the stairs, to the lower level of the country dive. Milos sat below a window with fake crystal glass that refracted light into purple rays. I did not sit right away, but walked past him, following arrows to the bathroom across a yard with a fenced family of sheep with muddy feet, who eyed me calmly. I walked back and sat at a round table about two yards from his.

He ordered lamb and a carafe of red wine in a perfect Zagreb accent. In Vukovar I remembered him using long Serb vowels, ironically stretching them. Maybe he was now afraid to be taken for a Serb. I couldn't blame him for that. Still, a man who could dissemble so well was dangerous, I thought.

I ordered the same thing. When I pronounced my order, I used the same wording as Milos, in my eastern Slavonian leisurely way, which to many people outside my region sounded similar to Serbian.

Milos looked at me for the first time and, hearing my voice, gave a start. The waiter, slumping in his greasy black jacket with a napkin hanging out of his pocket, eyed me contemptuously. His mouth was curled to one side, and one silver tooth gleamed over his shiny fat lower lip.

He brought one carafe to Milos and one to me along with empty glasses. Milos drank, I drank. He opened his magazine to the centerfold of a blonde with black pubic hair, and then he stared at me. What was the point? Did he pretend that he thought I was a homosexual stalking him and about to proposition him, so this was his way of telling me, No, I'm not interested? If he imagined he could confuse me this way so I would not be positive I had recognized him, he was dead wrong.

I had a postcard in my pocket; I pulled it out and began to write—I did not know to whom. To my ex-wife, who'd left me at the beginning of the war to visit her relatives in Belgrade? They had filled her head with nonsense about how Croats were going to kill her, and how even I might be a rabid Croat who would cut her throat. The nonsense actually served Miriana well; she got out right before the city was encircled by Serb troops and bombed. From what I hear she now lives with a widowed cardiologist whose Croatian wife died of a heart attack. Miriana used to visit Belgrade frequently even before the war; she had probably had an affair with the cardiologist. Her running away from the fighting may have been simply a pretext for leaving me. Anyway, I didn't have her address, so I couldn't write to her—no big loss.

I wrote to my dead father instead, although this made no sense either. He had died of stomach cancer last year in Osijek, perhaps because of the war. Without the anxiety he could have lived with the latent stomach cancer for years.

"Hi, my old man. I wish you were here. Not that there'd be much to see—in fact, Virovitica has to be one of the dreariest towns in Slavonia. But the wine is good. . . ."

My meal arrived. I folded the postcard and put it in my pocket. The meat was lukewarm. Who knows when it was cooked—maybe days ago, and it stayed in the refrigerator. I grumbled as I cut.

Milos swore too, as he struggled. He asked for a sharper knife.

"This is awful! They charge so much and give you only the bone!" he said to me.

If he thought he could engage me in a conversation and thus appease me, he was wrong, although I did answer. "Yes, they figure only travelers would eat here anyway, and once they get our money and we're gone, they can laugh at us."

He gulped wine.

I navigated my blade through the stringy meat.

"Where are you from?" he asked me.

I called the waiter. "You forgot the salad."

"You haven't asked for it."

He was probably right, but I still said, "Yes, I did."

He soon brought me a plate of sliced tomatoes and onions, with oily vinegar. That helped subdue the heavy and rotten lamb taste. Funny how finicky I'd become in a hurry—not long before, I had chewed on a sheepskin jacket, certain that I'd starve to death, and now I behaved like a jaded gourmet.

Milos bent down to search through his luggage. Maybe he's going to draw a gun? I thought. I slid my hand into my jacket.

Milos took out three dolls, the Lion King hyenas. What, is this possible? My torturer is buying toys for kids? He put the magazine and the hyenas into his traveling bag. Maybe that was his way of saying, I am not a guy who'd stab anybody, I'm a kind, family man.

He looked toward me, and I felt self-conscious with my hand

in my jacket. So it wouldn't look as though I was pulling a gun, I fumbled in the pocket and took out my pigskin wallet. The waiter eagerly came to my table. I gave him fifty kunas, certainly more than the meal was worth. "I need no change," I said.

"Excuse me, four and a half more kunas, please," asked the waiter. I gave him five coins.

"Preposterous, isn't it?" Milos said. "How can they charge that much for this? If I had known, I'd have controlled my appetite, could have bought another toy for my kids."

Was he appealing to me again? I had no sympathy for family men. My marriage failed perhaps because I had no kids. My business failed because the likes of Milos bombed my town, and here I sat as a twitching mass of resentment. I took another gulp of wine. I first used a toothpick and then whistled through my teeth to clean out bits of meat that got stuck there.

Milos looked at me with annoyance. He clearly didn't like my whistling. So what, I thought. If it bothers you, I'll do more of it. And who was he to complain? He slurped wine as though it were hot soup. And with his sharp knife, sharper than mine, he cut through more lamb, and I couldn't escape remembering again how he'd cut into my leg.

I scratched my swollen scar through the woolen fabric of my pants. It itched to the point of my wanting to tear it.

"Do you think there are fleas here?" I asked loudly, as if to excuse my scratching, but looked at nobody.

The waiter strutted and dumped tiny coins on my table ostentatiously, probably to make a statement that it was beneath him to take my tip. The rattle of the change scared two turquoise flies off my plate.

"Flies are all right," I said. Not much had changed since communism. I used to think that rudeness was a matter of fixed salaries, no incentive. But here, I was pretty sure the waiter was part-owner of this free enterprise establishment, and he was still rude, and did his best to disgust his customers. And, of course, customers hadn't changed either. They used to be rude, and I would continue to be rude. But before I could think of another insulting question, Milos asked one. "Hey, my friend, do you think I could buy a sheepskin jacket anywhere around here?"

This may have been a jab at me. But how could he have known I'd eaten a sheepskin jacket in Vukovar?

The waiter answered: "Maybe in a couple of hours. We are just getting some ready."

"Could I see them?" Milos was standing and picking up a thick cloth napkin that looked like a towel from his lap.

The waiter grabbed a large hair dryer from among plum brandy bottles on the shelf and waved to Milos to come along. Although I was not invited, I followed. They had identical bald spots on their heads.

Behind the sheep stall, in a shed filled with hay, on thick clothes wires hung two sheepskins, dripping blood into aluminum pots on the dusty dirt floor.

I wondered why the waiter collected the blood, why not simply let it soak the ground. Maybe he made blood sausages; maybe he drank it, like an ancient Mongolian horseman.

The waiter aimed the blow dryer at a sheepskin, filling it with air. Rounded like a sail full of wind, the skin gave me a spooky impression that an invisible sheep was beginning to inhabit it.

"This'll be a terrific jacket," the waiter said. "Give it an hour, if you can spare."

"But what about the pattern?" Milos said. "What about the buttons?"

"Fuck buttons. You can get those anyplace. But fine sheepskin like this, nowhere. Two hundred kunas, is that a deal?"

Milos stroked the sheepskin's tight yellowish curls.

"The winter's going to be a harsh one," said the waiter.

"Yes, but sheep won't save us from it," I said.

Milos quit stroking, and as he turned around, he stepped on the edge of a bowl, and blood spilled over his jeans and white socks and leather shoes.

"Seeing this is enough to make one become a vegetarian," I said to the waiter. I was nauseated.

"I'll be passing through town in two days again," said Milos. "Could I pick it up then?"

"No problem." The waiter walked back, Milos followed. The waiter pushed in a silvery CD, and Croatian pop came on, tambourines with electric organs that shook the speakers. The music was cranked beyond the point of clarity—blasted. No conversation was possible.

Milos walked into the backyard. I thought that his Serb soul wouldn't let him listen to Croat music. He gave me a look and winked. I wondered what he meant. The waiter smirked, perhaps thinking there was a gay connection established between Milos and me. Milos went into the toilet, an outhouse next to the sheep stall.

I went behind the outhouse. There was a hole in the gray wood through which I could see his back. I put the gun in the hole and shot through his spine. His body jolted forward and then fell back, right against the wall. I shot again. Blood flowed through the spacing between dry planks. Because of the music, I was sure the waiter couldn't hear the shots.

I rushed away from the tavern yard through the rear gate. A train was whistling into the station. I jumped on the train even before it stopped. I wondered why I was running away. I should have been able to explain my deed—revenge against a war criminal. I went straight into the train toilet and shaved off my droopy mustache that made me look melancholy and forsaken. Now in the mirror I looked much younger, despite my receding hairline and the isolated widow's peak.

I thought I'd feel triumphant after my revenge. And I did feel proud as I looked at my cleared lip. Great, I am free from my sorrow, from the humiliation. I won.

But as I sat in the soft seat of the first-class coach and looked around holes burnt into the velvet seat by cigarette butts, my heart pounded and I could barely draw a breath. The smell of stale tobacco and spilled beer irritated me. I turned the ashtray over, cleaned it with a paper towel, and threw it out the window. The awful mutton seemed to be coming up to my throat. I was afraid.

If I was caught, and there was a trial, public sympathy would be with me. Many people want personal revenge. Forget institutional revenge, forget the International War Crimes Tribunal in Den Haage.

When I got off in Zagreb policemen in blue uniforms with German shepherds strolled on the platform but they did not stop me. They probably did not look for me. The war was going on in Krajina; one more civilian dead in the North made no difference.

Drunken people frolicked all over town, beeping their car horns, the way they did when their soccer clubs won. As I walked I expected a hand on my shoulder, from somewhere, perhaps the sky. It did not happen. But what happened was worse. At the tram stop, I saw a man exactly like Milos. I thought it was him. Were my bullets blanks? But where had the blood come from? How could Milos have made it to the train? When he saw me, I thought I noticed a fleeting recognition, the cowlick on his head shook, but that was too little reaction for what had happened in Virovitica. It was not Milos from the restaurant. This man was a little shorter and plumper. He looked genuinely like the man from Vukovar who had stabbed me, more than my Milos from Virovitica did. What if I had killed the wrong man? We rode in the same tram car. I forgot to buy my ticket, I was so stunned. He had his punched in the orange box near the entrance and stood, with one arm holding on to a pole. What to do? I wondered, as the tram jangled us around curves, and slim young ladies with tranquil made-up faces stood between us. I could not just kill the man, although this was probably the one that I should have killed in the first place. He got off at Kvaternik Square. Now I could blame him not only for my injury but for the death of an innocent man, his double. But I could have been wrong, again. I couldn't trust my "recognitions" anymore. I hadn't felt particularly ecstatic after my first murder, not for long anyway, and I was not looking for ecstasy. So I did not follow this man. I was crazed enough that I could have killed him too, but I wanted to be alone. Enough stuffy trams, oily tracks, expressionless people.

I walked home, near the zoo, just south of the stadium. In the streets I saw another Milos look-alike. Was I hallucinating? It was getting dark, true, but I looked at this third Milos keenly. They all had the same gait, same graying and trembling cowlick, same heavy black brow. I was glad I hadn't killed the man on the tram. How many men would I have to shoot to get the right one? It was absurd, and I was afraid that I was going insane.

I watched TV in my messy efficiency. Crime, if this was crime, was no news. Only Serb mass exodus from Krajina and Croat mass exodus from Banja Luka and Vojvodina made the news along with Mitterand's prostate. I drank three bottles of warm red wine and still couldn't fall asleep.

Next morning, sleepless and hungover, on my way to buy a daily, I thought I saw a Milos look-alike, leaning against the window of an espresso café, staring vacantly, as though he were the corpse of my traveling companion from Virovitica.

In the papers I saw the picture of my man, "Murdered by an Unidentified Traveler": Mario Toplak, Latin teacher at the Zagreb Classical Gymnasium, survived by his wife, Tanya, son Kruno, and daughter Irena. Clearly, I got the wrong man. This one was Croatian, judging by his name. But then, even the man in the Vukovar hospital could have been a Croat. He could have been drafted. The fact that he did not kill me and did not drag me out onto a bus to be shot in a cornfield now gave me the idea that wounding me may have saved me. I could not walk, and since I gushed blood it would have been too disgusting for anybody to carry me onto the bus, so I was left alone. He may have been a Serb, and he saved me nevertheless. Why hadn't I thought of that possibility before? Maybe I should have sought out the man to thank him. But thirst for revenge makes you blind. Is this a real thought? I'm probably just paraphrasing "Love makes you blind." I'm filling in the dots in prefab thoughts. Can I think?

At Toplak's funeral there were almost a hundred people, so I felt I was inconspicuous in the chapel. His wife wept, and his son, about four, and daughter, about five, did not seem to understand what was going on. "Where is Daddy? I want my daddy!" shouted Kruno.

"He's going to visit the angels in heaven, so he could tell us what it's like there. He'll bring back some tiny clouds who can sing in foreign tongues, you'll see." The widow whispered loudly. Maybe she was proud of how well she was shielding her kids from the truth.

"How can Daddy fly to heaven from here?" asked Irena.

I could see why she worried about that. The chapel was small, stuffy with perfume—I detest perfume, as though breathing wasn't hard enough without it!—and too cramped for any Ascension to take place. Tanya looked pathetic, tragic, dignified with her dark auburn hair, pale skin, and vermilion lips. Her skirt was slightly above the knee; she had thin ankles, a shapely waist with round, sexily tilted hips. She was in her mid-thirties. After the funeral, I gave her a white carnation, which had fallen in front of me from a precariously laid bouquet during the prayer. (I wondered, could you make tea from carnations, at least for funerals?) "I knew your husband," I said. "I'm so sorry."

She took the flower mechanically and put it in her purse.

"Could I give you a call, to share memories of him with you?" I said.

"Not for a while. What would be the point anyway?" She gave me a look through her eyelashes, grasped her children's hands, and walked toward the chapel door. Kruno turned around, looked at the varnished casket, and asked, "How come the box has no wings? How will it fly?"

Toplak was in the phone book. I called her a month later but when she answered I put the receiver down. I was too excited, I couldn't talk. I feared that I wanted to confess to her. On several occasions I waited for hours not far from her house and followed her. Every Saturday morning she went to the neighborhood playground with her kids.

In the meanwhile, I had grown crazed and lucky in everything I did. I can't say that I was a shy man—I used to be, but photography, shoving my eyes into everybody's business and intimacy, freed me from that affliction. At the end of August 1995 I took on loans, sold a small house in Djakovo I had inherited from my father, rented a shop, and photographed a lot of weddings, funerals, births. I accosted couples in the park who seemed to be on the verge of getting married, got their phone numbers; I put up ads in all the funeral parlors, crashed funeral parties with my camera. I hired an assistant, made a lot of money. The country seemed to follow the same mood swings as I did. After Krajina was conquered, and all the transportation lines in Croatia were opened again, and there were no threats of bombing in Zagreb, everybody was on the make. Optimism, investment, spending— many people seemed to have money, while months before hardly anybody did. If I had talked to Tanya a couple of days after the funeral, I would have had nothing to show for myself, but just two months later, when I approached her at the playground while her kids were jumping up and down the slides, I could boast. It was a superb day, with leaves turning color and fluttering in the slanted rays of the afternoon sun.

I came up to her bench, camera slung around my neck, and said, "Hello, you look beautiful. Would you mind if I took several pictures of you?"

"Oh come on, that's an old line. Thanks for the compliment, but I don't think so." She did not even look at me, but laughed.

"I'm serious. I don't mean nudes, though I'm sure they would be wonderful too, but just your face, your figure, dressed. Your expression, your mood, that's art."

Here, she was taken aback by my speech, and she looked up at me, raising one of her pencil-defined eyebrows. I was standing against the sun, casting a shadow over her left shoulder but letting the sun blaze into her eyes—her hazel irises glowed with emerald undertones, like moss in a forest in the fall. Her eye colors composed well with the turning leaves, as the soul of raving colors. I wasn't lying—I did want to take her picture, and it would have been terrific.

"Do I know you?" she asked.

"Slightly. I came up to you at your husband's funeral and gave you a carnation."

"Oh yes. And even then you were about to offer something. What did you want to talk about then?"

"I was on the train with your husband that day," I said—actually, blurted out.

"Yes?" she said, and then looked over to the playground to see whether her kids were safe.

I waited and didn't say anything for several seconds. I did not want to give away any clues, but her husband was the only ostensible link I had with her—I wanted to use it, so she would not evade me and leave as a stranger. My desire for her was stronger than my impulse toward safety.

"We chatted briefly," I told her. "He told me how much he loved his family, you and the kids, particularly how crazy he was about you, how lucky to have such a beautiful wife. But that's not why I came to the funeral, to see how voluptuous you are." She grinned as though she understood that I was lying and waited for me to go on. "He went off to the restaurant, he was hungry. I was surprised when I did not see him come back to the train station, but I figured the meal must have been great if he'd miss the train out of that God-forsaken station for it. I hope, for his sake, that it was."

"Really, he talked to you about how much he loved me? I wish he'd told me he loved me. Anyway, I don't believe that he said it."

"Maybe he was shy with you."

"And not with you?" she said. "Maybe you're right. He was a moody self-obsessed mathematician. Anyhow, he was a homosexual. We hadn't slept together in two years. I don't know why

I'm telling you all this, maybe just to let you know that I have reasons not to believe you."

"You seem to resent him." I was amazed. I had thought Milos was defending himself from a possible gay stalker in the restaurant, but he was actually trying to pick me up. The waiter may have been partly right to smirk and think there was a lewd connection being established.

"I know, it's irrational, but in a way I blame him for leaving us like this. Now I have to work full-time, support the family, the kids are a mess, as though we didn't have enough problems."

"Did he serve in the army during the war? I've heard that in post-traumatic stress, many straight men go through a gay phase." I was bullshitting, just to appear natural, and also, to find out whether her husband was in Vukovar as a soldier, after all.

"That's interesting. Yes, he was in the army, in Zadar, and was wounded." She was studying me, and nibbling on a pencil eraser.

"What army?"

"Funny question."

"What work do you do?" I asked.

"Curious, aren't we? I teach English, mostly private lessons, and I teach at a school."

"Could I sign up for an intensive program?" I asked.

"That depends," she said.

"Don't you want to make money?"

"Sure, but there's something strange about you . . . I didn't mean it to come out like that. What I mean is, I don't know you."

"Do you have to be intimate with people before you give them lessons?" I joked. It was not a good joke, but she laughed, perhaps because we were both tense.

She let me take pictures of her kids, I took several lessons, and paid well. She allowed me to take pictures of her, in her funeral dress, with the red lipstick. She could not be as pale as she'd been during the funeral, so we touched up her face with white powder to intensify the contrast with her hair. I don't know why I hadn't taken pictures at her funeral; it hadn't occurred to me then.

That was three weeks ago. I've taken her and the kids to the movies, to the zoo, and now that the first snow has fallen, I'll take them skiing. Tonight I paid for a baby-sitter and Tanya and I took a walk in the old town, past the lanterns, in narrow cobbled streets. A cold wind chapped my lips, and they hurt, until I kissed her in a dark corridor, a moist, tingling kiss. We trembled.

When I got home, I saw that I had vermilion lips. I had forgotten to wipe them. I am still filled with tenderness, and I'm drinking red wine. I'm looking forward to another date, tomorrow night, hoping to make love to her.

I don't know why I'm having success with her—perhaps too many men are in the army, many have been killed, and there's a shortage that may be working to my advantage. Maybe she's stringing me along, maybe she's suspecting me and investigating the case. I think my guilt gives me extraordinary confidence— I have nothing to lose. I am tempted to expose myself to her, and this temptation thrills me just as much as the erotic seduction does. I am dizzy from her images—and his—swarming in my head. I should go back to the western Slavonian fields, and gather wildflowers, bury myself in their scents and colors. Then I would not need to remember and rave on the page from a strange desire to be caught. I would live like a fox in a bush of red tea.

A Woman Walks
through the Crowd

❧❧

Red roaches that could crawl into your ear and deafen you dug their tunnels below mine in wet sawdust that had remained after my father's carving clogs. Ivo, my older brother, didn't like the honey-colored sawdust, but I made a friend who loved it as much as I did.

I met him in the garden next to tall black cherry trees, rough-barked pear trees with cemented and whitewashed hollows, near a frog pond—over a barbed-wire fence. He had a large forehead shading his deep-set unhappy eyes, a prisoner-style crew cut, a thick nose and thin lips. Another boy, similar to him, but much bigger, faced my brother. Without a word, we stared at each other over the fence, reconciling ourselves to the fact that these not at all cultivated-looking boys would be our neighbors for half a lifetime, boyhood. "I am stronger than you," I said to Danko. "You aren't," he said. I jumped over the fence, wrestled him to the ground, and began to strangle him. At the same time the big boy jumped over the fence and choked Ivo. It was a wonderful day.

I invited Danko to the sawdust, where we played dead, burying each other. In summers we knocked down green-skinned walnuts, and smashed them open with pebbles, as though cracking skulls, and indeed, out came little brain hemispheres. We peeled off thin walnut skins from the little brains and chewed the sweet meat, feeling as unfettered as cavemen. The turpentine-like juice of tart-tasting walnut coats stained our fingertips. To soothe our bitter tongues, we broke into the larder where my father had locked his jars of heavenly honey—the bees revealing to him God's grace as set forth in the Sixth Book of Moses and the Sixth Gospel. But when Danko went home, his mother beat him because of his yellowed fingers, thinking that he had begun to smoke.

While we played, jumped off the walnut tree, and made castles, four eyes haunted us through a wire fence from a dank moss-covered yard wedged between three houses—faces expressively sad as though painted by Munch emerged from an unsettling background of black earth and permanent shadows. White fingers clutched the wire squares. The pale countenances hovered there as patient as cacti, growing in a cold climate, yet growing. The girl was taller than her brother, her hair silky and black, eyes glowless. The boy's eyes were large and livid. We were a part of their vision of freedom, and through their eyes, we lived; their eyes augmented us. When we spoke to them once, after a year of overtly ignoring them, they ran away, and came back later, and continued to stare at us, their eyes growing bigger and sadder. Their father, according to rumors, had been in the wrong army in the Second World War; nobody gave him a job, their mother worked, and the town, excelling in persecuting anybody different at all, isolated the family.

In an adjacent yard on the other side of ours walked an amateur nun who regarded her life a failure because she had not been a professional nun. Only her withered face, her veined hands, and worn-out leather boots peeped out of the cloth as she walked by heart, her eyes closed, around a spindle-well. She walked counter-clockwise, moving her bluish lips. Her dry swollen hands trembled in front of her, sliding rosary beads on a flaxen string, perhaps counterclockwise, although the direction could not help in fighting the fate of the clockwise march of time that leads us all, willy-nilly, underground. She moved around the yard in a trance of religious trust and terror, doomed to the same circle, a Christian version of Sisyphus.

Ivo, I, and several other boys played Robin Hood in our backyard. We built shacks in trees, held archery tournaments, fought with sticks and swords. I made wooden swords with the array of adzes and knives and rasps for clog making from Father's workshop, rejoicing in the smoothness and sharpness of the edges, proud of my woodcarving skill. Ivo was Robin Hood, I, Little John. Ivo, unlike myself, refused to recognize Danko as Will Scarlet. Ivo named somebody else Will Scarlet, so there were two.

For me, Robin Hood masculinity was backwoods masculinity. It was so vulnerable and wild that it had to hide. Robin Hood was Adam, who, when God asked him whether he wanted a companion, answered, Make one in my likeness! And when God created a woman, Robin Hood went deeper into the forest. After expelling Adam and Eve, God remembered Robin Hood and his answer, and created a man in his likeness, Little John. And by the sheer grace of the masculine God, the band of Robin Hood proliferated, and there was Will Scarlet, and soon the whole band, guarded away from the world of the fallen Adam and Eve by the flaming sword of the cherub at the entrance. To wish for Eve was to be expelled from a paradise of forests into the streets where beautiful women walked, a shameful fall.

My sister was a guardian of the indoor feminine world where she played with her pretty friends. They all collected napkins and pictures of Marilyn Monroe and Brigitte Bardot, MM and BB, secretively. When I could not be admitted into my sister's highly civilized world, I raided her room and kicked the tidy napkins while Nella ran after me to pull my hair. I stole several black and white pictures and kept them in the workshop attic among heels and soles of clogs. I gazed at an MM picture in the sunlight beaming through a crack in the roof—the picture blushed from small red particles of sawdust in the sun—certain that it was beauty I saw, for not only did everybody say that she was beautiful, but I

could see, I thought, the supreme delicacy of her nostrils and lips.
I stared at a picture of her on the ground in the grass, her eyes
nearly fully closed and her lips slightly, vertiginously parted, waiting for a mysterious event, a cataclysmic revelation.

Secretly I admired women, and I thought it would be a weakness to reveal my admiration. I stayed away from the streets, but,
on my way to the library to borrow a book on pirates, my eyes
turned obediently as a compass needle turns northward, toward a
woman who walked out of a house across the street from mine.

I followed her into the cobbler's and gazed at her, and before
my turn would come to be asked what I wanted, I left the shop
and waited for her at the opposite side of the street. When she appeared out of the darkness of the shop, I followed her, marveling
at how she walked without ever looking right or left, without
giving way to anybody. Before her the crowds of people moved
aside like the waters of the Red Sea before Moses, while I had to
move aside for anybody bigger than me, giving way even to dogs.

Every day I waited for her. She was most likely to appear in
the late morning. I was about ten and she was about twenty—a
real woman.

To make my pilgrimages easier, I volunteered to go shopping.
Mother was utterly amazed yet pleased that I was so considerate
to wish to help her.

Now I could pretend I had a purpose: If by any chance the
woman saw me cursorily, I would shift my eyes away from her and
hide behind my shopping bag as a good boy who was shopping.
Whenever I saw her, and that was two times a week, I would forget what I needed to buy and would buy, depending on what shops
she'd been to, something utterly unnecessary. Most often I bought
nothing when following her, because it would take a long while till
a shopkeeper would notice me; her he noticed straight away.

Her eyes shone out of the frame of dark hair that shimmered
as it lay on her chest and flickered blue on her back, falling
straight along her upright posture, and touched her graceful hips.

I followed her at a distance with a sense of the sacred in my blood until she would disappear noiselessly in the narrow door of her blue-washed home. Then I walked home. Having heard me push open the wooden gate, Mother stepped outside in loud wooden shoes to look at the thin shopping bag, about to ask, "Haven't you forgotten something?" I shouted, "Yes, I forgot to buy bread," and ran back into the streets toward the baker's, elated with the fresh image of the woman.

One night I dreamt that I heard three gun shots and that I saw her head covered with blood. I was startled out of my dream by three real gun shots, which made the window panes tremble. After a moment of dead silence, there was a shuddering scream. Loud leather soles were running away, less and less loudly, and another moment of silence was followed by hissing voices and shouts—her name and murder.

Soon the story was assembled. She had two lovers: a policeman and a young teacher of mathematics. The math teacher was kissing her in the hallway of her home that night. The policeman had followed them from the park. Listening to them through the door from the street, he aimed at the sighs and whispers, and killed the sighs as well as the sighers.

 ❧

After the slaying, I avoided the streets. And when I had to be in them, I shied away from the obituaries on doors and lamp posts, and shunned voices, lest I might hear her name and her death. I feared the letters on the obituaries below the cross, feared the page from the Book of Life and Death for there was only death on it.

The streets were empty for me. Missing her drew me to the door where she used to disappear after her strolls, and I was startled by three holes in it, filled with some silvery substance: In the tremendous speed, the bullet had left a silvery shine in the wood. I was never sure whether the night of the slaying I had indeed dreamt of her death just before she was killed. The overwhelming event could not fit into wakefulness nor into dreams, so that it had spilled from wakefulness into the dream and back to the wakeful horror. As she had ubiquitously strolled from one part of my mind to another, the first shot may have triggered a flash in my mind, evoking her image and my fear for her, destroying my sense of time, so that I had the illusion that I had dreamt the shots before they were fired.

I liked to think that I had indeed prophetically dreamt the three shots right before they had been fired. One day I touched the silvery holes in the door as a doubting Thomas touched the holes in the body of Christ. Touching them became my sacrament in Her remembrance, until the time, which I feared would never come, of Her appearing on the clouds in Her Glory.

I retreated into the sawdust, sifting its redness as though it were her hair, surprised that wood would give way to the ground, sawdust turn into mud. Is wood changeable, treacherous? True, wood changes in flames, burning in a myriad of radiant and evanescent orange and red motions, whimsical, furious, gentle and whispering, shouting, crackling, throwing out sparks, and when it tires, smoldering and smoking blue. White and black, moody. The Homeric properties of wood made me forget that wood could rot and sink into the monstrous underworld.

Wood contains the primal elements—water and fire, air and earth. And if I were a pre-Socratic philosopher, I would have claimed that the primeval matter of the world was wood, and that the creation of the world was a whim of the wood—joyously it burst into fire, sadly languished into decay and gave up its ghost, smoke and air. The archaic wood, mother of the earth, was now tired, and her own children conspired to destroy it—wind, fire, water, and earth bit it, gnawed at it, devoured it, and my sawdust was like frozen soil, through which I could not pass my fingers as through a woman's fascinating hair.

A year later I passed through the narrow door of the house where the woman used to live—and Danko's family now lived—to play chess with Danko. The narrow corridor was paved with red-brown tiles. An old unmoved air stayed there smelling as if it had been there for centuries, now too old and feeble to dare to move anywhere—the sort of smell one finds in almost all the narrow old houses of the rainy Danubian countries. In winter, with wood burning in the stove next to us, at a wooden table, on wood benches, Danko and I pushed carved pieces of wood. Out of thirty-two pieces, all were male, except two, and these two were the most captivating, the most dangerous: It was the ambition of every foot soldier to make a Queen and to murder the King.

After the games, my face flushed with the heat from the burning wood, or shame from having played badly, I stepped out into the chill and gloom of the corridor. I tiptoed over the tiles where her blood had been spilled, timidly, past the traces of bullets.

Out of the Woods

&⬦&

Dena's vision was blurry. The stucco on a brick house on the corner of Vlaska Street seemed to her to be detached from the walls,
as if it were the building's aura. She wondered whether being
malnourished during the Balkan wars had damaged her sight. She
looked for the offices of an ophthalmologist on Nazorova Street,
in the hills, past several embassies and an orphanage. When she
saw two men with patches of white gauze on their eyes, strolling
with sticks, back and forth in front of one building, she knew the
clinic had to be there. She walked inside and sat down in the
waiting room among a quiet group of people who stared ahead of
them vacantly. A man in front of her seemed to have no irises,
only large pupils, even though his eyes were wide open and sunlight filled the room. The light warmed her knees. She stretched
her miniskirt and was upset that she had forgotten to put on a
longer one. But then, what difference did it make among the
nearly blind?

It did seem to make a difference to the doctor, a tall man with
a few white streaks in his stark black beard. She crossed her legs,
but then felt that her thigh was exposed, so she uncrossed them,
but the doctor was now sitting straight ahead of her, and from his

angle he could probably see up her thighs. Not that that should be such a big deal—on a beach it would be normal. She brought her knees together and put her hands in her lap.

"Do you wear glasses?" His voice was a sonorous baritone. And she was struck by how pink his gums and white his teeth were—probably the result of German dentistry.

"No, I never have."

"And this is the first time that your vision has been blurry?"

"The first time that I noticed, and the first time that I had an eye ache and also a headache."

"Do you have any medical conditions?"

"I'm alive, that's a medical condition, isn't it?"

"Are you ill, allergic to any drugs, suffer from a chronic condition, such as asthma?"

"Not that I know of. But now that you mention it, I am breathing kind of hard, aren't I?" Her breath was almost a wheeze, and she looked down at her breasts, which rose and fell, with an effort, almost a pain.

The doctor shone an ophthalmologic light into her eyes, and she could smell soap on his hands. He poked an instrument into her ears, showed her the alphabetical and numerical charts, put her chin on a black plastic rest and kept giving her different lenses. Through some lenses, the picture blurred even more; through others, it became sharper, but smaller. "Yes, this is better," she said. "Better." Static electricity seemed to glide over her legs, and she wondered whether she was feeling his gaze. But how could a gaze project any photons, or whatever it was, that she could feel?

"All right," Dr. Glavni said, and stood behind her. He took off her glasses and touched her temples and forehead. "Close your eyes." His fingers passed over her eyelids and cheeks, and she remembered a priest putting his hands on her head, to dispense forgiveness after she confessed that she'd stolen her father's wine. That was a long time ago, in Glina.

"It's good to relax," Dr. Glavni said, "because a tense eye distorts the image more than a relaxed one."

"Are my eyes very bad?" Dena asked.

"No, they are beautiful. They do need a minor correction, though. Some astigmatism in the left eye, and myopia—minus one diopter—in the right eye. Good-bye."

Dena liked her glasses. They made her look like an intellectual— a professor of linguistics or a lawyer. She enjoyed thinking that the glasses decreased her attractiveness to the outside world and increased the attractiveness of the outside world to her. Her glasses made a statement to everybody around her. It's more important how you look to me than how I look to you. I'm the subject, you're the object. But she knew that the liquid clarity that the glass added to her dark blue eyes could actually make her look more seductive—veiled yet exposed.

While getting used to the sharpness of the world and to the tickle on the bridge of her nose, she walked into a photo shop in Ilica. She had a dozen pictures of young women, part-time prostitutes, all refugees from Bosnia, who needed work. She thought that she had good business sense. So she could work out of her two-bedroom apartment, two tricks at a time. The rent was high— seven hundred German marks per month, higher than an average salary. She wanted to buy the apartment so she would not have to pay rent, and then she could do something mellow and honest, like run a boutique.

In the shop she looked at pictures of a naked woman, lying sideways on a cement fence. Her thin waist ascended into broad hips in a bright line. Dena pulled several photos out of her deerskin purse. "Could you do these women, like your woman on the wall, in color? I want to make a classy catalogue. How much would you charge?"

"Hum." He bit the pencil eraser, and looked her up and down. "Not much. An hour of your time."

Dena took a swing to slap him. She missed, and a nail on her middle finger bent as it scraped against his nose. As she rushed out of the shop, he shouted, "I only wanted to take pictures of you!"

She was surprised at her reaction. After all, he was good look-ing, clean. Now she would have to look for another photographer, and it might cost her. She went home, and after taking a bubble bath, spent an hour looking for her glasses. She realized that she hoped that the lost glasses would warrant another trip to the ophthalmologist.

She called up her mother, a stooped old woman, who had aged terribly after her husband was executed in front of her. Whenever Dena was busy, her mother baby-sat Igor.

Dena took Igor, her five-year-old son, to get a haircut.

"I don't want a haircut," he said.

"But the hair's in your eyes. Doesn't that bother you? You'll go blind."

She did not cut Igor's hair, and she called Dr. Glavni. "I've lost my glasses. Can I come over right away and get another prescription?"

"Sure, but if you can wait a day, I can mail it to you."

"The mail is slow and unreliable."

"After work I've got to go downtown anyhow, so if you are around, let's say, at the Ban Café, I could meet you there, at six."

"Wow, that's like a date!"

"Would you like it to be?"

"To tell the truth, I don't remember how you look because my vision was so screwed up that day. I'd have to take a good look at you before I could tell you."

At six she walked back and forth under the sculpture of Ban Jellacic, the Croatian governor who had helped put down the Hungarian national revolution in the last century and who had partly inspired a Croatian national revolution in this one. The sculpture of the man in a tall hat pointed a saber to the south toward Krajina, where the Serbs had established their ministate. The original one—she remembered seeing pictures in the news-papers—had pointed north toward Hungary. And who knows where the sculpture would point next. East, perhaps. She looked up at the clock on a metal post on the western side of the square.

Since she left her glasses at home, she had to squint to make out the time, and that was not enough, so she pressed her eyelids together a little with her fingers, and that sharpened her vision. Six-fifteen. Meanwhile a man who looked slightly familiar kept walking back and forth, winking at her. To avoid him, she walked into the café, and there was the doctor, winding his pocket watch.

"Fashionably late, am I?" she said.

"No, that's no longer the fashion."

"Are you sure you don't need a pair of glasses yourself, if you couldn't see me from here?"

"Oh, that's fine. I was reading the newspaper. Here's your prescription." He handed her a blank piece of paper.

"Doc, are you kidding me? *You* need a prescription."

"I know I do, but I also know that I am giving you a better one now. Forget these damned crutches. If you keep losing your glasses, it'll cost you a lot and confuse your eyes. Take a trip, let's say a boat ride down the Adriatic, or a hike in the woods, where you'd have to look into the distance, and then if you still need glasses, come back."

"Are you kidding?"

"Seriously. You seem to be a natural kind of person."

"What's that supposed to mean?"

"Nature will heal you."

"Where do you get that, that I am natural?"

"The way you move. You are in touch with your body."

"In touch . . . that's a pretty loose connection to have with your body. I'm not only in touch—I am squeezing it, biting it, in fact, I *am* my body. And are you in touch with yours?"

"Yes, I like the way you move."

"You aren't answering my question."

"Yes, I am. The fact that I like how you move, how you breathe, how your lips pout . . . shows I'm in touch with my male self. Can I kiss you?"

"I didn't ask you whether you were in touch with *my* body."

"Well, I am." He leaned over and kissed her lips, softly. She kept her eyes open, and he did too. Their noses slid against each other. Their nostrils widened. Her lips tingled.

And then she burst out laughing.

"What's so funny?" he said.

"Your eyelashes are tickling me."

"Your place or mine?"

"I've heard that line before."

"Where?"

"Your place," she said.

"I mean where have you heard it?"

"No, you don't, silly hypocrite. But that is how barflies talk. Are you a barfly and a womanizer?"

"No, but it's not too late, is it?"

"Yes, it is." She pulled him by his brush-like beard with both of her hands to her lips.

They made love in the shower, on rugs, in chairs, on the kitchen counter. And they talked, and joked, pretending constantly to be misunderstanding each other. They were not only playful but serious, too. Nenad told her about his childhood, which he'd spent in the same house where he lived now. As a child he had spent entire weeks without anybody to speak to, in silence, without music. His parents did not talk to each other for an entire year and then got divorced, and the father went to Argentina, never to be heard from again, and the mother, who worked too hard as a teacher and tutor after hours, died of breast cancer when he was still in his teens. And there was more he could tell her, he said, but he would tell her once they got to know each other better.

Dena told him about the Serb massacre near her town, Glina. Her husband was impaled on a hot machine-gun barrel, and she was raped in a devious way. "An officer told me, 'I don't like rape. It's too dry, too much work. But I want to sleep with you. If you don't, I'll let the whole brigade rape you. And I want to see that you are excited. So let me first massage you, and we'll be real gentle.' And so the officer massaged me in exotic oils that he claimed came from the Caucasus."

"And you got excited like that?" Nenad paced, grabbed a plate, and shattered it against the wall. "Damn! Damn!"

"If someone had a gun to your head and massaged your ass, you'd feel excited too. The hairs on my body stood up, I shivered, and. . . ."

"Spare me the details."

She paused. She wanted to tell him how the officer had kept her in his barracks for two months, apart from her son, whom he took along on his rounds to the front lines to show him the artillery pieces as though he were his kid. She was not allowed to read, to watch TV, to walk, to see people; the officer put her into a sensory deprivation limbo, in a dark room, for days at a time, and when he visited, he poured honey over her and licked her, with an infinite patience and a determination to excite her senses, while she shivered from hatred mixed with lust.

"He kept his word," she said. "He didn't let anybody else rape me, and he put me on the bus to Bosanski Brod, from where we went to a camp in Opatija. It wasn't really a camp but a tourist hotel. Since tourism was dead, we were allowed to stay there, with aromatic pine breezes from the South Alps and the salty air from the sea." She wanted to tell Nenad that to get out of the refugee camp, she had resorted to prostitution—not exactly to selling her body, but renting it. There was absolutely no other way for her to get money, to get out.

As though Nenad could guess what she had not told him, he continued pacing, swearing. He drank a bottle of red wine without putting it down. She watched his pointed Adam's apple rise into his beard and fall out of it. The tip of his Adam's apple stretched the skin so that the skin turned white, bloodless. When he was done, his face was red, as though he had been choking. The wine made his lower lip glisten, and the wine flowed down his beard into his white shirt, and stained it. He was breathing hard now, and she was about to joke that perhaps he suffered from asthma, but she did not say it.

She had hoped that she could share everything with him. Probably there were things that he could not tell her—and perhaps things that he could not tell himself. She could not understand how someone could be like that, unwilling to hear the truth, no matter how ugly. Not hearing the truth was even uglier, and wishing not to hear it was a betrayal, self-betrayal, the ultimate adultery of diluting the truth with wishful thinking.

But she soon forgot, or nearly forgot, this day of confessions.

She and Nenad took a trip to Korcula, an island in the south of the Adriatic, and stayed in a hotel room overlooking a rocky beach and a round fortification with stone walls.

As Dena watched Igor shrieking with happiness and Nenad laughing with joy—far out to the sea—she realized that her sight had improved: She saw distant sailboats and seagulls in sharp detail. Her ocular crisis might have been caused by a dizzy spell. Since glasses would probably have ruined her sight, she felt grateful to Nenad for giving nature a chance to cure her vision.

Later, as they ate grilled squid with lime and tomatoes and onions, Igor slept in the shade on an air mattress, over crooked roots sticking out of the ground and smoothed over by feet that had stepped and tripped over them during three decades of robust tourism. A warm wind brought out the pine smell, and mixed it with the smell of the sea and olives and other scents that were hard to decipher, but which made one feel alert and curious. Perhaps similar scents had driven Marco Polo, who'd spent his childhood at Korcula, mad with curiosity and on to China. But these scents made Dena exceedingly happy, and started her dreaming of the happinesses that were still remote.

"We are having such a great time," Dena said, "just as if we were on a honeymoon."

"Don't mention honeymoons. We don't know each other that well."

"Well, how come you aren't married? You are thirty-eight—right?—and you've never been married. At this rate, you never will be. You'll let life pass you by."

"Life will pass anyhow. Just relax."

"I'm not proposing anything. OK, I won't bring it up again." She slurped lemonade until a lemon seed got stuck in the straw. She lifted the straw and squeezed the seed out of it, and said, "You think you're something, don't you?"

"You do. Obviously. I don't. I know I'm not stable enough to take care of myself, let alone others."

"Do you tell that to your patients?"

Igor moved his arms in sleep as though he were swimming, and Dena and Nenad laughed at him.

After the trip, Dena did not answer the phone for a week, exasperating Nenad, who rang her doorbell every evening. On the eighth evening she missed his company, and answered the door. They took a walk, and Nenad told her the new jokes he'd heard at work. They laughed, and soon they made love, like adolescents who have no place of their own and no money for hotels, in a lanternless and narrow street, against a wooden gate, and in a park, leaning against a windstruck tree that showered them with smooth round chestnuts that bounced on the cobblestones with dull thuds.

Dena conceived, and told him that they were expecting. If he did not want a family, he should pay for the abortion, and they would never see each other again.

Dena and Nenad got married, and she and Igor moved into Nenad's house on Nazorova Street.

Nenad was busy. After hours, he spent time at meetings of the Croatian Social Liberal Party, the second strongest party in Croatia, which held about 30 percent of the parliament seats. He could become a minister of health, or an ambassador to Germany, or mayor of Zagreb.

Dena, who stayed home, cooking, tutoring Igor, and reading, had developed new ambitions. Now, she wanted to become a physician, and so she studied chemistry and physics for the university entrance exams.

They were both overworked. After a month they did not have sex frequently. Dena thought, That's what men are like—once the conquest is certified with a signature, they yawn.

Sometimes, when she was anxious, she went to the attic and smoked. Because of her pregnancy, however, she did eventually manage to kick the habit, for the time being.

During the final month of her pregnancy, Nenad took off from work and stayed home with her. In the hospital, he held her hands when she had powerful contractions. The labor went on for more than a day and a night. Dena sweated, panted, moaned, and said, "You'd better love us after all this."

He delivered the baby and wept. He described the sensation to Dena as a surge of fear and joy, with a unique worry for another life, a little crying, red-faced life, which opened its milky blue eyes at him in blank wonder. They named the child Robert, and soon, Bobo.

Bobo was breast-fed for a year. Dena formed an intimacy with Bobo that demoted Nenad to the periphery of her affections. Bobo slept with them in the same bed, and climbed all over her, sucking and slurping loudly. Dena could see that Nenad felt left out of all this. He often watched them with a frown before he went to his office, or the parliament, or wherever he went, away from home. Dena did not worry.

As soon as Bobo stopped breast-feeding, Dena felt left out, too, and now she wanted to be with Nenad. But he was busy with his politics, and he ignored her, and the little time he had at home he spent playing with Bobo.

In May, Zagreb was cluster-bombed, and Dena had nightmares: She's trying to get out of a burning house. And she's hanging down with ropes above a barrel of hot oil, and as her pelvis sinks in and burns, the officer says, Now you'll be hot and smooth.

And, she's running through the woods, and she falls into a pit where a white tiger is puking hundreds of purple fingers with golden wedding rings.

When she shrieked, Nenad turned the lights on, and they drank tea, and she leaned on him, her ear against his beard. Her anxiety attacks kept her fidgety even during the day. Whenever he went out, she smoked in the basement, or in the attic, or in the street.

He discovered that she smoked and kept tabs on her budget to prevent her from buying cigarettes.

One evening when she got back from a brief get-together with her girlfriends, he said, "Where were you?"

"At my mother's."

"Why do you smell like a tavern? Like booze, tobacco, and lousy coffee."

"Because that's what we drank."

"You are lying."

"You are impossible. Why would I?"

"I mean, look at your clothes! You wear miniskirts, high heels. And why do you wear that scarlet lipstick? Who do you need to wiggle your ass at? I've seen how men look at you."

"I need to stay attractive for you, so you won't look at other women. You think I don't see what you look at? Double standards."

"Double standards. For a man it's natural to look at different women."

"So it's natural for men to look at me. Why are you so upset about it!"

"Because you've got a whore hormone floating around," he said.

"You are a brutal asshole."

He slapped her. She kicked him. He pushed her down into an armchair, and said, "Don't ever kick me again."

Once, when Nenad was away at a conference of his political party in Split, Dena ran into a man who used to visit her—a computer programmer, an ex-hippie with long hair, who treated computers as a mind-expanding drug. She went with him to his apartment, and they kissed fleetingly, drank wine, and watched cyberporn. Pretty soon they had sex. He kept staring at the screen behind her during sex, and she felt as though she were a computer accessory, an inflated mouse for him to move his cursor around, or, more likely, a bit of physical to augment his virtual reality. Dena enjoyed the sensation of freedom, of being frivolous despite marriage; and she thought that she was having sex to spite the marriage in which she could not be free enough to do such an innocuous thing as to smoke an occasional cigarette. Her marriage was threatening to become a bondage situation, a little like being a sex slave in the Serb army, except that there was hardly any sex in her marriage. And now, because she felt so free she even accepted the money, the hundred German marks that the programmer offered her—so the programmer would not owe her anything and she would not owe him anything, and moreover, she would have money to do with as she pleased, buy cigarettes and makeup. But she had not enjoyed this casual sex and afterward had a hangover. The memory of the programmer's bad breath disgusted her.

The programmer called her in the morning and wanted to get together again, and she said, "No, never again."

"Unless you get together with me, I'll let your husband know what we did last night."

"That's not a persuasive argument. You mean, if I don't sleep with you, you're going to tell him that I sleep with you. That's silly. Get lost, and don't ever call here again."

Afterward, when Nenad came home from the party conference, Dena felt both guilty and free enough to know that she was not missing anything out there, and certainly not anything from her past. She wanted to make her home life work. She put flowers in vases around the apartment, taught Igor to play chess, and read baby books to Bobo.

Nenad also seemed to be trying to make the marriage work. He bought Dena a present, a gold necklace with a large ruby. He cooked now and then so Dena could study. She thought that he probably was a good man.

But mostly he was busy, and when they sat at their dinner table, she looked across and wondered who this man sitting there was, and what they had together, and thought of asking him, "Excuse me, have we met before?" but she didn't.

One evening when he got home from work, Nenad said, "I smell cigarettes, again!"

"Here you go again. I didn't smoke inside."

"But you smoked. It's like a man saying, I didn't come inside, to prove that he did not have sex after visiting a prostitute."

"A beautiful analogy."

"And not inappropriate. Guess who I saw today."

"I hate guessing," Dena said. She had a feeling of panic in her chest, she was short of breath, but she maintained an exterior calm. "This city has a million people in it. You could have seen anybody."

"And so could you, from what I found out—the photographer told me about your wanting to make an album. You wanted to be a madam!"

"So? You believe him? And what if I did? That doesn't mean that I'd sleep with the clients."

"I've heard rumors before. And I was blind to them. Deaf. I thought I was the only one, but I was the only one who did not have to pay. But I paid, of course."

"So what's the problem? That was all before you. I couldn't talk to you about anything that happened during the war, let alone after it. How do you think one gets out of a refugee camp?"

"You could have stolen, that would have been better."

"You've been spoiled; you've had it too easy. Good degrees, good jobs, politics."

"Well, forget politics now. You've ruined my politics. In the Balkans, a man with a wife like you is disqualified. If I can't run my own house, what can I do?" He sat down, and poured himself a shot of Black Label on ice. "On the other hand, if we were in the States, it would be the same; a wife with a bad reputation, that would ruin me. Can you imagine if Hillary Clinton moonlighted on the side as a whore?"

"But wasn't he a slut, and he was still elected?"

"Here, there's no difference between the past and the present. Once a war, always a war. Once a whore, always a whore."

"I quit before I met you. You were proud to marry me—weren't you, you?—you thought you were a damned patriot, saving a war victim, a raped woman—you were saving the continent, you were so full of yourself, you did not even look at me as a person but as a war case, probably as a stepping stone in your political ambitions."

Nenad gathered all her lingerie and set fire to it in the furnace. The clothes crackled, and burned blue and orange and hissed.

"What are you doing that for?"

"You have to ask?"

"We have a family together. You have to behave respectfully toward me, if only because of them."

"Oh, yeah? I think we should get a divorce."

"Do as you please. But I'll sue you. I need to take care of the kids."

"I'd take them with me."

"I'm not so sure."

"I have political influence."

"During the trial, you'd lose your political influence. You've said as much yourself."

"Hmmm . . . I'll give you three months to prove yourself. You really feel no guilt, do you?"

"For what? For surviving?"

From that day on, Nenad did not speak to his wife. When they drove to town, he sat in the front with Igor, and she in the back with Bobo. The children talked, played, cried, but Nenad did not talk to his wife. He pretended that she did not exist. They did not sleep together, either. They never looked into each other's eyes.

Sometimes she talked to him, without knowing whether he listened. Dena complained: "In the Balkans, apparently, women are nothing. The woman is the last hole on the flute. Except when men get horny." She considered the option of divorcing him, and although she would have liked it, she decided that because of the children she was not free to be impulsive. She would bear it, and maybe the crisis would be over one day.

Nenad stayed at work more than usual, and at home he read children's books to the kids. When she read to them, she could see that he was jealous. They loved their kids, and hated each other, but their love for the children was stronger than their hatred for each other.

One evening, however, Nenad did talk. He pulled out a letter, addressed to her. It was a pornographic letter, starting with "Don't you remember?" and ending with "Let's do it again."

She read it. "I've never known anybody by that name. It must be one of your political competitors trying to screw you."

"But I am not in politics anymore."

"They're making sure that you won't be. How come you're so blind? You're a fucking blind ophthalmologist."

"Don't you know it! Aren't you scared of disease, disgrace, dis—? . . ."

Nenad slapped her hard, several times. She fell into an armchair and cried. The children cried and held on to each other and trembled in the corner of the room.

"Don't hit Mom," Igor said.

"He's right," she said. "You are scaring them."

As he looked at the children, he was startled. Their teeth were chattering.

"My dear children. Everything will be all right." He approached them to hug them, but they ran to her, and she embraced them.

"All right. This must change," he said. "We've grown too selfish. Let's make a happy family, let's pretend, maybe even join a church, sing cheerful songs, for their sake."

He was still too proud and vengeful to sleep with her, or to look into her eyes, and he easily lapsed into days of silence. He clearly suffered and tried to change his stony disposition. He suggested that they take a trip, to the Plitvice lakes, in the recently liberated Krajina.

And so they did take a trip, in the middle of October, when the leaves turned and each tree became a giant wildflower, as though the earth had reverted to an earlier era, where forests were God's garden.

"Boys, let's go fishing," Nenad said.

"And Mummy, too," said little Bobo.

"And Mummy, too," Nenad said.

They drove, and Nenad whistled. When they got to Plitvice early in the morning, the mists hung over the lakes.

They paddled in two boats—Dena with Bobo, and Nenad with Igor.

"Dad, I won't fish," Igor said. Dena could hear them talking on the water, the sound carried. "I don't want to hurt them."

"What shall we do then?" Nenad asked.

"Let's gather mushrooms."

"No, you can't do that," Nenad said. "There are mines in the hills."

Dena put Bobo in his car seat in front of her and paddled gingerly, so as not to wake him. She enjoyed the sight, or rather, the lack of sight, when she reached the middle of the lake. She could not see the shore or any color, just gradations of gray, as though she had sunk into a penciled drawing. She did not know whether it was mist or rain, but mused dreamily that the mist was a rain that had forgotten to fall, or a cloud that had forgotten to rise. Or if the mist was a rain, it was a fine one, one that fell so that you could not see that it did, because it had forgotten to make drops. The particles floated, touched her face, wandered through her hair, soaked her shirt, and drifted away from her, and she drifted away from them. The mist silenced the water, except for a waterfall in the distance, and the water lay still, unwind-blown, unruffled. Baby dragonflies flitted and zigzagged on the surface. A seagull, exiled from the sea, glided and landed on a rock that stuck out of the water near the boat's path.

She dipped the varnished paddle into the lake and when she lifted it, the paddle ladled and spilled the water, to be tasted by her knees, ossified tongues.

Several drops fell on Bobo's cheeks but did not wake him up. He lay tranquil, smooth, his little hands clasped in fists. When she neared the shore, she saw many downed trees. Their roots brought up circles of dark earth. Some trees may have fallen the year before and were still sucking at the earth, as at a breast.

One fir tree had fallen over together with the large rock it had grown on. The tree roots clasped the rock and wouldn't let go. Another tree had peeled away from its rock, leaving the rock clean.

After the mists had drifted away, the sky turned intensely blue, evergreen trees grew dark green, and beeches and oaks began to sing in red and orange keys. Among the colors, clouds clashed—black and gray and white, like an old photograph, merging into the new colorful one.

As she landed against the wooden dock, and stood on the canoe unsteadily with Bobo in her arms, she heard Nenad's shout, "Stop, don't go any further!" And then she heard crackling branches, running feet. She climbed out, and without tying down the canoe, rushed toward the woods. "Where are you, Igor, where are . . . ?" She heard Nenad shouting, and his call was cut short by an explosion. It echoed from the hills, so that it sounded like a cascade of explosions. She feared it could be her son, and even that it could be Nenad. She ran toward a scream. Over a hump of soil, she saw Nenad kneeling among orange leaves stained with scarlet blood. Bobo woke up and cried. She panicked.

"Oh my God, he's dead, dead!" shouted Nenad.

Dena put the car seat with Bobo on the ground, and fumbled

through the leaves, but could not see Igor. She only saw streaks of flesh. Nenad gripped her from behind, and said, "Stay still. There could be other mines!"

"Let me go. I hope there are. Let me go!"

She stumbled and vomited, and the red and orange turned green in her head, and she could see nothing but the green, and wondered whether she'd gone blind. Now it did not matter. What mattered was that Igor was dead, scattered, ungatherable, probably not even a resurrection could piece him together. Nenad held her up, and he picked up Bobo.

Dena kept groaning. Nenad wiped her face with his white handkerchief, and said, "One thing is strange. I haven't seen his shoes, his clothes, not even a scrap of them, as though. . . ."

He left her with Bobo in her arms and searched further, in widening circles. "Don't," she said. "There could be more mines around."

"That would be all right" he said. "It's all my fault. When he was far enough so that I could not catch him, he said he was running away from home."

Dena's larynx rose up toward her mouth as she was about to shout at Nenad in rage, and only a quiet choking sound came out. Nenad shrieked something she could not understand, and he held up a foot with a hoof. "It's a fawn! Maybe he's alive!"

They found the tail of the fawn, as well. And then Nenad moved further away, and she stood with Bobo in her arms. She looked up at the sky, to pray to God, but she did not know how.

She looked up an oak tree, and there she saw Igor, high up, and grinning.

She shouted with joy, then said angrily, "You saw us down here? Why didn't you say anything?"

"What was there to say?" he said. "Dad did not speak, and I did not want to speak to *him* anymore, to show him what *that* was like."

"Come down, you rascal."

And Igor did, chuckling.

There was another explosion, far away, and it echoed against the mountains. Before Dena could decide whether she should worry about Nenad, or whether the explosion was too far for that, Nenad emerged from the woods slowly. When he heard Igor, he lifted his head and squealed, like a delighted child. Now they all huddled together, and talked eagerly, as one joyful family, amidst light-refracting, dank particles that drifted from the nearby waterfalls and shrouded them in the graceful spectrum of vision and sound.

The Devil's Celluloid Tail

Daruvar, Croatia

⚵⚵

My older brother, eight, and I, six, arrived at the movie theater a little late to see our first movie. As we looked for seats in the dark, a huge train rushed straight at us, gushing steam and hooting louder than any train I'd heard before. We ran for our lives out of the theater. Nobody else came out, and we concluded that the train had killed the entire audience. When we reported the tragedy at home, our father and sister laughed. Then our father took off his belt and gave us an instructive beating. "Don't you ever go to the theater again! The devil teaches sin there." Though glad to have escaped death, Ivo and I did not have a good first-movie experience.

For a year I wouldn't hear of movies, for they reminded me of my stupidity. My sister, Nella, on the other hand, went to many movies, against father's wishes. She collected pictures of movie stars from tabloids and glued them in her notebooks. Gregory Peck, MM, and Gina Lollobrigida were her idols. For Gregory Peck I did not have much use, except that his pictures suggested to me that American dentistry must be much better than ours, for hardly anybody his age in our country had such glaringly white teeth.

Almost every evening the theater tickets sold out. At the time, in the mid-sixties, TV sets weren't a living-room staple, and our town could receive only one channel; half of the programming was devoted to the news, documentaries, and Yugoslav Second World War movies, in which a handful of partisans defeated German divisions (these simplistic movies were extremely popular in China). Our family had no TV set because Father believed that TV bred decadence, so even when he could afford it, he did not buy a set. Instead he wanted us to read books—although, according to my mother, books too—except for textbooks—wasted time. Mother did not set a good example. Whenever I borrowed novels from the library, she'd read them, sometimes all night long.

A new movie theater opened, named after Tito's fictitious birthday, 25th of May, "The Day of Youth." (Tito was most likely born on May 8 but did not want to compete with May Day.) On opening night the red-brick theater with padded doors and a thousand varnished seats was full. Nella and I sat on the carpet in the middle. The lights dimmed and a skier flew downhill, splashing snow, with sunrays streaking across the screen. This was a French romance, and nothing scary happened, indeed nothing at all seemed to happen, except that I saw many elegant people with thin eyebrows and exquisite nostrils and teeth not much better than ours.

Soon after the theater opened, our minister delivered a sermon against the demons of cinema. "Somewhere in the U.S.A., a Christian promised to God he'd never go to the movies again, but the Devil seduced him and he went. As he watched a scene of adultery, lust from hell flamed in his heart. The floor opened under him, and he fell through, straight to hell. Several witnesses saw it. The man was never seen again. He's in hell. That's what'll happen to you if you go back to watch the Devil's celluloid tail." At that he glared at me, and went on, "And if the earth does not swallow you into its fiery stomach, you who watch movies will at the very least become liars, adulterers, thieves—petty criminals."

None of his prophecies (about Christ's coming in a certain year, about a Yugoslav civil war erupting in a month) had worked before, but this one, strangely enough, did, at least in my case. I became a petty criminal in order to watch movies. When I did not manage to steal enough from my mother, I'd slip into the middle of the thronging crowd and pass through without a ticket, until I grew too tall to pass unnoticed.

With several boys I collected a hundred keys, and one key worked to unlock the theater basement door. We sneaked through the basement, stumbling over coals and piles of wood. We came up behind the screen and read the subtitles in reverse, which at first was harder than reading the Cyrillic alphabet (once a week our composition classes were held in Cyrillic, the rest of the week in Roman alphabet). The screen cloth's grains sparkled and refracted the light, dazzling us. We waited for a loud and dark scene, and then, still blinded by the previous bursts of light, we crawled down the stage stairs, into the audience. We stumbled over feet and knees, falling into large laps. We wanted to be in a crowd because, if you sat in a row alone, a guard would catch you, drag you out, and kick you. But in the crowd you were safe, partly because of events like this: Once, in a silent scene I heard a resounding slap, and then another one twice as loud and these words in a guard's voice, "Oh, sorry Doctor, I did not know this was you. I'm deeply sorry. Please forgive me."

"Get lost."

Instead of finding a boy who sneaked in, by mistake the guard slapped a respected citizen. (Of course, knowing the doctor, I would not put it past him that he had snuck in.) Because of risks like these, the guard left us alone once we were in the rows.

We often broke in from the street. With a furnace stoke we could jack one door-wing high enough to open the door, but that made too much noise, and the guards quickly caught on to the trick. Then our group of ten boys often gathered enough money to buy one ticket. One boy went in and opened an exit door, leaving it slightly ajar. The rest of us peeped through a crack, and during a dark scene ran in, scattering all over the cinema. Many boys got their ears boxed and arms twisted, but a couple of days later, we'd be back for more—more dark heaven. *Doctor Zhivago* dragged us around in the ice of Russia to kiss beautiful women and rot in lousy trains in anti-revolutionary zeal. Italian movies with Laura Antonelli's plentiful body taught us to stare voyeuristically at older women, our teachers, committing adultery—to our regret, only with our eyes. In *Cleopatra,* Caesar praised Cleopatra's hips, broad as the river Nile, for they would bring forth children with ease. Henceforth, broad hips became our canon of feminine beauty. We walked out of the dark, into the starry streets, dizzy from the world shot into our brains through our eyeballs. My eyeballs were as sore as if I had absorbed a drug through them by osmosis, or as though needles had scraped—through my pupils— the back of my skull. The spiked light from the screen hurt like a porcupine thrown into my face. Even though the porcupine had fallen back into its hole, the needles stayed, somewhere inside.

Movies left such strong impressions on us that we spent hours walking around the town, recalling good moments, wondering what each detail symbolized, and what psychological and political statements were made in the films. Movies gave us a way to connect abstract theories to the world. The ideas did not need to stay chained to the leaden letters on the page. Cinematic light revealed them, made them closer to the world, more imaginable.

Besides thieving, breaking in, gate-crashing, truancy, adulterous lusting, subversive thinking, and lying, movies taught us forgery. If money could be forged in movies, why not tickets in order to see movies? In a store we bought sheets of paper in different colors—pale yellow, pink, purple, and blue—that matched ticket paper. On a sewing machine with a fine needle we made holes along the lines where ticket stubs should detach when the guard at the door pulled at them. We did not do a perfect job, but were never caught. In the dim light dozens of hands stretched out, and the bored guards kept tearing the stubs and tossing them in the large pockets of blue workers' overcoats. It's possible that they knew what we were doing, but nabbed us only when our break-ins were blatant, and they had to do it for the sake of their jobs. (Even when they caught us, their blows were never harsh, not like our math teacher's. If you neglected to do your homework, the teacher would tickle your chin, and when you lifted your jaw he'd knock you down with his heavy hand.)

One movie was most educational. After the last showing of *How to Steal a Million* a friend of mine, Velyko, and a friend of his managed to break into a bank next to the theater. They found no money and took several boxes of documents, hoping to find cash. They climbed on the asphalt roof of the cinema, and sorted through the boxes, tossing checks, promissory notes, contracts, and records of transactions into the wind. The following morning these documents floated in the streets like exhausted leaves. Velyko's father beat him with a heavy chain, so that Velyko was bedridden for a month. He was no longer interested in crime or cinema after this, only in reading books and playing the piano.

Under the influence of the movies, my brother, a friend of his, and I stole several hundred lightbulbs and a mile of wires from a visiting circus. We used the spoils to illuminate our backyard and play outdoor soccer at night.

I thought that if I was brave and clever enough I would become a professional criminal. I saw all the James Bond movies that came to town. A newspaper printed Roger Moore's address, and when I was twelve I wrote my first letter in English, to the actor, in calligraphy, using a dictionary. Two weeks later I got Roger Moore's picture with his signature. The signature was not forged: When I tested its tail end with hot water the ink dissolved. I had not expected to get a response from 007. I continued with minor thieving. In a Zagreb philately store I stole a series of rare stamps, and cashed them in with a local collector for an impressive sum of money. Now I could go to the cinema like a gentleman, buying tickets. Every day I stole something—money from an Italian car, a watermelon at the marketplace, a pair of black gloves at the store. I believed that while stealing I could achieve a state of invisibility, as long as I was natural and nonchalant enough.

But once I got caught, stealing a brandy bottle from the self-service store; the store manager twisted my ears and kicked me. Hitherto I was an actor, stealing with precision and calm, but now inglorious beating among sacks of sugar and salt brought me back to my pedestrian, adolescent limits. I lost the cinematic confidence and savoir faire. During my next theft—a Russian fur cap at the town fair—I hesitated a bit too long. My heart skipped, my palms began to sweat. I did not know whether to put the cap back on the stand or not, but unwilling to concede that my career was over, I ran off with the cap. The stand keeper, whom I hadn't seen at all, ran after me. He was tall and athletic, growing taller at each step, and closer to me. I had the impression that all the marketplace was watching, that they all knew I was a lousy petty thief. Some shouted, "Catch him! Kick him! Box him! Maybe they did not shout, but in the noise of the market I was sure I heard all these angry voices. I was brimming with shame and fear. The man would catch me any moment now, and break my arm or smash my face. Sure enough, he caught up to me and tripped me. I flew over the gravel. He lifted me by my shirt, leaned into my face, and studied me, waiting for me to calm down, while I trembled from fright. He did not hit me. He took the cap from my hands, and saying nothing, walked away. He seemed to be saddened. His reaction amazed me, but it deepened my shame, for clearly this was a good man trying to make a living.

After this incident, I concluded that I was not clever enough to become a good criminal. Whether because of this debacle, or because of reading *Crime and Punishment* and falling in love with literature, or because of something else, I lost the moviegoing addiction. Occasionally I did watch movies, as a detached spectator, not as an imaginary participant.

A Whale's Throat

❧❧

My roommate Sultan introduced me to an old man at the Hungarian Pastry Shop. "This is Herr Franz Heim, one of the best living pianists." Sultan tended to exaggerate everything, so I didn't rush to be impressed. If there was a discussion about Italy, Sultan claimed to be not only Italian but a direct descendent of Petrarch; if about Spain, he was a descendent of Goya; if about Georgia, he was a Georgian prince; if about poor and oppressed Turks, his grandfather was a poor and oppressed Turk; if about Ukraine, why, Khrushchev was his uncle. So why now to believe that Franz Heim was a great pianist?

Sultan listened with humility to what Franz had to say. I couldn't make out what he did because of his thick German accent, but I was still impressed, by how he spoke—with emphasis, theatrically, with his hands, eyes—sitting upright as though in front of the piano. I asked him, "Do you miss Berlin?"

Heim sighed. "What a *wunderbar* city—I'd never visit it. Of course, I play German music every day, I erect the destroyed city in my memory."

"You should listen to him play," Sultan said to me. "Just lean your ear on the piano."

It snowed, Mr. Heim coughed and picked up his stick, and I decided not to ask for a private concert.

After meeting Mr. Heim, I spent six months like an old man—reading philosophy. What a luxury, to be an old man amidst your youth, and then to come back and say, I am still alive and I claim it! I would laugh in the spring—and then I'd listen to Mr. Heim's piano rumble and buzz, and he'd tell me something startlingly laconic and wise, in a distilled artistry of words of which only those who have spent their lives in thought are capable. At the university I missed the image of an old professor with a terse wisdom of Diogenes or Socrates. Instead, I saw many people with bad posture adjusting their glasses on their sweaty noses, losing places in the texts from which they quoted.

Actually, I had nearly forgotten Mr. Heim, until the day I met a woman pianist in the subway. The crowded F train was somewhere between and below Brooklyn and Manhattan. I read from *The Singer of Tales* about a young Bosnian peasant who quit work and married—so his wife would till the fields and support him while he studied the craft of singing and improvising epic poems. I laughed and, wishing to share the laugh, showed my neighbor the passage. She eagerly read and said, "I don't think it's funny. What does it tell about you that you do?"

"That I don't have your sense of humor." We talked.

She told me that her piano teacher was not only a teacher, but a guru to her—he taught her life through the piano. It turned out to be Mr. Heim, and his figure presided over our conversation, and over our date the weekend afterward. Our evening, instead of under the spell of our presences, was under the spell of an absence—a séance of admiring the pianist, the saint who taught the poor for free, and charged the rich one hundred dollars an hour.

Every morning at eleven o'clock Mr. Heim walked to a pizza place as punctual as Immanuel Kant on his rounds, and every evening at eight he walked to the Hungarian Pastry Shop and stood in front of it, gazing in, breathing hard, hesitating, and then he stepped in, to find his disciples, several young pianists, who listened to every word he said. When I saw him, he was usually on the other side of the street, and I did not want to impose. Would he remember me, anyway? I decided he would—that would flatter his memory, and me, and we'd live in the best possible world.

On a cool summer day, I took a walk with a friend of mine from India and his baby, and we ran into Franz waiting for his pizza. Ram worked as an investment banker, and it was a miracle—on a level with the immaculate conception—that he could spare a moment to see my new apartment. Though I had a deep respect for old age, I was in awe of babyhood, and so I walked on with my friend and his baby. The baby behaved quite well—didn't cry at all—and at one moment her father and I had enough cause to discuss seriously the possibility that she smiled or that she was contemplating the paradoxes of infinity as well as the limitations of paradoxes. We walked past the pizza place, and Mr. Heim was still there. I greeted him, and asked, "Do you remember me?"

"*Ja,* I remember you," he said. "You are . . . what do you do?"

While I looked for options how to answer or avoid answering, my countenance must have born a mask of humility, for Mr. Heim said, "So sorry—it's an impolite question."

"I study philosophy and theology."

"At the Union? What demon . . . denomination?"

"At Columbia, purely theoretical."

"What, theocracy?" Mr. Heim cupped his ear and then asked me to walk around him and talk into his better ear. He took out a wad of cotton—with an air of doing me a great favor, for he rarely honored non-musicians by opening his ear. "Let us go to my home, and I'll play for you a series of chords, I'll show you theocracy! But we'll need cream for coffee."

"I drink it black."

He raised his white eyebrows in surprise, and I remembered that when I met him I took cream in my coffee, but that was before my conversion to the anti-cholesterol religion.

"I too drink it black," he said proudly. "Has the bread come in yet?" he shouted to a Syrian shopkeeper, who answered, "In one hour."

"And the rolls? Are they fresh? You baked them?"

"My brother did." The shopkeeper pointed out an older version of himself cleaning his teeth with a toothpick.

"Then it must be good," Mr. Heim said. "You—not a factory—made it." And he stared at a curvy girl at the cash register. "And this is your daughter?"

"Yes."

"Then the bread must be excellent."

We walked out and Mr. Heim leaned on his stick and, having filled his big chest, said, "Lord, I love my neighbors!" with a terrifying vigor. "And where do you live?"

"One hundred and twelfth."

He pointed toward West End, the richer, more solid end of the street.

"No, that way," I said, "on Morningside."

"Ah, so we are neighbors. We have to be good to each other."

We walked past the Hungarian Pastry Shop, and there sat my roommates with a colleague, a complete string quartet. "We'll have coffee here before we go to my flat," Mr. Heim said. He seated himself, heavily, leaned his walking stick against the wall and the table, and admired a waitress, her clavicles, her neck and lips, and said to her, "If I were ten years younger, I would ask for your hand."

Eight of us—Franz Heim, the quartet, I, and a couple of Heim's disciples—walked up and down the windy Amsterdam Avenue in front of St. John the Divine. We huddled around Mr. Heim, holding on to our French berets, hats, jackets, so the wind wouldn't steal from us. "At my age," he said, "to see a beautiful woman, it's a huge thing. It keeps me alive."

"And philosophy?" asked an unshaven disciple.

"*Ach,* philosophy," he said with an air of deflation. "Philosophy keeps me old—and alive."

"And music?" I asked.

Mr. Heim didn't forget his promise that he would play for me; and besides me he invited the party to his apartment as though challenging them for a duel at the OK Corral.

We climbed the stairs of his building to the fourth floor. The front of him was convex, like Brahms' body, and he stepped heavily, wheezing, and wiped the sweat from his eyebrows, which had two levels: one high loop and one straight line. The high loop, like a roof, deflected the beads of sweat to roll down his sides and stumble into his white stubble, in front of his large hairy ears. His blue eyes beneath heavy eyelids seemed to breathe, expanding and contracting in the rhythm of his chest's heaving. The swollen circles under his eyes showed colossal exhaustion. Two bold creases sank down his cheeks from the nostrils past the lips pursed in the manner of Beethoven. Bluish hues emanated out of his lips as though he were cold, despite the summer—the winter was in his bones.

Before his apartment, he apologized for the mess we would see. "I am a bachelor. My stomach makes it hard to bow, so I don't pick up everything after myself, and I hate the idea of cleaning ladies—too much like servants."

Large curtains were drawn almost all the way in his living room, and the sunshine slid into the room most respectfully and gently, renouncing its usual summer boisterousness, and spreading its hairs over the brown carpet with a reddish glow, mostly yellowish, light, soft, intertwining in a subdued wind. Near the top of the ceiling, darkness found its refuge, comfortable, creating an aura of a firmament, a sky, that magnified the light below, giving it aura, depth. I was not aware of the angular, sextilateral nature of the room. The threadbare Persian carpet absorbed my steps. And along the wall ominously slumbered two brown pianos, one small and one big—like a son and his father. The father piano spread his opulent structure, like a piece of a Concorde that had flown between Europe and America and could now tell the oceanic tales. Mr. Heim wanted the string quartet to play first.

The young men played a Haydn quartet—the more they

studied, the more they respected the old—in a highly precise way. Mr. Heim interrupted them. "Enough. Too timid. Where are your balls?" He clenched his fist and shook his forearm. "With the vigor of a bull climbing a cow! *Ja*. Try now." They did. He was dissatisfied again. The conservatory students argued with him, in favor of technique, precision, discipline, restraint.

As Mr. Heim listened to them and made his points, five sharp creases undulated on his forehead with the waves of his upper brows. If he controverted what you said, the waves ruffled and rushed from left to right—the direction I read in. And when he made his point, the waves ran from right to left, the direction in which he, as a reader of ancient Hebrew, could think. The two waves crashed in the middle of his forehead, rising into a pillar. And at the end of discussion his creases straightened into the calm of an empty music sheet. But, scrutinizing his forehead, I noticed two moles making a long fifth. "You need character, all of you," he said to the string quartet.

"Character, what is character?" scoffed the ex-Soviet.

"Character is the way you simplify, cut through, get to the point. Maybe your nations can help you? There you have a ready-made character that can live through you—your ancestral culture has become your instinct. Let the instinct burst out. Tell me—all of you—your ethnic backgrounds." The roommates mentioned their nations and countries.

I was surprised when he reciprocated. "It would be too simple to say that I am a Jew. My father was a petty French bourgeois. My Dutch mother died giving birth to me. My father, angry at me, gave me up for adoption, and a petty German banker from Munich adopted me and raised me as a German. When Nazis started persecuting Jews, I converted to Judaism, out of protest. Circumcision at an adult age, without painkillers! *Ach!* I learned Hebrew, read the Talmud, I emigrated to New York, and here I've been ever since. And do I feel Jewish? Dutch? German? French? A German stepson, and a chosen Jew—not by God, by me. But, I don't believe in nations." He sighed and wiped his strained forehead. "Character. That's what you need. I have to show you."

In front of the piano was a long bench, over it a thin pillow, a seating mat. When Mr. Heim played, he slid over the seat toward the area of the general activity on the keyboard—he kept his arms close to his body, to concentrate his power. The arms were a part of his self, and not emissaries to be flung into the periphery, into the lonely provinces. His arms expressed his breath, his lungs, as though he were a singer. Actually, he hummed, humanizing the buzz of the chords, putting the pastel into the metal.

In the quiet between fragments, he sat straight, as a man without a nation, without fame, family, money, yet with the vigor that neither nation and family nor money and fame can buy—as though he himself were an independent country, a nation of one.

He played out a fragment from the "Sonata #111" by Beethoven—it sounded like jazz. "God revealed jazz to him, a century before it would happen!" he said.

Herr Heim sat humbly before the large piano—an oceanic monster, a gasping whale, with its nose flung in the air, teeth bare—begging it for mercy, in its very throat. And yet, despite the humility, the musical Jonah had the gall to pluck the strings right out of the whale's throat, helping it to explain its hunger. Pain seized his face. The strings shook him, made him tremble.

I stared as though I could see the music, and above his head, in darkness, I saw a lean mummified cat, an Egyptian three thousand years old. The resonating wood made the mummy move, slide, shake, as though it would come to life any moment and leap at a mouse hiding in Sultan's violin.

But the waves of terror subsided, and after a lyrical calm, in which the cat respected its being dead, they came back, first tiptoeing, and then stampeding. In some passages, the enemy's encampment was close at hand, and Mr. Heim was going to knead out of the enemy the last living breath, crush them. At other times, the tide reversed—as in *The Iliad,* where now the Trojans and now the Achaens gain the upper hand—and the whole bunch of the enemy pursued him, and he, running a fugue, shouted in terror. One more move, and they would throw a javelin through his one good ear and it would come out through his eye.

But, he went on bravely—no matter what eschatology would come out of the music—a murder, a suicide—he had to hear it out, to the end. Willfully, he struck the new chords, and waited ashiver for the answer. The strings had the power to electrocute him—with his own electricity. When he finished the last chord, he kept his hands above the keyboard, like a priest blessing a newborn child, while the piano, a large casket, echoed with eternal life.

Bread

☙❧

Cries of cricket wings came astride frogs' voices on damp winds and drowned in the grease of Ivan's ear, scratched the eardrum, bounced around in the cochlea, and entered through the eustachian tube into his throat, where the cries were hard to swallow, thick with the blood of the prisoners slain the night before. That his army, Croatian Home Guards, protected *ustasha* execution squads sickened him. As he paced around the storage barracks, his sweat glued his shirt to his skin, he shivered despite the heat as though he could shake off the clothes, the sweat, and even his skin, and emerge into a cleansed world.

"Tomo!" Ivan startled his sleepy fellow guard. "It's going to rain." He laughed although it was hard to laugh through the heavy phlegm of his throat. "Your nerves are thin! Don't worry, so are mine."

A blue lightning silently spread through the humid air.

"The Germans are beginning to lose in the East," Ivan said. "They'll drag us down to hell with them. Let's run away, save our asses!"

"But how? Where? Partisans shoot Home Guard deserters."

"That's what we are told so we won't run over."

Far away a steam engine train whistled, like an owl without a mate. Ivan's hands trembled as he wrapped some ham and a kilo of salt in a newspaper.

When the rain turned into a waterfall, as though a sea was sifted through a perforated sky, Ivan and Tomo ran across the soccer field outside the barracks. German shepherds neither smelled nor heard them. The deserters walked through a torrential ditch, through muddy cornfields, over the train tracks, into the sylvan mountains.

They walked all night. The morning was so lucid that they squinted at the mountain peaks near Zagreb eighty miles west, which resembled a hunter's cap without a feather. They sat on the outskirts of a whitewashed village, on the smooth bark of a thick beech that had apparently fallen that night—not because the winds had been powerful but because the waters had loosened the ground so much that the tree fell like a tooth pushed by the tongue out of an old abscess. The rain had washed the soil off the roots so that the blind, naked limbs silently groped in the air, black against the turquoise of the emptied sky. The deserters squeezed water out of their shirts and socks. Ivan took out the wrapped salt, which had become petrified in the wet newspapers, and rubbed smoked ham against the salty stone before he chewed the meat. He and Tomo gazed at old women in their black skirts and wooden shoes herding geese with sticks down the only street of the village. Noticing the men, the women crossed themselves. Soldiers, no matter from what army, meant a good likelihood of pillage, rape, drunkenness, and house burning. Tomo and Ivan picked up their rifles, clicked them ready, and said, "Calm down, we aren't going to shoot you."

Tomo went into the nearest house while Ivan stood guard outside. They went through several houses in this fashion, picking up two suits and two sheepskin jackets. Then they poured gasoline over their uniforms, burned them, and ran into the woods.

After wandering for two days they found a band of partisans. They buried their guns in the leaves and walked to the camp. The guards kept them at gunpoint and called the captain. The captain walked out of a tilting tent, picking his teeth with a thin branch, which he kept thinning with his thumbnail before having another go at his molar. His small narrowly set hazel eyes, made green by the forest, scrutinized Tomo's and Ivan's lips and teeth, as he interrogated them, as though the truthfulness of their words could be mirrored in their teeth. Ivan became self-conscious of his two silver incisors. Perhaps all would not have gone well if a partisan from Byelovar had not recognized them and said, "They are all right. Ivan Toplak is the town baker, and Tomo Starchevich, the basket weaver. I know them from the time when we pissed together making mud out of dust."

"What else do you know about them?" the captain asked.

"Ivan is some kind of new believer, I guess a Methodist, and Tomo is a gambler and whoremonger."

"Eh, that's no good," said the captain. "No need for God in this war. If there's one, he's hiding now, and then in peace, he'll come around and ask us for money. No, boys, that won't do. We got a new religion, us and freedom. Brotherhood and unity. What else?"

"After the German invasion, when *ustashas* burned down Serb Orthodox churches outside Byelovar, Ivan Toplak went around collecting protest signatures."

"You are a Serb?" The captain turned to Ivan. "Not enough of your people here—and we should be international."

"No, not a Serb—a Croat—but since I am a God-fearing man, I did not want to see any churches burn."

"All the churches should burn. And what else?"

"*Ustashas* looked for Ivan, but he fled into the woods, and that's the last I heard of him." The man either did not know that Home Guards captured Ivan one night at home and conscripted him, or he did not want to make it harder for Ivan to be accepted. Probably the latter, for he winked at Ivan after he'd finished telling.

"And you, what was your name?" The captain kept talking. "Tomo the Whoremonger? That's all right with me, but remember, no rape, not while I am in charge. Hmm, Ivan the Baker, you say—why not a smith, or something more vigorous?"

"Why not?" Ivan said. "During the Depression, blacksmiths had more apprentices than they needed. I really wanted to become a doctor, but I had to quit school after fourth grade to help support my younger siblings. My parents convinced me that being a barber would be almost like being a doctor—so at first, before becoming a baker, I was a barber. I learned the trade in a couple of months so that when my boss went bingeing in the taverns he'd let me run the shop. It was all right until one day when my neighbor Ishtvan came along for a shave. I place a white apron around his neck, sharpen the switchblade on leather, and lather him up nicely."

"All right, all right, speed up the story, we all know what barbers do—so what?" The captain grumbled.

"Foam touches Ishtvan's hairs, which stick half an inch out of his nose, and he sneezes.

"'Do you want your nose hairs cut or plucked?' I ask. He does not answer but sneezes again, blowing the foam down all over the shop.

"'*Gesundheit!*' I say."

"No German words allowed here," the captain interrupted. "Don't do it again!"

"All right, 'God bless you!' I say."

"No, that won't do," the captain said. "No God around here, isn't that clear once and for all?"

"But," Ivan was losing his temper, "I am trying to tell you how it was. Ishtvan sneezes again, for the third time. I say 'To your health, neighbor Ishtvan! May you outlive many wives!' But Ishtvan does not say 'Thank you!' though he is a famously polite man. Instead he keeps his hand in front of his nose. He waits for the sneeze to come up and out. After he hasn't sneezed a minute later, I say, 'Should I hit your back?' As I raise my hand, his hand drops in his lap. His head nods to one side. I take a look at him and shake him, until I realize that he's dead. I fetch his wife. She runs in and says, 'He's going to get rid of his mustache? Is that what the fuss is about?'

"'Just look at him,' I say. 'Don't you see? He's dead!'

"The woman gasps, and shouts 'Oh my God! *Wie schrecklich!*'"

"I warned you!" the captain said.

"So I ask the lady, 'What should we do? Should we carry him back?'

"'Wait, what should I do, what do you say? Tell you what, why don't you finish the shave?'

"'But what good will that do?'

"'A lot of good,' she says. 'He'll need a clean shave for his wake.'

"She liked the shave so much that she made me promise that during the wake I'd give him two to three more shaves because the hairs of the dead grow fast. As soon as we carried him back home, I closed the shop and ran off. Not that I was horrified or anything—actually, I was so surprised by how calmly I took it that a guy died while I worked on him that I thought I should become a doctor. But I did not want to be a barber!"

"So, in other words, you deserted," the captain said, "A bad sign, a very bad sign." But the partisans, drinking, swearing, and laughing overshadowed the captain's comment.

The mood was festive. An unattended herd of pigs ran down the mountain slope, as mad as the pigs possessed by demons that ran into the Sea of Galilee and drowned. Partisans shot several. They found it hard to start a fire because all the wood was wet. Tomo suggested that they strip the pork-belly fat because it would burn like gasoline. After they put the fat and a sheepskin jacket among the branches, the fire caught on and sent up a cloud of smoke and steam so that the meat was both burned and steamed. The soldiers ate heavily, soaking bread in the grease that dripped into pots, and drank plum brandy, sang, told jokes. There was so much grease that they polished their shoes and greased their guns with it.

They feasted for four days. Ivan was scandalized by the disarray of the army—clearly they avoided combat but talked about imaginary battles, which grew greater and greater day by day.

One morning Ivan sat on a rock in the sun and read his Bible. The captain snatched it. "Why were you so stingy? We could have started the fire with your book! My, what silky pages! Good, I'll use it to roll my cigarettes." And he tore a hundred leaves, and tossed the rest into the glowing coals beneath a piglet. The paper burned blue and, as the fat dripped over it, changed to red, hissing. When the Bible had burnt, the ashes retained its shape; Ivan could see between the fine pages into the pink middle. A slight breeze shifted the ashen pages of the book as though it wanted to open to the right page to find its golden verse, the guide for the day, which would tell it where and how to blow next. And then one large drop of fat fell on the silhouette of the Bible, piercing a hole through it. The ghost of the book collapsed into flimsy ashes. Above the camp the transparent gray paper floated, the millennial letters falling apart midair.

Just as the biblical words had all scattered around the camp and fallen softly on the trampled ground, the partying mood came to a close. Two couriers informed the captain that a detachment of Germans and *ustashas* had taken Raven's Peak and built a bunker there.

The captain said, "We have to take the bunker, that's all there's to it."

At night the partisans marched through beech, pine, and oak forests, crackling branches and sliding over last year's leaves that had rotted but hadn't turned to soil yet. After they set up their position in a cave, the captain selected three soldiers—Ivan and two other novices who had come over from the Home Guard—to creep up to the bunker and take the machine-gun nest. "Go up and prove yourself. If you bring back the machine guns, I'll know you aren't bullshitting." (Tomo was not chosen for the perilous task because he had already proved himself as a soldier of integrity with his arsenal of bawdy jokes and appetite for brandy.) On a misty morning, as low clouds drifted beneath the peak, and the forest steamed under the sun, the three soldiers crawled up the mountain.

Ivan was enraged. If he succeeded, the captain would get the credit. If Ivan failed, the captain would continue to party, as though nothing had happened, while Ivan would be left dead to rot like the last year's leaves. As they crawled up the slopes, they caught glimpses of a machine-gun barrel sticking out, like the damning finger of an iron god above the clouds. The finger pointed far above them, to the horizon. When Ivan was a hundred yards away from the bunker, the machine-gun barrel turned toward him. He fired at it. A series of bullets came out from the bunker, in smoke and steam. Ivan rolled down the slope, like a child over a meadow, except that there were stones sticking out of the grass here, but that did not matter. Death was after him, casting lead and fire. A bullet struck him on his left side. He rolled on, wondering whether he was still conscious. The sensation that he was losing it, that he was hit, comforted him. No more of this. Bullets swished the brush and tall grass, cracking stones, sinking into tree bark. A verse resounded in his head: *The earth is utterly broken down, the earth is clean dissolved . . . The earth shall reel to and fro' like a drunkard.* One of his comrades rolled past him, red, missing his face. Ivan stood up and ran, feeling no ground. He was not running back to the partisan positions, but away from both the bunker and the cave.

He stopped to examine his wet wound; the bullet had blasted away his skin, a layer of fat, and the muscles above his left hip. He tore a sleeve off his jacket and held it tight over the wound, but the jacket kept drinking his blood the way an inkblotter draws ink out of a fountain pen.

Should he run back to Bjelovar? That would not do. He had deserted two armies, and the soldiers of both might soon be looking for him. Should he look for another army? No, he'd had it with armies. But could he make it alone? He wished he had his Bible on his body, although he wondered whether his religion had misled him in these dark woods. He walked into a pine forest, with a magnificent calm in its cool darkness. Treading softly, he stepped over the carpet of pine needles half a foot deep and, light-headed, inhaled the aromatic air.

Beyond the woods, he crawled into a deserted, burned village. He crept into a house and fell asleep in ashes. Several days later a wet sensation on his forehead and eyebrows awakened him. A purring cat was licking him. He was not sure whether he was awake—and he did not resist the raspy tongue, which now covered his eyelids and pushed them open. That seemed to please the cat, so that she ceased to lick him and rolled up against the side of his face, warmly purring, instilling the rhythm of life into his neck. He tried to move, but a thick pain in his left kidney dissuaded him. He felt his side—a rough crust covered his wound. There was no wet blood there anymore, no great swelling, no abscess. Lying in a burned-out house helped because there weren't many bacteria around, and so there was no danger of gangrene, he thought, though he was not sure what exactly caused gangrene. Was the cat dangerous for his wound? Did she lick it, too? Now the cat licked and tickled his ear as though to tell him, You'll never know.

When he got up, the cat walked into the yard toward a large brick bread oven. She lifted her tail straight up, letting the tip of it wiggle out a code of satisfaction. She invited him to a nook where she must have spent her days.

In the woods Ivan gathered wild strawberries, mulberries, cherries, wild onions, and mushrooms of all kinds. In the bushes he found a nest of lark eggs, and made an omelette.

When the tabby cat vanished at night, he missed her purr. He woke up to a choir of nightingales, which had flooded the forest with a brilliant melody. The cat appeared after sunrise, dragging a young rabbit nearly her size, to the oven. He started a fire with two stones and hay, and roasted the rabbit. He felt a little selfish doing it, until the cat caught a nightingale and ate it ostentatiously. The following morning Ivan sharpened several twigs, and went down, below the village, to the creek, which was so slow that it formed a pond. The cat loved sharing carp with him.

The summer went quickly. Leaves began to turn red and cold winds blew from Hungary. He would have perhaps managed to spend the winter in the village, had the sounds of gun battles not come close. Detonations, machine-gun fires, air strikes burnt the life several miles away from him and drifted in dry, biting smoke. From a crack in his oven one day he saw partisans walking through the village, and a day later, Germans, and on the third day, Serb Royalists, Chetniks. Alone, he would be a sitting duck for these armies in the winter—but despite that, he might have stayed, had his cat not vanished. He wondered whether soldiers had shot her.

Walking westward, outside a village, he found a Golgotha monument. The statues of Christ and the two robbers were torn off and thrown onto thick heather on the side of the road, and instead of them, three corpses were nailed to the crosses. Two were circumcised Muslims, and the third, occupying the place of the talkative thief, was a Catholic, with a tattoo of the Virgin Mary on his forearm. Now and then their blood, still turning brown, emitted a sparkle of ruby red in the sun. Every head had a hole in the pate—a Chetnik signature—with a thick trail of blood curling around the neck onto the chest.

Near another village, in a pit of dried mortar, Ivan saw corpses of ten young men, stomachs slashed. Their murderers had thrown them with open wounds into the wet mortar to be eaten by it. The bodies turned into white sculptures, their fists sticking up, groping for the bank, for tree roots.

Ivan avoided people and stayed in haystacks—and when he couldn't find any, in ditches, even in late November, when a terrible winter gripped the continent with an excessive ferocity. Near Chazma, his shivering eyes bulging, Ivan plucked ice out of his beard, and daydreamingly recollected glimmers of his childhood: Every Sunday after church when he was thirteen he would walk in a field, where a shepherdess bared her breasts and let him squeeze them with his tremulous hands. Now the recollection protected him from ice until he fainted.

That night he was caught by Home Guard soldiers. They wrapped him in a rough woolen blanket and drove him to their barracks in Zagreb. They gave him hot tea with aspirin, which dissolved in his throat before he could swallow it, and there it spread its dusty bitterness of bleached charcoal, a mock Eucharist, which recalled the ten slain men metamorphosed into mortar sculptures. Pneumonia filled Ivan with fevers and nightmares, and he replied to no questions and no answers, until he saw the sun in the spring and recovered. By that time, several Home Guard soldiers had recognized him. The guards kept him in jail for three months, and after that, employed him in their bakery.

In 1945 as the Red Army advanced from the East and the partisans from the South and the North, many Home Guards deserted to join the partisans or to hide, but Ivan stayed. A colonel gave him a rifle to be a regular soldier once again. And so when thousands of partisans surrounded his garrison, and his regiment surrendered because of a promise of amnesty, Ivan became a captive of the army he had once served.

At gunpoint, he climbed into a cargo train among many soldiers. The train went through Maribor to Austria. A partisan had told them that Croatian armies would be handed over to the British and French troops, who would treat them according to the Geneva POW Convention.

But as the prisoners exited from the trains into a field, fire from a hundred machine-guns strafed them down. Partisan officers on tractors ploughed the twitching corpses into the soil, disking it over and over again. When it was Ivan's turn to step out, the machine-gun fires quit. Partisans pushed bayonets into the captives' ribs, and said, "You want to go home? Fine, we'll show you your home, croaking Croats." A partisan pumped a machine-gun round into the group of captives, as if to punctuate the speech, but nobody fell to the ground, because the captives were so squeezed that those who were bleeding to death remained standing among them.

For two hundred miles—from Maribor, through Krizevci, Virovitica—the prisoners were forced to march. Whoever asked for water or leaned on a fence along the way was bayoneted and left in a ditch, his eyes spooned out or ears cut off.

The second day was scorchingly hot. The partisans sang. Many disappeared in the villages they passed, to chase girls into the woods, wink at them, court them, and if that did not work, to rape them.

By the time the captors and the captives reached Vocin, one half of the captives had perished. The old partisans left, and the new ones joined.

At dusk, a partisan poked his bayonet into Ivan's kidneys, on the healed side. "Long time no see!" Tomo, his old comrade, laughed. "How in the hell did you get stuck here? I thought you were dead and gone. I bet you wish you were!" Ivan did not say anything. Tomo passed an open bottle of *slivovitz* under Ivan's nostrils. This style of torment was the usual—a cheerful soldier tantalizing a POW of his choice—so that nobody paid any attention to Tomo's pushing, jostling, and nudging Ivan: not even Ivan did until Tomo slid a flask of water into Ivan's pocket. When clouds covered the moon, Ivan gulped all the water and tossed the flask during a crack of thunder.

The clouds grumbled, cleared their throats, but did not spit out a drop of rain. They gathered low, furrowed, trapping heat and moisture, making the air musty. In the morning Ivan sweat, salt from his forehead sliding into his eyes and biting them as though they were open wounds, and that they were, with dust specks, gnats, sand, grating them almost as much as did the sight of his colleagues collapsing, with partisans crushing their heads with the wood of the rifles, brains flowing out like borscht.

By noon of the new day his lips were cracked dry and swollen. The villages they passed seemed deserted, for the survivors hid as though witnessing the procession would be a horrendous burden to carry into peace—peace that was upon the land, blown from Russia, as a putrid stench, and from America and Britain, as a deodorant—and beyond peace, to the grave, to hell.

As the partisans grew thoroughly drunk another night, several

POWs managed to sneak out of this Trail of Crosses, but Ivan did not try. He trudged on, stumbling over stones. The insides of Ivan's groins bled from the constant friction and sweat, but that may not be right, for by now there was no sweat because he was so dehydrated. He could barely swallow whatever was in his throat, but it was not spittle, it was dust.

At night he tried to urinate, stealthily taking out his penis. Nothing came out, except scorching pains, burning from his kidneys down his penis, into his fingers. He put his penis back and remembered how, as a little boy, he loved to piss in public, even in the churchyard, until his mother taught him modesty. He had just pulled out his winnie, proudly, when she said: "Put it right back. A cat will snatch it and eat it like a sardine." After that, he used bathrooms. This memory made him smile and his smile widened the cracks in his lips so that blood oozed down his stubbly chin.

The captives made it to Osijek, where they were allowed to eat beans. The partisans waited for a two-day storm—a tremendous outpouring—to end, and then they pursued their captives for 150 miles more, to Popovacha.

Past a burned-out and gutted steel mill, the decimated regiment of Home Guards stumbled through a field of craters that bombs had dug. Water filled the craters, out of which rough-skinned gray frogs leaped as beating hearts that had deserted the bodies of warring men and now roamed the doomed landscape. Ivan found the sudden leaps of so many hearts out of the gray earth unsettling. He could not see any of them, until they were in the air, so that it seemed to him that the earth was spitting up useless hearts and swallowing them back into the mud.

In Popovacha, having made the whole stretch, Ivan swooned and collapsed. After he recovered in a Zagreb hospital as much as was in the power of his damaged kidneys, he was drafted into the Yugoslav People's Army for a correctional service of two years, as a baker, for even this army loved bread.

Bruno

☌☌

1948
Hrastovac, Croatia

At the Kamenars, there was a festivity. Pero Kamenar had just returned from serving in the reserves of the Yugoslav Federal Army.
He had been stationed on the Danube along the Romanian border; since Tito's break with Stalin there was a constant threat of
Soviet invasion.

"I tell you, my dears, when I saw across the river hundreds of
tanks aiming at us, and a green square lake of soldiers on the march,
I was sure I'd never see you again. I'm amazed that I'm here!"

He drank the last swallow of pale brandy, rakia. Neda, his wife,
brought out a jug of steaming milk, fresh from the cow, who was
still mooing, perhaps from the surprise of being milked that late
in the day. And along with the low moo, there was a high one—
the calf was probably protesting being deprived of her afternoon
meal. "Too bad we don't have a lamb to roast for you," Neda said.
"We've even run out of chicken and geese. Nothing left to roast."

"To tell you the truth, I prefer our milk. Beats the beans we
had every day."

He sliced a bundle of garlic and mixed it with cool white cottage cheese, poured paprika over it and salted it, and ate it. His dark eyes watered. His long, gaunt face turned red. The skin around his eyes glowed so that the irregular dry creases around them vanished for the time being. "That's life!" he exclaimed and broke a thick slice of brown bread into pieces, which he dipped in the milk and chewed slowly. "And how are my boys doing?" He slapped Toni, an owly eight-year-old, with broad cheeks, and a little hooked nose—his and Neda's son. Then he glanced at Bruno, a pale ten-year-old with a large cowlick and a wide nose. Bruno came from Pero's first wife, who had died of typhoid fever. "You look mighty thin. You don't like that cow of ours?"

"Oh, he does," said Neda defensively. "It's amazing how much milk this boy can gulp down. Stand up, show your dad how tall you've gotten."

Bruno didn't say anything, but he stood up, aware of his big knees and thin bones. He was shy—this father of his, for whom he had been waiting for months, was now a stranger to him—much louder and somehow less genuine, less believable.

His father pinched him on the cheek and pressed a slobbering kiss over his eyebrows. Bruno wiped the kiss away with his forearm and blushed.

"This milk, that's something else. If we sell our little forest and buy several cows and a bull, pretty soon we could have a big milking operation. That would be better than my lousy lumberjacking. " He stood up and pushed a split log into the brick oven. "But then, this wood has its uses too." Smoke came out of a crack in the bricks before the fire caught on, and then no more smoke came out; the wood crackled in the flames.

Sitting next to the stove, Bruno sweated and coughed. His father looked at him critically and Bruno covered his mouth and suppressed another wave of coughing that was coming. "The smoke irritates you? Tomorrow we'll cut some trees and chop them, so you'll feel like a man, you'll see." He tickled his son under the ribs. "You've become all effeminate in my absence!"

"Let's play chess," Bruno said to Toni, and Toni said, "Tomorrow. I want to hear our dad's stories."

Bruno yawned and went to sleep under a thick down cover in the little room he shared with his brother.

At night, Toni woke him up. "Listen," he said. "Our mom is having nightmares or Dad's choking her or something."

They listened. Their mother moaned, father groaned, the bed squeaked.

"They are having fun, that's all," Bruno said and laughed.

Soon the house was quiet again. Toni snored—an amazing snore for a kid. For a long time Bruno couldn't fall asleep—the sounds of his father and stepmother making love disturbed him and strangely exhilarated him, and he didn't know whether it was because of that excitement or something else that he found it hard to breathe. He had to think of breathing, or else, he had the feeling the breath wouldn't take place. He didn't dare draw a deep breath and he trembled minutely. When he fell asleep, he had nightmares—he was hanging from a gate frame, on a rope, while soldiers sang a joyous hymn in a high pitch. With his hands he tried to free his neck, but the rope was too tight, and he kept choking while the pitch of the hymn rose into a prickly buzz.

"Get up. Milk the cow!" came a voice. He thought this was still the dream, and the oddity of the request that he, who was hanging from a gate, should milk the cow, perhaps more than the fright of the nightmare, woke him.

"No time to waste!" said the stepmother.

But Bruno couldn't get up. His muscles ached, he trembled. Neda pulled him up, threw an overcoat over him, slid wooden shoes on his feet that dangled over the edge of the hay-mattress bed, opened his squeezed fists, and pressed the wire handle of a lantern into his palms. The flame in the lantern wavered, and from the side, Neda's little eyes blinked hazel under her scarf, and her shadow darted jerkily over the whitewashed ceiling, like the profile of an eager and blinking eagle. Bruno gripped the lantern.

"What's the matter with you?" the stepmother said.

"It's cold."

"No, it's not. I put wood in the stove." She pushed Bruno out of doors into the chill of the fall twilight.

In the cow pen Bruno put the lantern on a log and sat on a three-legged chair; one leg kept sinking through the soggy soil. As he couldn't support his weight, he leaned against the taut and warm belly of the cow. Past the cow's side, he saw a worried calf—a beautiful dark red animal with a white forehead—peeping through wood planks from another stall. Bruno relaxed and stretched his hands to the cow teats, and pulled, alternating, now one, now the other. Milk squirted with a shush into the wooden bucket, and the steamy smell of rich fresh milk climbed between his chin and the cow's belly. He usually loved the smell—sometimes even squirted the milk directly into his mouth—but now it made him wretchedly and retchingly nauseated. He slid below the cow's belly and knocked down the bucket of milk. He thought that he was passing out—he hoped that he was because he couldn't stand this weakness and nausea—but as he stretched in the steamy and stale hay, he realized that he was terribly lucid, the way one is supposed to be before the moment of death, while falling, or just before being hit by a train. Now he could be squashed by the huge cow, shifting above him in her disenchantment and irritation that her teats had been teased and left full to the bursting. The cow mooed a slow moo, and this moo, Bruno imagined, spoke—I've had enough feeble human hands, give me my calf, with her strong mouth, to free me from all this milk. The famished calf yelled out and tried to climb the fence.

Bruno crawled from beneath the cow gingerly.

His stepmother shouted from the door. "Oh Heavens, you spilled the milk! How could you? How will we buy bread?"

"Those are good questions," said Bruno. "I fell. I don't know how. "

"And how do you think we're all going to feel if we starve? Get up! Back to the cow!"

"Don't torture the boy!" his father shouted on the porch

beneath cracked gray wooden beams, blowing out the haze of his morning pipe. "He must be ill."

He came over and carried Bruno back to bed. "Some milk?" he said.

"Where would we get that?" Neda said.

"How, where? There's more in Milkitza. "

"And who'll milk her?" Neda said. "I'm sure it won't be you."

"How come you're always right?" said Pero and laughed merrily although this didn't seem to be a happy occasion, but almost anything was bound to be better than a new eastern front.

"No, I don't want milk," Bruno said. Seated in the house, leaning his elbows on the table and supporting his head with his palms, he declined rose-hip tea.

"Milk is life," repeated the stepmother. "Only if you drank more, you wouldn't be so thin."

Bruno burped up some milk and groaned in bed, unable to vomit.

When he felt better, he drew tiny drawings in pencil—since he couldn't get much paper—realistic and precise pictures of cats, dogs, horses, and the village faces.

"That's wonderful," said Pero, "but it would be even more wonderful if you ate."

Bruno was surprised that now he could draw better than usual, as though his illness had given him endurance for painstaking concentration.

Later in the day a doctor from the nearby town visited in a yellow ambulance with red crosses. Bruno saw the car from the window. A tall thin doctor without ears—they had been cut off in the war—showed up in his room, took off his hat, and placed it on the bed post. He felt Bruno's temperature on his forehead and then insisted on taking it anally. Neda pinned Bruno down. Bruno kicked the doctor, and now they were trying it again, when Pero came in. "What's the ruckus?"

"He won't let the doctor take his temperature!"

"What kind of temperature taking is this?" Pero asked. "Anybody would be feverish under this pressure!" He laughed. "Isn't it good enough to put the thermometer in his armpit?"

"No," said the doctor. "He's running a high fever, and the most precise measurement, unfortunately, can be obtained from the anus."

"Isn't temperature only a symptom, and you already know that he's got it?"

"Temperature, of course, is an accompanying symptom but it can also be the cause of all sorts of troubles—even death."

"He's not dying. The two of you can't subdue him."

The doctor looked into Bruno's throat with a flashlight, depressing his tongue with a light aluminum spoon. He pressed one finger on Bruno's back and knocked at it with another. "Hm, no hollow spots, that's good, but perhaps the sound's too dull; hopefully the lungs aren't filled up." Then he listened with a stethoscope and asked Bruno to breathe deeply.

"Bronchial disturbances. Now can you cough? Cough!"

Bruno did.

"Do you have a white towel, a sheet?" asked the doctor and turned around toward the kitchen.

"Of course we do!" said Neda, as though this question insulted her. She brought out a white bedsheet.

"May I tear the edge of it?" The doctor asked, and without waiting for an answer, tore a foot-wide strip and cut it in half.

"All right. Cough again, clear your throat, and spit in this sheet."

Bruno did as he was told.

The doctor inspected it. "No blood in the sputum." He folded the sheet and placed it in a metal box that he brought along with his black bag.

"Now, can you blow your nose?"

Bruno did.

The doctor stared at the green snot with streaks of blood in the shiny sluggish pathways. He folded the sheet too, and put it together with the other one in the box.

He drew blood from Bruno's forearm into a little vial. "We should know in a week what it is. But for now, since it's most likely a bacterial infection, we need a shot of penicillin." He took out a large syringe and fitted a thick needle on it. "It won't hurt. Now, bare just a bit of your behind." Even Pero helped to hold Bruno and stripped his threadbare pajamas down. The doctor slid the needle into the left buttock while Bruno screamed. "We're almost done," said the doctor and slowly kept squeezing the liquid into the flesh while grinding his teeth. When he withdrew the needle, he placed white gauze soaked in pure alcohol over the bleeding skin.

Bruno drank a glass of water with two aspirin tablets. The tablets got stuck in his throat and melted there, becoming bitter chalk powder. Through tears he saw the disfigured features of the assembly of adults closing in on his body. He tried to kick them, but as his foot flew in the empty space, he realized that the adults were not as close as they had appeared through his tears, and their features were not even disfigured, for they were neither frowning nor smiling but looking at him intently.

The doctor was one of those people who couldn't whisper, so while he was attempting to keep his voice down, it still carried through the walls, and Bruno heard it. "He's got pneumonia. Whether pneumonia is a secondary illness here, I can't tell yet, but for now, don't let him go out and mix with people. I'll need to draw your blood samples too."

"What could it be?" said Neda.

The doctor didn't say anything. Nobody said anything any more, but even Bruno, though only ten years old, knew the feared unspoken disease, and "could it be" echoed as "TB." TB or not TB.

With that consonance in his ears, he coughed loudly with paroxysms, as though he had just got the license to do so. He shivered with pride as he coughed—self-important, for he partook of the terrors of fate, despite his youth. He wished the wind that rasped through his throat were even louder, and that like a gun the blasts of air could kill at least the doctor. And then he understood that they probably could kill.

At night Bruno heard his father's radio—he listened to the short waves, Voice of America in Slavic languages and various German radio stations, because he was obsessed with the movements of the Soviet army.

Bruno fell asleep and woke up at night with the same nightmare of hanging, surrounded by singing soldiers, and in the soldiers' uniforms were his father, the doctor, and many people with mustaches. Trying to fall asleep again, he buried his face in the down pillow and muffled his coughs.

Bruno woke up before dawn in wet pillows that were sticky with his coughs and droolings. Though he didn't like to be seen in his misery, he waited for company. In twilight he walked out to the cow and leaned against her warm belly to get some heat. The cow sighed, steam came out of her nostrils, and she gently rubbed her side against him, perhaps wishing that he were the calf, who was separated from her. When Bruno was leaving, she looked at him with glassy and liquid eyes calmly. He walked back and coughed into the feathers in the dank down pillow—he coughed his sorrow into the plucked sorrows of geese.

Pale and disgusted he waited for hot tea, made bitter by aspirin. His stepmother woke up after him, and she understood it to be her duty to impale him with the long and oval mercury thermometer stick. He refused the first morning, but the second he felt particularly weak and willingless, and he let her roll him over and push, and even though it hurt, he didn't object, but waited for the trouble to pass. That pain was minor compared with his chest pains and worries.

Later that second morning, he sat up in bed and looked out the window. Toni was out on a grassy slope (the grass was green and young with a second life)—in Bruno's overcoat, which dragged on the ground, in the mud—cowherding Milkitza and her calf. Milkitza grazed slowly, while the calf, her head tilted, nudged the teats with her wet and pink nose. She pushed so hard that the cow's large belly swung.

In the afternoon, his father brought him a box of watercolors and brushes with a lot of paper.

"Thank you, Dad," he said. "This must be expensive."

"Not too bad. I just won't smoke for a month."

"Can that be done?"

"You should have clean air to breathe anyhow. Maybe we'll figure a way to move to the Slovenian Alps or Gorski Kotar."

Snow fell early that evening and it snowed all night in slow, large, and blue flakes. The next morning, Toni, who now slept in the room with his parents for fear of catching Bruno's disease, went out sledding with other village kids. Bruno watched, his head leaning against the window of old glass that in places elongated and thinned images and in others fattened them, in waves. He rolled his forehead over the window, enjoying the undulating changes in his view. His forehead bumps left grease spots above his eye level. With his breath he hazed up the image of children sledding so that for a while the scene appeared as though the children were up in the clouds falling through with the snow. He was tempted to envy the children, but realized he had no desire to sled; the thought of snow melting behind the collar of his shirt onto his back sent a violent shudder through him. He preferred drawing the scene in watercolors, against the background of a Catholic church, which he saw, and of a funeral procession, which he imagined, with red horses drawing a sled-hearse through a sparse alley of bumpy-limbed and trimmed lindens. Each tree had a couple of thin soldiers hanging and dozens of crows pecking on them.

The doctor was back four days after his initial visit. He talked to Pero outside, but again so loudly that even Bruno heard what he knew must be the case with him anyhow, that it was TB.

He gave Bruno another penicillin shot—in a ceremony of violence, sticking the needle in the buttocks. "It's not the perfect medicine but it will prevent many secondary infections from developing. Americans have developed a great medicine, streptomycin, but we don't have it here yet, and it would be very expensive."

"How about the rest of us? Are we ill too?" asked Neda.

"No, he's the only one. I think he's vulnerable because he's so thin. Even now, the best therapy for him is to eat a lot of protein. You have milk?"

"Jesus, do we have milk! You want to see our cow?"

"Actually, I do."

They walked to the sty, and the doctor picked up an aluminum bucketful of fresh milk and cheerfully drove away in the yellow ambulance.

Pero sought streptomycin in Zagreb, but he couldn't find it. At home on the short waves, on a Swiss radio station, he heard that the Swiss government had offered a supply of streptomycin to Tito, to help curb TB, but Tito replied that Yugoslavia had everything and that it needed nothing. Pero was enraged. He went to a bar and got drunk and reported the story to the drunken patrons.

As a consequence of that, several days later, three policemen came to the Kamenar house and arrested Pero. He was sent to a penal colony, the Goli Otok (the Naked Island) in the Adriatic, for malicious spreading of false information and for undermining the Proletarian Revolution. In climate, the island may sound much better and balmier than Siberia, but in practice, with brutal guards and heavy labor, it was a match for the Soviet penal colony—and one's saying that openly warranted one's being sent to the island colony.

One morning as his stepmother was about to take his temperature, Bruno got a hard-on while she undressed him and with her cold hands pressed his buttocks aside and squeezed one thigh. He lay on his side. Neda laughed. "At least he looks healthy. Do you play with him?"

He covered his penis, and said, "What do you mean?"

"Big boys often do. They squeeze it and pull at it."

"What for?"

She pulled the thermometer out of him and rolled it around in her fingers against the petroleum lamp. "Hum, it's at 41 Celsius again. Poor boy."

Another time when he got a hard-on, she asked him whether he'd played with it. He said he still didn't know what she meant by playing with it, and she said, "Well, I'm not going to show you. You'll figure it out soon enough."

She leaned over him to get the teacup on the other side of the bed, and her breasts came out of her poorly buttoned shirt, and brushed over his face. On her way back, her breasts stroked his cheeks again. He felt warm in her bosom. Even when she stood back with the cup, he sat up and tremulously leaned his cheeks onto her breasts, listening to the beating of blood in his ears or in her, he couldn't tell, and after that he'd be pleasantly dizzy for several minutes. From then on, she let him lean like that many times. On such occasions, he loved being weak and sick and cared for, like a baby and, illicitly, like a man, but not like a young boy. Though his illness, he was everything but himself.

Bruno's health grew worse. Fresh bright-red blood appeared in his sputum. By the end of January he had wasted away and was close to death.

One day, a grim and tall doctor, with a high forehead, thin lips, and sad, heavily eyelidded lightless eyes, came accompanied by a short French UNICEF doctor. "Could we see your son?" he asked Neda.

She showed them in. "Where is our old doctor?" she asked.

"Oh, he came down with TB himself. Actually, he's already dead."

"You think he picked it up here?"

"It usually takes a while for the disease to kill you. Anyway, there are so many places with TB, it's almost a plague. But everything is possible; he may have gotten it here."

Bruno was drawing pictures and muttering to himself, sunken with bulging eyes. Everybody in his pictures was emaciated and elongated, like in El Greco's paintings. He was drawing a picture with several altars, and at each altar, there was a thin and tall Abraham look-alike, not with a customarily thick beard, but with a goatee, and with his bony hand up in the air to stab a goat but the Abrahams had no knives in their hands, and some, instead of goats, had calves spread out on wood piles. The angels, instead of holding the hands back to prevent the slaughter, were rushing down from the sky, and some were already at hand, passing large daggers into the hands.

"Wow, that's marvelous," said the grim doctor. "And where are the Isaacs?"

"They are the angels."

"Does that mean that they are already dead or that they are saving themselves from death like this?"

"I don't know. "

"Hum," the doctor said and studied the painting, with his finger pressing against his canine. He turned to Neda. "Mrs. Kamenar, your son is an unconscious genius, the only kind there is. I'd like to buy this painting from you, young man. What do you ask for it?"

"Streptomycin."

"You know everything. That's why we are here. We have brought it for you."

"Really? Is that true?" Bruno cried. "Does it work?"

"Yes, we'll give you your first shots in a minute and then an even better drug, PAS, a Swedish miracle. Together the two drugs will cure you in two to three months, I am sure. And what do you want for the painting?"

"Are you serious? I can't believe it."

"Of course, of course."

And he turned to the Frenchman, who watched the paintings with admiration, and exchanged several sentences in French.

"I asked him whether the paintings would work for UNICEF

and he says that they are a bit too morbid for that, but he, too, would like a painting from you. How much do you want?"

"I'll give you all of my paintings. I don't want to look at them."

The doctors looked through his collection. The grim doctor handed Bruno a bundle of banknotes in the color he had never seen in money before, purple. "Enough to buy yourself buckets of paint and bushels of sausages!"

Bruno, who usually hated injections, welcomed them. "In order to keep up with the treatment, we'll take you to Zagreb. You are one of the first people in the country to get them."

"How did you choose me?"

"We can't tell."

In the hospital, in Zagreb, by February, Bruno had almost fully recovered.

Neda and Toni visited him. While he drank tea from Neda's hands he blushed. They didn't look each other in the eye; he was himself again, a nearly healthy boy, who no longer had the privileges of stepping over the boundaries between boyhood and infancy and adulthood. Neda had a story to tell him. "You know, the calf died. It got thin and just wasted away. It had all sorts of diseases, and the vet says it didn't die of TB. He tested the calf for TB, and she had the TB bacteria, and so does the cow. The vet thinks you got it from the cow's milk. "

Several days later, Pero showed up in the hospital, his head shaved, with a big knife cut over his face, but glowingly happy. He had a letter of pardon from Tito, in which Tito thanked him for drawing his attention to the need for obtaining new medications for TB from the West.

Pero had heard that TB is often spread through cows. He asked the grim doctor whether that was true, and the doctor, surprised, said that of course it was. "What, you haven't had your cows tested before? Why, I thought that all the villages tested their cows and destroyed those that had the bacillus!"

"Well, now we can see just how far behind God's back our village is, I guess," said Pero.

That summer solstice, the Kamenars, in their festivities, did this. They tied the cow in chains in the pen. Since the hay and the dung and the very ground in the pen was thoroughly infected by the TB bacillus, Pero wanted to purge everything on the ground. He filled the pen with hay and poured gasoline over it. From a distance he flung a torch, and the pen burst into an explosive flame. The old creature bellowed, its flesh hissed and cackled, the beams fell, and when the night fell, there were only glowing embers and ashes left, and among the ashes, white bones with black hollows where the infected marrow had lodged.

Bruno had watched, smelled, and listened with horror—there was the unconscious creature who had comforted him so much and so often, who had fed him since his infancy, who had raised him, who had warmed him in his weakest moments. Who had nearly killed him. He had thought that he had loved the cow, that he would be sorrowful, but as the flesh hissed and shushed in the flames, he shivered, and it was not from fever that he did, but with relief. In the morning, when all the ashes were out, he was so filled with strength that he felt he could fly over the village in his muddy overcoat on the warm smoke of the burned-out cow.

On Becoming a Prophet
A Tale

&⅋&⅋

One evening Stephan watched from his window his neighbor's wife taking a bath in the blue moonlight, glistening with soap, and later with oil, in her flower garden. Like David, he lusted. His lust grew stronger night by night, and he wondered how to find an escape from it. Whether to kill his neighbor and take his wife—is it certain she would have him? Her bosom and thighs, oiled in olive, glowed in his mind, even on the night as dark as a coal mine when the moon eclipsed and clouds covered the other celestial luminaries. There were no gas lamps in the streets of the poor Slavonian town. Ears overshadowed the eyes.

No snoring could be heard although many windows were open. Therefore the steps of the Reverend Absalom Strahovich, who knew the streets by heart, resounded on cobbles. He pulled and pushed the handle sticking out of the wall next to Stephan's gate. On the other end of the hallway, the bell rang as if summoning for matin prayers.

No answer, for a while. The gate opened without a squeak since Stephan, a carter, had greased it.

"Praise the Lord," said the two men to each other.

"I knew it was your Reverence."

"I suppose you can recognize my way of tolling the bell. . . ."

"And your time of doing it. What brings you here?"

"Listen to what I have to say."

"I am listening."

Silence.

"Is there a place, brother, where the walls don't have ears?"

In the secrecy of four whitewashed mud-brick walls, a maple floor, and a crumbling ceiling, the minister spoke: "Brother Stephan, in my dream I heard a voice. 'Stand up and go to brother Stephan and say unto him: Thus says the Lord thy God, If thou looketh at thy neighbors' wives with lust and schemeth to please thy flesh with them in the fields, thou shalt surely go blind.' My brother, the words are not mine. Hearken unto them."

Several months later, during a luminous night—full moon, crisp air heightening the brilliance of stars—people strolled in the streets or gazed through the windows, and their eyes feasted in the blue light. A lone man, however, trotted slowly, feeling his way with a stick, probing forth with a borrowed limb, uncertainly, awkwardly, unlike the way the blind usually do—obviously, lacking the routine. He came to the door in the church attic where the Reverend lived with his wife. He pulled the bell, once, twice, thrice, and the door opened.

"Praise the Lord, Stephan."

"Good evening, Reverend. I came to tell you something."

"Please come into my office. Oh I see! You cannot see your way. Let me help you."

"My Reverend, don't sound so triumphant, for I have bad news for you! I was awakened from my sleep early this evening, and I heard a voice. I thought it was you calling me, and I was scared. I smelled and listened through the window, went to the door, opened it. Nobody stood there. I went back to bed, and heard, 'Stephan!' And I replied, 'Here I am. Where are you and who are you?' And the answer came. 'I am He whom you cannot know. Stand up and go to the servant of the church, Absalom, and tell him that not one week shall pass and his wife will become a harlot in a big city, and that he'—that is, you Absalom!—'will live alone, consumed with demons of lust.'"

"Nonsense! What gives you the authority to say this! You are slandering. . . ."

"My Reverend, I am curious to find out whether it is only you who can prophesy in this town."

"Did you really hear the voice?"

"I swear by all the dead ones."

"Though shalt not. . . ."

". . . be a pedant. Good night."

Several years later, a series of droughts and military campaigns exhausted the land, sinking it into dusty poverty, so that many people sold everything they owned for tickets to America. The evangelical churches in America and Britain failed to raise enough funds to support the minister and his wife—neither the members nor the foreigners could contribute enough, and so, unbeknown—for a while—to the minister, his wife took up the oldest profession, secretly, in Agram—or Zagreb—not far from the Slavonian town. Through her, the minister contracted syphilis, which began to dim the light of his brain, and one night, blind, he walked to Stephan. "My brother," he said. "How right you were. Tell me one thing. Why haven't we listened to each other?"

"You were too proud and I too low for you. But worse is yet to come. Last night I heard a voice. . . ."

"No, I've had it with voices."

The minister didn't mean that as literally as what followed. He went deaf. So did Stephan. Both of them lost all their senses, but their gifts of speech strengthened and gained them fame.

As two prophets of doom, they sat together in a candlelit room, their lips moving incessantly, now and then uttering something understandable. Hundreds of sweating people thronged around them. The congregation increased day by day, fed the prophets, and in fright listened. They foretold that brother would kill brother, son mother, granddaughter grandfather. Not one illness and death in the town—and in the whole region of Slavonia—went unforetold.

Crimson

⇛⇛

The sulfurous red tip of Milan's match tore trails in the wet matchbox and fell into a puddle that filled a large boot imprint. The match tip shushed, and a little frog leaped out, young, brown, and merry. Milan threw away his wet cigarette, spat into the puddle, thumbed his aquiline nose, and pressed his knuckles into the eyes beneath the high-arching brows, but he couldn't get a sensation of alertness.

This tedium was not what he had expected. The war was supposed to be over in two weeks, and the Pannonian Plains of Eastern Croatia would become part of Serbia, but this was the army's fourth month of lingering in the woods and cornfields.

Most nights the Serb soldiers, who had crossed the Danube into Croatian territory and now encircled the town of Vukovar, fired from mortars, tanks, and cannons into the town. They aimed wherever the Croat soldiers could hide, and they also fired randomly at the houses. "Don't pay any attention to what you hit," said the captain. "They are just Croats, *ustasha* children, *ustasha* parents, *ustasha* grandparents. If you don't wipe them out, they'll wipe you out." As he talked, the captain's disheveled silvery hair shook, and beneath thick black eyebrows, his eyes blinked quickly.

Half of the cannons did not work because they were rusty and soldiers often forgot to oil them. When the weapons would not fire, the soldiers played cards, and watched American porn movies on VCRs hooked up to tank batteries. And they sang: *Oh my first love, are you a bushy Slav? / Whoever you rub and mate, don't forget your first hate. / Oh my first hate, who should I tolerate?* He wondered why so many songs dealt with first love, lost love, why all this nostalgia? His first love was only a childhood thing—on the other hand, childhood was perhaps the only genuine time of his life, the time to which all other experience was grafted, like red apples on to a blue plum tree, where apples grow stunted.

At the age of fifteen he'd had a crush on a girl, Svyetlana. For a New Year's dance party, he had put his shoes on the stove to warm them and gone to the bathroom to shave, though he had no need of shaving yet. The rubber soles of his shoes melted, but he didn't have another pair, so he went to the dance in them. Waiting to meet Svyetlana atop a stairway, Milan dug the nails of his forefingers into the flesh on the edge of his thumbnails so deep that several drops of blood dripped onto the ochre tiles of the floor.

He had then followed Svyetlana to the gym, where the dance had begun. To avoid stepping on her feet, he stood away from her. Her friends whispered and giggled—probably about his melted soles. Like Svyetlana, they were Croats and the daughters of engineers and doctors; to them he was just a Serb peasant. He slipped out of the room, his cheeks brimming.

Several days later he and Svyetlana talked in front of her house. He walked around her, desiring to touch her and kiss her, though he knew deep down that he could not. His tongue probed several cavities from which the fillings had fallen. He feared that his breath was bad, and he cursed the dentists at the people's clinic.

Thinking back on it now, he felt ashamed again. He drank more *rakia*. At the beginning of the campaign, they had had fine *slivovitz*, gold colored and throat scorching, but now only this rotten, pale *rakia,* made from doubly brewed grapes. There was no coffee. The captain had thrown a sack of it into the river, saying, "No more stinky Muslim customs and Turkish coffee dung here—is that clear?"

"But coffee originally comes from Ethiopia," Milan said as he watched brown fish surface and open their yellow mouths to swallow the black beads, which looked as if they'd spilled from rosaries used to pray for wakefulness.

"That's Muslim," the captain said.

"Didn't use to be, and it's Coptic too—that's very similar to Orthodox."

"That doesn't matter. We don't have any filters, and if you don't filter the coffee, it's Turkish."

"You could filter it through newspapers," Milan said.

"Yeah? You'll get lead poisoning."

"You will anyway," Milan mumbled, thinking of bullets.

"What did you say?"

Milan didn't respond. The captain was edgy, and Milan thought he should be quiet.

To recover from drink, Milan and many other soldiers drank more. The soldiers were festive, although the festivity seemed forced. Milan did not want to be there. But going back to Osijek, his home town in Croatia, would not do. Once, he might have lived there unmolested; now, after being a Serb soldier, he certainly could not. Officially, he was in the Yugoslav—mostly Serbian—reservist army, but the Croats would not make that distinction. To them he would be just a *chetnik,* a Serb loyalist striving to create Greater Serbia by subjugating Croatia and Bosnia—just as to the Serbs all Croat soldiers were *ustashas,* striving to purify Croatia ethnically. He had heard that Croats had burned his home, and now he hated them. He ground his teeth, but carefully, because one of them hurt. He resented the Serbs around him as well.

One night, three Serb cops had come to his home and asked him to join the army. When he hesitated, they threatened him with knives. The Serbs would soon conquer the town, he was sure. Still, he could have stayed back. His brother, older and stronger than Milan, had not joined. Neither had a friend of his, who'd spent his young days in fights. Most of the violent and brave guys had stayed behind, and nothing had happened to them. Croats respected them for remaining in Croatia and not joining the Serb armies. The strong guys had the courage to say no. Those who had no courage, the yes men, would be the military heroes.

Many soldiers had deserted, and several companies from Serbia had left. Still, with twenty thousand well-armed soldiers surrounding a city with two thousand poorly armed and untrained Croatian soldiers, the Serb army ought to be able to take the city in a day. He did not understand what they were waiting for, launching thousands of bombs every night. What would be the point of taking a devastated city, a mound of shattered bricks? But when the tanks had gone forward, heat-seeking missiles had blown up many of them. The Croats had smuggled in some arms.

By the middle of November, the Serb ring around Vukovar seemed impenetrable. Vukovar hadn't received any supplies from Zagreb, the Croatian capital, in weeks, and the Serb guards would not allow the UN ambulances through for fear they concealed weapons. The Croats had run out of food and bombs. The tanks and the infantry made steady progress, taking a suburb of Vukovar. Milan's company moved from house to house, block to block, smoking people out of their cellars with tear gas. No water flowed through the pipes and most of the sewage system was empty, so the people had lived like rats, together with rats, and the rats waited for them to die, so they could eat them.

Serb soldiers killed men, even boys. Milan's captain said, "Just shoot them. If you don't, someone else will, so what's the difference—as long as there are no journalists around, and if you see a journalist alone, shoot him too." In a dark cellar, Milan stumbled as he leaned against a dank, sandy wall and slid forward. The captain shouted from above, "What are you waiting for? Keep going. There's nobody down there." Milan saw a man's silhouette against the light of a window in the cellar. The light fell in shifting streaks, hurting his eyes. The man was quietly crawling out the window. "Stop or I'll shoot," Milan said. The man slid from the window, the sand shushing. Facing a tall, bony stranger, Milan felt neither hatred nor love, but he did not want to shoot him. Could he save the man if he wanted to? He could not escape from the army himself. Still, he said, "Do you have any German marks? Give them all to me and I'll get you out of here."

"I have nothing."

"That's too bad."

"If you know God, don't shoot," the man said in a tremulous voice. "You have kids?"

"You'd better come up with better reasons for me not to pull the trigger."

"I can't harm you, why should you want to harm me?"

"Let's get out of here, with your arms up." They walked up the stairs, into the light. Milan's captain said, "What's taking you so long? Shoot him." Milan raised his rifle unsteadily and stared at the Croat's widow's peak and the deep creases separating his cheeks from his thin mouth.

"You haven't shot anything in your life," said the captain, "have you?"

"A bunch of rabbits and birds, that's all."

"You must start somewhere. What kind of soldier are you if you're squeamish?"

Milan said nothing. You can't be in a war and not kill. Although Milan was scared and embarrassed, he suddenly became curious, not so much about how men died but how they killed, about whether he could kill. Who knows, from a distance some of the bombs he had handed to the cannon man might have killed, probably had. But he had not seen it. Maybe killing an unarmed man was wrong—of course it was wrong, what else could it be—but he thought that to be a soldier he needed to pass the test: to be able to kill.

Milan still could not shoot. He imagined this man's grandchildren, and how much misery his death could mean to the people close to him. If they exchanged places, would anybody miss Milan? Probably not, he thought, and that thought irritated him, and he pitied the man a little less.

"Do you want a cigarette?" Milan asked.

"What, are you doing the last-wish bullshit?" the captain said. "If you don't shoot the bum, I'm going to shoot both of you." He lifted his pistol. "You got to be able to pull the trigger."

Several other soldiers gathered to watch this initiation rite. "Come on, Milan, you can do it!" a voice shouted. "This guy probably killed your grandfather in the world war!"

"He's only about fifty-five," Milan said.

"Then his *ustasha* father did," the voice said.

"My father was a partisan," the tall man responded.

"Yeah, right—now you are all partisans," the captain said.

Milan abhorred this public performance. His hand trembled and he tried to hide it. He used to have stage fright when he addressed audiences; holding a glass of water, his right hand would tremble, simply because once, during his high-school oral exams, it had. He was scared of groups. In that way, he and the man had more in common than he did with the other soldiers: They both were outside the group. The man could do nothing about it; for him, this was fate. Milan, on the other hand, could pull the trigger or not pull. Not pulling would be the right choice, obviously. But in front of the deranged group, it would be the wrong choice. Whatever he did or did not do would work against him. He should not have the illusion that he had a choice. He breathed hard, as though he was about to have an asthma attack.

"I know you're a good man," the man said hopefully, in a shaky voice. "You can't kill the defenseless, right?"

Milan thought that the man saw through him, through his anxiety, through his thin guts, straight to his shit. Milan saw that the man's knees shook; the man spoke out of desperation. The man's green pants sagged. There was a streak of urine on the pants, growing bigger and bigger. When Milan had been in the second grade, the teacher had called him up to the green blackboard to subtract numbers. Out of Milan's fear that he could not do it, crap, solid and dark like cattails, slid down onto the floor and smoked while the class laughed, and for a whole semester, he could not look anybody in the eye.

Milan pulled the trigger, three times, quickly.

The man fell. His hazel eyes stayed open while blood gushed from his neck onto the brick-laid yard, the narrow yard between two three-story buildings, the dank, dusty smell blowing from out of the cellars, as though the Danube water had softened the clay beneath the cracked cellar cement, and the river mud exhaled its old air of rotting caviar yolks. Uneven over the melted soil, the rain-drenched bricks darkened slightly in the new blood.

Milan breathed in the gun smoke and coughed. So that was it. It did not feel like anything as long as you concentrated on the details. He watched the crushed snail houses on the bricks, and red earthworms sliding straight, unable to coil, in the cracks between the bricks.

The captain poked his finger into Milan's buttocks. "Good job. I was worried for you, that you were a sensitive Croat-loving homosexual. You passed the test."

Milan cringed and thought he wouldn't mind shooting the captain.

"See, you passed the test." The captain's laughter smelled of onions and cigars.

Accordion music, a bass, and shrill voices came from around the corner, from a tavern with a burned-out, red-tile roof. Milan waited for a long while, then walked in. Water leaked through the ceiling, and beads of precipitated steam slid down the walls, like sweat on a harvester's back. In their muddy boots, disheveled bearded soldiers danced the *kolo,* the Serb *rondo,* more slowly than the accordion rhythm called for. They yodeled derisively and fired their guns into the ceiling. Mortar was falling off the reeds and thudding onto the wooden floor. They tilted gasoline-colored bottles of *slivovitz* and emptied half-liter bottles of beer into their mouths, pouring some of the liquid down their chins, beards, shirts.

Milan gulped down half a liter of beer and then heard a scream in the pantry. He kicked the door in with his boot, and saw the hairy buttocks of a man above the pale flesh of a woman. Milan's lips went dry with a strange excitement: Was he appalled, yes he was; was he lustfully curious, yes he was. He grabbed a bottle of pale brandy from the shelf and gulped, tasting nothing, but feeling a burning on his cracked lips. The woman's face was contorted in pain, but even so, he was sure he recognized the stark, pale skin, the black eyebrows under streaks of wet brown hair falling across high cheekbones: Svyetlana. And the man was his odious captain, who turned to look at him and said, "After I'm done, you go ahead too, dip your little dick, and enjoy. *Hahaha.* You'll have a complete education today. You know, Stalin recommended rape as a way of keeping up the aggressive impulses. You'll make a soldier yet."

"Don't worry about my aggressive impulses," Milan said. He lifted the rifle and with its wooden butt struck the captain's head. The captain's head collided with the woman's, driving hers onto the brick floor. Milan kicked his head away from hers, and when his rifle struck the captain's skull again, the bones cracked. The man bled from his mouth onto the woman's belly. She had swooned. Milan dragged him away from her and covered his head with an empty coffee bag. What to do with her? How to protect her from the bar? His heart beat at a frantic pace, and his windpipe wheezed.

This was she, his childhood memory, Milan thought, as though all that singing about first loves and hates had summoned her. He gazed at her parted scarlet lips, thin vertical lines ruffling the shiny skin. The swollen lips were shapely, twin peaks of a long wave, a wave of blood, whipped by internal winds from the heart, and netted in the thin lip-skin, which prevented it from splashing out, onto the shore, onto Milan. Only the thin membrane, the lips, separated his rusty plasma from hers.

He remembered how Svyetlana's lips had looked when he had leaned forward to kiss her. Her lips had parted like now, but when it was clear that he would not lean closer, she chewed her bubble gum loudly and, it seemed, challengingly, disrespectfully— her saliva gluing and ungluing foamily beneath the blue belly of her tongue. Coldly she stared at his lips through her deep brown eyes with their black stripes. And then she vanished without a whisper through a large wooden gate, into a dark garden with vines of ivy and grapes. As he gazed after her, his heart bounced in his chest like a wild dog on a chain. After that, they were strangers to each other, but he continued to yearn for her.

Milan suspected that his longing had been unrequited because of his cowardice. He had not had the courage to declare his love to her. In a dangerous world, wouldn't a woman be attracted to courage? She went to Zagreb, graduated from the school of architecture, married a doctor, and stayed a class above Milan. Perhaps out of despair, he was loud and unruly and flunked out of the engineering school at the University of Belgrade. Once, when it was his last chance to pass an exam in thermodynamics, he'd stayed in the chess-club room because he thought he'd figured out a mate in five. He stayed for the romance of it, for the sake of freedom, saying in his way, *Fuck you!* to school, ambition, and class—instead of going to the exam, which he thought he'd flunk anyhow. After that, he became a subdued engine man, driving cargo trains all over the damned federation: a blue collar worker, the most despised in the socialist worker's state.

All his failures had to do, Milan was sure, with Svyetlana's aloofness. She could have seen what he was up to and could have helped him approach her. And now he had killed a man, two men, for her, for himself.

He stared with a sorrowful glee at the woman lying at his feet, her skirt and bra ripped open and her supple breasts tilting downward and trembling with her uncertain breath. He felt a thrill and a shudder. Below her blood-smeared ribs, her thighs, ample, curvaceous, defenseless, loosely stretched before him.

Milan carried the woman outside and gave her aspirin and water to drink. She looked at him disdainfully and asked: "You saved me or something?"

"I don't know whether anybody saved anybody, but you could thank me. Maybe I saved you."

"Will everybody be free to rape me now?"

"No, you can go. Nobody will rape you."

"I have a horrible headache." She blinked.

"The captain's head knocked against yours pretty hard. Just a concussion would be my guess."

As he escorted her to a bus crowded with Croat women and children, she stumbled alongside him, but refused his support. He wondered if the rusty bus with bullet holes would make it or if at some drunken sadist's whim a sulfurous bomb would strike the bus on the road and burn up all the passengers, including her, and if—the way things were going—he would be the one throwing the bomb. He felt sorry for the woman and asked, "What's your name?"

"What difference should it make?"

"Come on, aren't you Svyetlana?"

"No. Olga."

"Are you sure?" Milan gripped the woman by the shoulders so he could look into her face and compare it with his memory of Svyetlana's—and so he could lean on her, because he was stunned.

She pushed his arms away. "Sure I'm sure, at least about my name. Probably about nothing else."

"Olga in the Volga. And I'm Mile in the Nile," he muttered drunkenly as she stepped onto the bus. How was the confusion possible, he wondered. But the woman was not lying: Her voice was higher and her eyes darker than Svyetlana's.

In a ditch, Milan took the uniform from a dead Croat soldier. He walked into the tavern, where his comrades still danced. In the pantry he dressed his captain in the uniform, and then he carried his body out and dumped it on a horse-drawn carriage, onto a pile of a dozen corpses. Milan shifted uncomfortably because the blood had soaked through his cotton uniform and shirt, gluing the fabric to his skin. A dark orange horse with strong round buttocks stood, his head bent to the road, which was covered with empty gun shells. His hoof screeched over shards of glass. The shrill sound shook the horse's ears, reddened and pierced by the sun's rays so that a thick vine of veins stood out. A round fly sat on an ear, filling up its green belly on a vein. Milan was jittery, as though he'd had delirium tremens. Who knew what diseases lurked in this city, where cats had been eaten and rats frolicked in the walls; where cat and rat skeletons lay entwined together; where maggots formed shifting gray mounds over loose flesh detached from bones. He did not dare take a deep breath, for fear of inhaling a plague. Piles of bodies lay on almost every street corner, yellow eyes looming out of purple faces. Soldiers—some with their teeth chattering as though they suffered from hypothermia—poured gasoline over the piles and burned them.

After taking Vukovar, Milan's army progressed north to surround Osijek. One night while on guard duty in a far-flung trench beneath oak trees with long branches and water-darkened trunks, Milan sat on a sack of sand. Loud rain was knocking the last brown leaves off the branches. Drops hit the mud, splashing it. The wetness carried the smells of poisonous mushrooms and old leaves, not only the leaves that had just zigzagged to the ground but also the leaves from the last year, and from hundreds of years ago, with mossy, musty whiffs of old lives in the soil, and new lives that slid out of the cloudy water and soiled eggs: snails, frogs, earthworms. When the rain let up, the leaves sagged and a cold wind swayed them, and water continued sliding down in large drops, which hung glittering in the moonlight before falling onto Milan, into his shirt and down his hairy neck.

The other guard on duty snored. Irritated, Milan stood up

and then realized there was nobody else in sight. The series of events in Vukovar had changed him: He no longer feared what would happen if he were caught deserting the Serb army or if he were apprehended by the Croat police. Milan crawled out into a cornfield, threw away his gun, tore off the army insignia, and by dawn walked into a village near Osijek. He went to his brother's place, where his brother let him sleep on the sofa.

When Milan walked in the streets, those who recognized him merely looked at him suspiciously, as they did everybody, more or less. Milan joined the citizens who placed sandbags in front of all the shops and windows, and while doing so he wondered whether he was sandbagging his conscience more than the buildings. One afternoon three months after the fall of Vukovar, Milan had just finished piling sandbags. Dusty and sweaty, he walked past the scaffolded red-brick cathedral, where masons plastered up grenade holes in the bricks. Wet cement kept falling and thudding like hail. Listening to the thudding and to the ringing of a tram, he noticed a graceful and pale woman with black hair and a full figure walking toward the Drava River, frowning, her eyes glassy and luminous. Milan recognized Olga, and at first was surprised that he could have confused her for Svyetlana, then scared that she might jump off the bridge. But she had survived Vukovar, so ending her life now, when it was no longer threatened, would be absurd.

"Hello," he addressed her, "what a fine day, isn't it?" She shrank back as she recognized him. He was thinner than before, and white streaked his oiled brown hair. Still, his face had to be unmistakable: the eyes set deep and wide apart under the brows; large ears that stuck out the same way they did when he was a boy. He thought that he still looked like a boy, had the same expectant, big-eyed look, of desire, hunger, envy, even love, perhaps: He had been dreaming of Olga many nights.

"What are you doing in Osijek, of all places," she asked.

"I'm looking for a job." He was so nervous he could hardly breathe.

"That's brave of you, after what you've done."

"What have I done?"

"You know best . . ."

"Where do you want me to go? To hell? Where isn't it hell these days?"

"Go to Canada or Britain, and give them a story of how oppressed you are here. They love those stories."

"Why shouldn't I be here? I killed a Serb officer. Anyhow, the Croatian government wants to prove to foreigners that Serbs can live in Croatia, and I'll test them. I can't live in Serbia. In Belgrade, from what I've heard, if you are a Serb from Croatia, the police look for you where you live, in cafés, bars, and even churches, to draft you for the war in Bosnia. And the Belgraders, you think they'd be grateful to someone like me? They'd say, 'What are you doing here? You brought the sanctions and poverty upon us, and now you want to sit on your butt, sipping espresso? Go back to the war, get the hell out of here!'"

"That's not a particularly touching story."

"I know it."

"So now you want to live here as though nothing had happened."

"What else?"

"It might be easy for you."

"I saved you from . . ."

"I guess. But I'm pregnant—since then."

"I thought I killed him before he could do it."

"Sorry, but I have to rush. It's almost two o'clock—the abortion clinic will close."

"Don't do it."

"Why not? Who'd take care of the baby?"

"I will. I don't mean that we should get married. But then, why shouldn't we?"

"Why would you do that? We don't know each other."

"We do."

They stood in front of a café, and in silence they looked at each other. With blue lines under her eyes, she looked tired, but she was also curious, scrutinizing him.

She motioned toward the café and they walked in. They sat by the window. "I replaced the windows here." Milan proudly knocked on the glass. He didn't like his part-time job fixing windows, but he could bear it full-time, he thought, if he lived with Olga. He enjoyed looking at her mouth as she answered his questions about where she worked (taught high-school science), whether she had other kids (didn't), parents (mother died a while back, father was killed in Vukovar), a house (no, but apartment, yes). He had kissed those crimson lips while she was still unconscious in Vukovar. He thought he should tell her about it, but he was certain that if he did she'd leave right away, and he wanted her to stay. Still, he thought that he should tell her, but instead he said, "What kind of music do you like?" and decided to tell her later.

"You want to make small talk? Years ago, that's how people talked—wasn't it nice? I don't like to listen to music anymore, but I play it on the piano, mostly Bach."

He clasped his hands, which seemed to want to touch hers of their own will.

"How many people have you killed?" she asked, staring into his eyes.

"Yes, I've killed. I don't know what counts. Feeding bombs into cannons that I didn't fire myself—how do you count that?"

"There'll be an accounting formula in hell, I'm sure." She grinned at him.

"Come on, that's not funny. You're right: I'll pay for it somehow. I wish I'd run away sooner. But then I wouldn't have met you."

A waiter with a round tray and a black apron came by, and Milan ordered a bottle of red wine. He looked through the crimson wine at his thin fingers. Her glass beads below her long neck glittered through the wine like rubies.

They gulped the wine.

"Don't go to that abortion clinic," said Milan. "I got divorced because my wife and I couldn't have kids—we were married for a year. Since my twenties I've always wanted to have a baby. Wouldn't you love a little wet infant to crawl between us, and look up at us, with hazy, filmy eyes, to see the world for the first time—a world that would be new, innocent, big, admirable, imitable, and that we would be a part of? Wouldn't you like those astonishing little fingers to grasp your finger, barely closing around it, and to tug at it?"

Olga smiled and did not say anything.

Milan imagined the power of a new life sleeping with his dreams inside her, and the dreams caressing her. He had not dared to think so concretely about a baby. Now he liked imagining a biological happiness with her, more with her than with any other woman, more than with his lost childhood loves or pretty young women.

She pursed her lips. "But the kid's not yours."

"We wouldn't tell him. Or her."

"Mixed marriages aren't exactly in fashion." She stood up as though she'd had enough nonsense.

Leaving behind a crumpled blue bank note on the tablecloth, he followed her into the windy and darkening streets. "Eventually Serbs and Croats marrying each other will be all the rage," Milan said. "You'll see. People will want to prove they're not nationalists."

They walked to the river bank, then looked into each other's eyes, calmly, and listened to the ice in the Drava River cracking. They watched floating ice pieces piling on top of each other, breaking, sinking, rising, colliding, exploding—sharp, white, jagged, glaring in the sun like gigantic glassy swords clashing with slabs of marble. He imagined that the ground they stood on floated north like an iceberg while the river stayed in place.

"You think the ice comes from Austria?" Milan asked.

"And Hungary."

"And it's flowing down to Serbia. See how we are connected."

"Who is? The rivers?"

"Our waters, we."

The wind that blew chilled them, and they walked past an aluminum kiosk with postcards, cigars, and a saleswoman who yawned with her gleaming silver teeth. From behind them, the wind pushed Olga and Milan, and they walked effortlessly, with their chilled ears red and translucent against the sunshine, which shone in thick rays through black branches of leafless acacias. They pulled up their collars, and stepped into the tobacco cloud of a tavern, listened to the Hungarian *chardash,* and drank more red wine. They walked out into the sleety winds, with lips purple from the dried wine, and they huddled against the weather, against each other, making one standing mound, a man and a woman against each other.

Milan now worked full time as a glass cutter. Because of occasional shelling and frequent low MIG jet flights, which penetrated the sound barrier above the town with loud explosions, there was no shortage of broken windows. He and Olga enjoyed each other's company, and he moved in with her. When the baby was born, he held her hand in the hospital, and cut the cord with a pair of scissors. They got married, and lived happily—almost. Milan had rat and war nightmares and ground his teeth in his sleep, and during the day, if he wasn't playing with Zvone or working, he'd sit in the armchair and brood. He couldn't talk about all that happened in the war. Not saying wasn't good; saying might be worse. In a way, it was the same kind of bind he was in when he shot the poor man in Vukovar. And, to a large extent, it was the poor man who troubled him, until one evening at home, two years later, when Olga showed Milan her family pictures while their boy slept with a light snore that made them both laugh.

"This is my dad, see," she said, pointing to an old, brown photo. "Here he's teaching me how to walk. Today would be his birthday, is his birthday." Tearfully she looked at Milan, who winced and bit his lips.

"So still no word on him? Do you think you'll ever know

what happened to him?" His voice was barely coming out of his throat.

"He was in Vukovar when you were there—maybe you saw him?" she said.

"Such a tragedy—it really saddens me to think about the loss you've suffered." He paused. "Is there any brandy?"

"You drink too much."

"Or too little." She ignored his request and showed him more pictures of her father.

"This is awful. I don't know how to say this. But I must— I killed him in Vukovar."

She dropped the family album on the floor.

As soon as he'd spoken, he regretted what he'd done. After all that had happened, why did he feel the need to be honest? Why not keep secrets to himself, live lovingly, and cling to the bit of life that he had left?

"I didn't want to kill anybody, least of all my future father-in-law. I didn't know it was your father, at the time I didn't know you either, but the man I shot looked exactly like the one in that picture."

"Oh my God."

"The captain had me at gunpoint, and if I hadn't done it, he and the soldiers around us would've killed us both. So it's just a technicality who pulled the trigger. I would've been forced to pull the trigger on my own father."

She moaned.

"I can't say I'm sorry—it wouldn't make sense to be sorry for something I had no control of."

She moaned and lowered her chin to her collarbones.

"That's amazing bad luck. How many people lived in Vukovar? Thirty thousand? Two thousand men in their fifties? And to chance upon your father . . . But not to chance upon anybody would have been even more unlikely."

"Why didn't you tell me sooner?"

"I only saw a small, hazy picture of him before, and while I could tell there was a similarity, I couldn't be sure—there's often a similarity. I'd even mistaken you for someone else. I'm no good at recognizing faces. Even if I had been sure before, how could I have simply come out with it: 'Listen, I killed your father.' Why wreck a family—for we have been reasonably happy, haven't we?"

After this, Olga would not allow him to stay in the bed with her and Zvone anymore.

One evening while Milan brooded, Olga said, "All right, we can't live like this—you can join us."

But he continued sitting and sulking.

"What's wrong?" she said.

"There's always something," he said.

She stood above him, and said, "Why are you talking in riddles? I know what else there is. That captain of yours who, you said, raped me? Strange that we never talked about it."

"It's not strange. I didn't think women liked to talk about such things. Yes, he was doing it when I bludgeoned him."

Lately she had remarked several times that Zvone looked like Milan: He had the same kind of drop-off between his forehead and the rest of his face, and his broadly separated, large hazel eyes peered hungrily from beneath his brows.

It angered Milan that, no matter how hard he tried, just one hour out of whack made it impossible to live the rest of his life honestly and peacefully.

She paced the room, kicking her way through plastic cars, trucks, and animals donated by UNICEF, Caritas, and German Protestant churches. "Zvone looks like you. How come?"

"Isn't it obvious?"

"I can't believe it."

"Listen, throughout the war, I was shoved around. Once I killed your rapist and my rapist, I felt free for the first time ever, and I was in a frenzy, beside myself, and I couldn't control either the drink or the lust. I couldn't handle anything consciously anymore. And I didn't know that I could have children—I was told my sperm count was too low. So later, I didn't think it made any sense to tell you; I thought it was either the captain's seed or, who knows, there could have been people before him. But when I noticed the similarity, I thought that in a way we should be happy: We are the biological parents."

"So you killed the rapist, to rape me, and you never told me!"

"What could I tell you? At that time I was unconscious, drunk, and there you were. I just lay with you. I did not force anything. I did it in some kind of dizzy grace period, when I was free from everything, even from the past and the future—lucky to be alive, and unlucky, doomed."

"But I was unconscious!"

"So?"

"That's rape."

"No, rape is done against a person's will, not without the will."

"That's a sophism. You raped me."

"Come on. If we were both unconscious, how could it be rape?"

"But you weren't."

"I wouldn't be so sure. Anyway, I put you on the bus. If I hadn't, the whole bar would've raped you and they would have shot you after it."

"So you're saying I should thank you?"

He didn't respond, but threw up his arms in despair. What could he do about it—about going off the edge for an hour of his life? Suffer for the rest of eternity? Kill himself?

She was wearing a gold necklace with a cross. She grabbed it, tore it from her neck, and twisted the cross in her fingers. "If it weren't for the child, I'd kill you."

She wept. He came close to her and put his arm on her shoulder. She shuddered and pushed his arm away.

They paced the room. Lightning filled the room with flashes of blue light, and he saw her as if she were in a series of blue snapshots. In silence they stumbled over chairs and walked on toys, crushing them.

Milan thought how strange it was that he should be held responsible for the past, three years ago, when he was conscripted, enslaved—when he wasn't even himself. "We all have multiple personalities," he said. "One of us is the past, and another the future, and there's no present me. We are vacant right now—spaces through which the past and the future disagree." He sounded academic, but he was trying to articulate his alienation—and while alienation and displacement usually troubled him, now he wanted them to help him. Yes, it would be good to be as alienated from Vukovar as possible.

"What nonsense. Don't philosophize. Philosophy is an excuse. You have no excuse," Olga said. There hadn't been a lightning flash in a while, but thunder grumbled and rattled the loose windows. Zvone cried in the bedroom, and Olga went to him. Milan watched from the door. Zvone sucked eagerly, kneading a breast with his little fists, sinking his untrimmed nails into the opulent flesh. Milan could see that she did not mind the scratchy nails, the little loving kitten's claws, nor the raspy tongue. Letting one of his hands roam, Zvone caught the other venous breast and smiled when he got it to squirt.

Milan undressed and went to the sofa. The baby, as though sensing the tension in the room, kept sucking for an hour, and Milan heard Olga say, "It's empty, they are both empty—can't you stop? Do you want some bread?"

"No. Milk, I want my milk," he said.

"Time to go to sleep," she said and turned off the light.

"Light. I want light!"

She switched the light on and read him a book about happy bears and happy eagles eating happy fish.

The lightning storm resumed, and the thunder rumbled the silverware on the table. "Lions are fighting," Zvone said.

Loud raindrops hit the windowpanes. "They are crying too," Olga said. "They are knocking for us to let them in."

After a while Milan's mouth was sticky, tasting of plum brandy and onions. He didn't want to walk to the bathroom to brush his teeth, in case Olga slept, and he wondered how much she must hate him at that moment. She probably wanted him to die in his sleep. He dozed off, then awakened to a stabbing pain. Olga was lifting a hand that held a large kitchen knife, and before he had time to realize that he was not dreaming, she drove the knife down into his abdomen. She leaned hard on the knife until the stainless steel ground against his rib.

The pain scorched him. He pushed her and then kicked her against the wall. He stood up and staggered, bleeding, then collapsed, but stayed half-conscious in the burning pain. The boy woke up and screamed, "Mama, I'm afraid. Lions are biting! Where's Dada?"

Now she panicked too: The cold blue lightning revealed the spooky aspect of her deed—a man in a black puddle. She called an ambulance and went to the hospital alongside Milan, with Zvone at her breast. She did not know her husband's blood type, so finding out took time. The hospital was out of supplies of his blood group. As she belonged to group O and was thus a universal donor, she gave as much as she could: three pints of blood, enough to keep him alive until new blood came, and enough to exhaust her. Now her blood would stream through him. Zvone wanted to suck, but she was empty.

As Milan came to, Zvone cried, "Milk! I want more milk!" Zvone sucked hard.

Milan's body hurt and his ears buzzed, but he listened in elation to Zvone's voice, which he'd thought he'd never hear again, and the voice cried, "Milk!"

"No, no more milk," Olga said. "Maybe blood, if you like. Keep sucking, it will come. There's some left."

Ice

❧❧

A while back, in the Croatian town Nizograd, Ivan, ten, and Tomo, eight, went out into the streets in a snowstorm because they had heard that Coca-Cola had arrived. The rumor had spread around Nizograd in whispers, shouts, and the veracity of the news was disputed at the street corners near bullet-riddled buildings with peeling mortar. Photographs of glistening mouths with dazzling white teeth had heralded Coca-Cola as tremendously refreshing. Forget apple cider, plum cider, apple juice. Humans had made a drink that God should like to drink. JFK had drunk nothing but Coca-Cola.

In front of Hotel Slavia stood a white truck loaded with curvaceous bottles in the form of hand grenades. Crowds gathered and gazed at the precious reddish darkness, resembling the darkness of breathless venous blood. The boys, Ivan and Tomo, crawled on their knees through melting snow, between the legs of adults. Like two dogs off the leash they sniffed quickly. Ivan had heard Coca-Cola was coming, but he did not believe it. He had waited for Christ for years and years, and Christ was not on the clouds yet. But the Coca-Cola was there in the snow.

"They are going to start selling it next week," said a voice. "First they need to see whether it's real."

"What does it taste like?" Tomo whispered into Ivan's ear, and Ivan said, "I cannot tell you right now."

"Why not?"

"It's a state secret."

"But everybody's going to know how it tastes. It will be sold next week!"

"That's doubtful," said Ivan. "The drink is reserved for the Mayor and his guests. Maybe we'll even see Tito in our town!"

Late that night the boys tiptoed to the hotel yard, and stared at the truck through the cracks between the planks of wood in the fence. With trepidation, they crawled beneath the fence, grabbed a box of Coca-Cola, and rushed home.

"Let's drink right now!" Tomo said.

"No, not yet. You are supposed to drink it with ice. Without ice it doesn't work."

"But it's cold enough!"

"No, it has to be icy. We'll leave them in the snow overnight."

"But why not pour it into a cup, and put some icicles into the Coca-Cola? See, there is enough ice!" Tomo pointed to the roof of the house—icicles hung like straight transparent mammoth teeth. Tomo cracked one from the roof, broke it into pieces and chewed them.

"Don't do that, your teeth will crack," said Ivan.

"Please, let me drink Coca-Cola! I have the ice!"

"No, the ice has to come out of Coca-Cola. You mustn't mix outside ice with it.

"But why not?"

"If you do, it won't be real. There'll be plain water in it."

The bottles were lined up in the snow. Ivan and Tomo watched the bottles, shedding flashlight over them, as if over war prisoners—imprisoned little Americans whose caps soon would be twisted off and brains drunk. They shivered, partly from the cold, partly from the thrill, the cosmopolitan thrill. You need not go to America to feel like an American; just drink Coke with ice, the Eucharist with the blood and the flesh, the wine and the wafer, of the United States of America, the land that touches the Moon.

After midnight when Ivan seemed asleep, Tomo stole out of the room and went barefoot into the snow. But Ivan heard him and caught him just as he was about to touch a bottle. Ivan tied him to his bed, so that Tomo was now like a dog on the leash. Like a sad dog, Tomo squealed, until he fell asleep.

In the morning Ivan untied him, and they rushed out. The bottles had burst, and icy, light red Coca-Cola, like fresh arterial blood in the shape of the bottles, stood there, slanted. The boys separated the bits of glass from the coke.

Tomo moaned.

"Shut up," Ivan said.

"Why, how are we going to drink it now? It's all ice!"

Tomo couldn't wait. He put the Coke ice into a pot and was about to place the pot on the stove.

"Don't do that. If the Coca-Cola melts too fast, it will lose its flavor."

Several hours later with tears of impatience in his eyes, finally allowed to drink, Tomo gulped liquid Coke and chewed ice at the same time, with fear, as if he would be transubstantiated at the end of the cup. At first Tomo felt nothing except the icy anesthesia in his lips and tongue. But as the contracting tart taste reached in, he spat it all out on the floor. "Why, this is cough medicine!"

Ivan chewed slowly and gulped, his eyes closed, and his face twisted into an expression of beatitude, as if the inner certainty of salvation sweetly permeated his cheeks and eyelids. And then he coughed, shuddering. And he coughed so much that a doctor was called in.

"Yup," said the doctor. "The boy's got it again!" And that winter Ivan had a more acute bronchitis than any year hitherto. He stayed in bed for two weeks, reading, and Tomo served him a glass of Coca-Cola every six hours.

Fritz: A Fable

꙳ ꙳

Lipik, Croatia
Fall and Winter, 1991

Fritz, a gray German shepherd, who in his pointed face and thick tail resembled a wolf, howled so terribly that his owner, Igor Lovrak, went into his larder, greased his great-grandfather's rifle, and thumbed gun powder and bullets into the barrels before he dared to walk out into the yard. And even then he trembled, expecting bears or a band of thieves to be closing in. Just when Igor stumbled out in his wooden clogs, Fritz leaped so violently that he tore from the ground the thick pipe to which he was chained and with a terrible din jumped over a hedge. A cat leaped onto the lamppost, barely escaping the dog, and climbed to the tilted and capped lightbulb, and placed its paws over the lamp hook. Once settled, the cat didn't move.

Although usually obedient, Fritz wouldn't listen to Igor's shouts to stop. Igor, who was built like a weight lifter, dragged him by the chain, but almost all the ground he had gained he lost with Fritz's leaping toward the aloof enemy.

Igor locked him in the basement—Fritz knew how to open

unlocked doors—but that didn't prevent Fritz from howling most unpoetically his ugly song of hatred all night. Igor couldn't sleep. He marveled at Fritz's voice box. After so many bullets of wind from the lungs into the vocal cords, you'd expect the cords to snap. Igor's nerves did, so he took up his ancestral gun to walk into the basement. His frizzy-haired wife, Dara, who couldn't sleep either, stopped him. "Hey, leave that gun alone. What good could you do with it?"

"Shoot the devil."

"Once the cat goes, he'll be all right."

"Are you suggesting that I shoot the cat? I could."

They sat up on the edge of their bed with their feet on the cold cement floor. It was past twilight. Against the paling sky, the lamppost appeared stark black. On the post was the silhouetted cat, in the same position as the evening before.

"The damned cat hasn't moved at all!" said Igor.

"Are you sure it's alive?"

"Maybe it died of fright. Cats are such cowards that probably most of them die of heart attacks."

"I wouldn't call this cowardly. Maybe he's got himself electrocuted in the wires."

In the slanted, streaking sunlight, frosted branches of the hedges sparkled; in the hills, the bark of beeches glistened. Loud sighing and intermittent snoring came from below, through the drains in the bathroom and the kitchen. When Igor turned on the faucet, even the water seemed to flow a sleepy sorrow of a groaning hunter—or Igor's ears still murmured in the aftermath of the howling. Now he couldn't stay alert, although he had to go to work as a plumber of the spa hotels, where ladies from all over Croatia and Hungary came to improve their complexions in iodine mineral water; they languidly coiled in pink oval marble pools, and when adjusting pipes, he sometimes caught a glimpse of them— born-again embryos in halved and steaming eggs with ossified shells. Now he thought that if he wasn't alert at work, he might cause some damage, cut his fingers off.

Igor walked out and called the cat, but the cat didn't move. Its turquoise eyes glowed, independent of the sunlight.

Igor whistled like a bird, but the cat's ears stayed unmoved. He didn't want to let the cat remain suspended dead above his house. If a cat crossing your path spelled bad luck, a cat crossing your wires and looming lifeless in your window spelled doom. Would crows eat the cat? Maybe pigeons? Owls? He got a ladder and climbed, shakily, up the cracked post that smelled of oil and tar. When he reached for the cat, in a sudden blur the cat's claws and teeth lashed at his stretched hand. He lost balance, dropped the cat, and gripped the post. After the cat, his ladder fell. Slowly, hugging the post, with splinters needling his palms and sliding between his skin and his flesh, he descended to the ground. The claw swipes had made the back of his hand look like a fragmented music sheet, brownish with age; and two bloody canine marks coagulated, captured, and for now silenced two disharmonious notes of fear and hate—but the notes kept the frequency of the song that sooner or later would find throats to grip.

"What happened to the cat?" Dara asked.

"That interests you more than what happened to me?" He poured plum brandy over the music sheet that the back of his hand had become, and winced at the wet melody of scorching pain his nerves were hearing. Then he pinched splinters from his palms. The splinters hadn't provoked a flow of blood while under his skin, but once they were removed, blood flashed in the emptied lines like comets in the sky.

"Well, that'll teach you to pick up a strange cat without gloves. Where is it now? It must be starving."

"I'll go pet the dog and let him run after the cat."

"Let him stay down there—and I'll feed the cat."

She walked out. Igor, pouring plum brandy down his throat, saw a gorgeous tabby with thick black stripes—a veritable black and gray picture of a tiger—scratching its back against Dara's thin ankles, which were in thick woolen socks. Her heels, he noticed, even now formed a dancer's right angle; she never forgave him for living in the provinces where she couldn't become a professional dancer. The cat lapped milk, rubbed his back against the socks, lapped more milk. The cat's tail went straight up, and grew fluffy, perhaps from the static that flared up from the socks. The tail tip waved joyfully above round testes. Dara picked him up, scratched his tummy, and the cat licked her palm and put his paw pads on her cheek. And so they stayed for a whole minute, gazing at each other with an interspecies sympathy.

"That cat's so thin," Dara said as she poured milk into a tea cup. "We should take care of him."

"Is that up to us to decide?"

"Fritz will just have to get used to it. When he realizes that the cat is here to stay, he'll accept him and even love him."

But Fritz couldn't get used to it. At night he barked mercilessly. He chased the cat into roof pipes and into the hills. Once, when the cat fled onto a thin birch, Frtiz peeled the layers of bark with his teeth, and then gnawed on the wood, like a beaver, until the tree fell. The flying cat barely touched the ground before it bounced over the dog, up a huge beech. Fritz kept digging the beech roots and tearing them, perhaps with the design to bring down that tree, too. And maybe after a month of labor he would have succeeded if Igor hadn't found him and chained him again.

Fritz's hatred for the cat grew legendary. (And so, this story could have started like this: In a spa town there lived two mortal enemies, a cat and a dog. Now this was not unusual—there were many cats and dogs in the town, and they were all mortal and the hatred between them frequently entertained the inhabitants, Serbs and Croats, and the laughter of the inhabitants was loud. However, the hatred between most of the cats and dogs was amateurish compared with the hatred of a gray German shepherd and a gray tabby. The night the tabby appeared in the hedges on the edge of the town, the dog howled so terribly that his owner went into his larder and oiled his grandfather's gunpowder rifle . . . Anyhow, the story didn't start—nor will it end—this way.)

Fritz chased Bobo all over the hills and treed him up many trees; and yet, when he dragged his feet home exhausted and disenchanted, unable to lift his hanging tongue into his mouth, he'd see Bobo strutting across the yard to his bowl of milk, in the old barn's rafters. Fritz would yawn, while Bobo lapped his white nirvana of peace. Once, after a day of chasing, Fritz fell asleep, and Bobo came up and cuddled with him. Bobo licked his nose, purred in his ear, then left. Pretty soon Fritz awoke with a howl; he sniffed himself all over and even bit himself trying to get rid of the odious odor, and he kept sucking and chewing his fur as though he'd been infected with cat-flies. However, usually Fritz needed only a catnap to recover, and soon he'd be up against the barn howling and digging holes under the wooden wall. Once, in a corner, he surprised Bobo, who had been absorbed in the joys of tossing a dying mouse over his head. He flew at Bobo with predatory certainty. Bobo flew even faster past his face and tore his ear. Before Fritz had time to understand what had happened, Bobo was up on the wall, ostentatiously ignoring him. Fritz would have a V-cut in his ear for the rest of his life.

The inability of the two beasts to get along complicated the Lovraks' lives. They slept poorly. Fritz had been a passionate hunter even before Bobo showed up. He had leaped on anything that moved. But nothing matched this monomania for the cat.

"He hates life," Dara joked.

It was a miracle that the cat did not seek another home; but, as theirs was the last house in the town, this may have been his last chance.

Who knows how much longer this would have been going on if people hadn't begun to behave like—and worse than—cats and dogs. Lipik was one of the first towns to be surrounded by the Serb armies. When rumors of approaching Chetniks with their bared knives reached the town, and even more concretely, when a mortar shell shattered their roof tiles, the Lovraks rushed away. They couldn't find Fritz and Bobo to take them along—and besides, how could you take two such enemies in one little car?

Many cars, tractors, and trucks drove out of town—Croats north to Bjelovar, Serbs south to Banja Luka.

Igor and Dara stayed in a basement belonging to Igor's brother in Bjelovar. Igor feared to walk out into the streets, lest he should be drafted and forced to run at Serb tanks armed only with a rifle. His sense of masculinity was insulted—for he saw himself as a brave man. In his youth he had been a bar fighter. That is how he had met Dara when she worked as a tavern waitress. A giant drunk stalked her and, when she had finished her shift, attempted to rape her. Igor jumped at the giant and nearly strangled him. Dara had been grateful to him, and he had been proud. And now he was reduced to living with a bunch of onions and potatoes that in the winter sprouted their offspring; out of the old, shriveling fruits of the earth grew new pristine lives. And what could grow out of him? He tried to do some good—he fixed all the plumbing and rewired the house—but once he was done, out of his bleak moods sprouted only cynicism, which Dara couldn't take for long. She abhorred the fact that Serbs were attacking, but she also detested listening to the venom Croats, including Igor, spewed at Serbs—she was a Serb. When Croatian bands began to burn out houses of the Serbs who had left—and presumably become soldiers in the Serb army—she stepped on a train to Hungary. Weeks later she sent Igor a card from Belgrade, telling him that she hadn't felt safe in Croatia.

He was enraged. He had worried about her for weeks, and now she didn't feel safe! And who was responsible for that, if not the Serbs in Belgrade, whom she now served, cooking bean stews in fast food dives, feeding past and future murderers? He read the card while watching pictures of Lipik in the newsreel.

In the war only a dozen elderly people remained in Lipik. Serb soldiers lobbed mortar shells into the town for weeks without a break. Croatian policemen—there was no Croatian army at first—defended the town, entrenched in the schools, churches, and hospitals.

In the old Austrian spa buildings, rocketed many times, now loomed large holes, so that the ruins looked like skulls with empty eye sockets, with bricks and tiles on the side, like broken teeth. Many tree trunks, cut in half from stray howitzer hits, resembled the broken legs of tubercular patients, their yellow bones sticking out of crusty skins; the rest of the patients' bodies, which should have been above the broken femurs, was missing; the bodies may have hidden in iodine vapors or slid into the ground under the moss. Shards of stained-glass windows with peeing angels lay in the gardens and in pastel blue tiled swimming pools. The shards sank in a heap of dead crows, leaves of weeping willows, and oaks.

The gloom notwithstanding, most people could take care of themselves. At least they could run; they understood what was going on. But how were animals to understand war? They trembled as though a natural calamity were taking place—thunder, earthquake, fires. And all of these were taking place. A Lippizaner stable (from which Lipik got its name)—where for more than a century one of the original lines of the Austrian white horses kept going—had been firebombed. A white horse was seen running into the hills, with its mane and tail and penis ablaze. Another stepped on a cluster of mines and flew into the sky as a geyser of blood, iron, and hooves.

When that Christmas Eve Croatian soldiers broke the siege and took over the town, several of them wanted to enter the Lovraks' house. But on the threshold stood a wolf-like dog, and next to the dog, a tabby, leaning on the dog. The dog's paw gently and protectively lay over the tabby's shoulders. When the soldiers came closer, the dog growled most threateningly and the cat arched his back and hissed. The soldiers, who otherwise may not have felt any qualms at shooting an inimical dog, were touched. They didn't insist on entering the house, even though that may have been imprudent—Serb snipers could have crouched in there, but the captain of the unit decided that that was highly unlikely, for the house had a large tank hole gouged into its middle. On the way out, the Serb tanks had blasted holes in many houses, according to the dog in the manger fable: If we can't have this, neither will you.

Later, when Igor returned, Fritz wouldn't let him into the house.

"Don't you know me?" Igor shouted. "I'm your master."

But Fritz didn't acknowledge him. And when Igor wanted to pet Bobo, who showed no resentment but a great deal of indifference, Fritz growled jealously and nearly bit Igor's hand. Igor backed off, and Fritz's tongue washed Bobo.

With the help of the United Nations, Igor built a cabin in his yard. He was lonely. Not even his dog liked him. Not even the cat did.

He took photographs of Fritz and Bobo, and captured the images of the two souls cuddling. Igor sent the pictures to his wife in Belgrade. He wrote a letter, and among other sentences, he wrote these:

"During multiple-rocket-launcher fires, the two shell-shocked trembling creatures forgot to hate each other. Who knows how many nights they spent together, embraced. Who knows how they survived. I imagine that the cat hunted and fed the dog pigeons, mice, little rabbits. And when the cat couldn't catch anything, perhaps Fritz did. Or maybe they ate horse carcasses, or even human corpses. I don't want to imagine that but I just did. I am sure they didn't—they hunted. I see Bobo hunt in the yard in the morning. But the strange thing is, they don't let me approach them. They don't let me into the house, either. Anyhow, all I want to say is: If Fritz and Bobo get along, why couldn't we?"

That was a rhetorical question. Igor didn't expect an answer, but three weeks later—not much longer than it took the letter to reach Belgrade—Dara arrived on a seemingly empty train. The train wasn't in fact empty. People didn't dare to travel at night in the trains, and if they did, they lay on their seats and on the floors for fear of snipers shooting them from the woods.

Once she closed the squeaking yard gate of her old home, Dara hugged her husband. Fritz and Bobo came out of the house and growled at them.

Rye Harvest

I won't tell you my name. I don't know who you are; maybe you'd pass my name on, and there are many whom I fear now. I would love it if I had nothing to tell you. I have lost nearly everything—country, family, name—but I have retained my honor and gained a story, to my detriment, that I've retold in courts, where I was constantly interrupted and reduced to *yeses* and *nos*. I'll give you a more unhalted version than you would have heard in the court.

In the spring of 1991, just before Croatia's Declaration of Independence, the mayor of our village—I'll initial the village as V (for a generic village), although it didn't start with a V (and wasn't generic, to me at least)—went from house to house to tell us that after Croatia declared its statehood, the Yugoslav People's Army and Serb Chetniks would try to drive all the Croats out of the region to create a pure Serbian Republic of Krajina. "What guns are you comfortable with?" the mayor asked. "What did you do in the Yugoslav People's Army?"

I didn't believe him. I expected him to be locked up by the Yugoslav police any moment. I looked toward the door and was surprised that it was all quiet out there, except for a pair of cats fighting or making love.

"Infantry? Artillery?" He leaned over me, and I could see the hairs in his nostrils and atop his nose bulb, like sparse grasses on a shiny rock. This man had stolen my two goats that I'd let roam free in the grassy ditch in front of my house. They'd disappeared, and a month later I recognized them tied to the lamppost in front of his house. He probably made cheese out of my goats' milk. He smelled like chèvre even now. Anyway, I had gotten over the losses, and I answered, "I worked in radio communication. I did spend three months in training, and I can handle a basic rifle."

"Oh, good. Others can handle guns. You'll be in charge of the radio tower."

Soon I spent nights in the postal relay tower on a hill above the village, typing Morse code, jerky alterations of long and short beeps, and talking on the radio. I developed a network of people to chat with—radio communicators from Croatia, Serbia, Bosnia— and to trade in plum brandy, CDs, produce, medicinal plants, mushrooms (I collected them in the woods). Sometimes I picked up warnings when Serb jets were about to fly over our area to bomb. Then I'd call the priest by phone, and he'd toll the church bells and burn incense as though to hurt the devil's eyes, and some- times he'd burn up so much incense that it smelled as though the village was burning. People hid in the basements, but some didn't bother. Jets flew over us on the way to factory towns, to demolish the factories and terrorize townspeople so they'd run away. Once, before dawn, when I was already home, sleeping with my cat, the jets bombed—burned down the mayor's barn, struck the tower foundation. The electricity went out. Next day we brought in new cables, and were back in business, but a hole gaped in the base of the tower so that it looked like an old rotten and branchless oak that had grown a couple of huge mushrooms on top.

Everybody was more alert than usual—dreading what was to come, suspecting, being suspected, yet energized to work, talk. There was a solidarity among us; we would defend what was ours. I talked even with the mayor, about the habits of the red fox, what mushrooms you couldn't eat while drinking brandy, and so on. I cooked my favorite mushrooms for him and his wife, and when he went out to get blood sausages to go with that, without any thought, his wife and I embraced and made love, standing, next to the stove, and we continued on the sly, in haystacks, at least once a week. There was something erotic about the fear in which we all lived, and an incredible amount of spontaneous screwing went on. I won't get into all that, other than to say that I actually enjoyed myself, for a while. I was now twenty-five, felt clever, expanding my horizons beyond my village through the radio—I just didn't know how far these horizons would stretch me.

Now across from us over a river valley sat a Serbian village, and on the other side over another valley a Croatian village, and in the distance you could see blue Bosnian mountains, from where Yugoslav troops—supposedly neutral but fighting for the Serb side—fired projectiles into the Croatian villages. Ours was mixed ethnically and, thanks to that, rarely bombed. I had never worried about ethnicity, but now we were forced to think in those terms, and I still didn't bother to, much. In the village of about two hundred, I'd say there were eighty Croats, seventy Serbs, some Hungarians, Czechs, and Italians. Before World War II, half the village was German and Italian, but only one German remained. The partisans left this one German because they'd eaten the bread he'd baked. The bread was so good that the captain said, "You've got to stay here and keep baking that bread of yours for the rest of your life!" And the old stooping German did just that, with his large cracked hands, cracked from the heat of crusts and yeast.

Once Serbs encircled us, I felt strongly that I was a Croat. I was proud of it, felt offended by the aggression and all that. Now, I'm neither proud nor ashamed of it. The identity is certainly useless to me. I get nothing from it, and I have nothing to give it. If you come from some wonderful country like France or Italy, you gain immediate prestige with an aura of culture, but if you come from some godforsaken place like Croatia or Slavic Macedonia or Latvia, what do you get? Nothing, except to be categorized as an alien, a collaborator. Abroad, I'd be inclined to be ashamed of being a Croat if I didn't see that this system of grading ethnic identities wasn't a bunch of chauvinist crap even if under the guise of anti-chauvinism, such as, for example, to say that all Croats, Azeris, Armenians, and so on are hotheaded chauvinists who don't deserve respect, unlike the wonderfully cosmopolitan and tranquil Swedes and the Dutch. Anyhow, I cleaned my rifle every night to make sure it would fire smoothly at the invading Serbs. Still, although I hated the Serb armies, I didn't hate the Serbs around me.

My best childhood friends were all Serbs. I had grown up alone with my grandmother and spent most of my time with my friends; my father had left for Sweden in the first wave of worker migrations, and we never heard from him again. There were rumors—that he'd been killed by the Yugoslav secret police, that he'd married an old billionaire, that he was a drug lord. My mother left for Germany and cleaned office buildings there; she came home for a month every Christmas, but after she remarried, I saw her only two or three times. Now and then she'd send my grandmother a check, to cover school supplies for me. Since I grew up without a family, friendships became extra important.

Even later, when I went to Germany for a couple of years as a Gastarbeiter, with my Serb friends I hung around and drank my daily beer and played soccer on Sundays. When the war started, we were all back in the village, and sometimes two of them, Jovo and Dragan, visited me in the tower to play cards. They were part of our village army, along with most other male Serbs who were drafted. Only a few—those who probably were Serb nationalists or who felt threatened in Croatia—drove off to Bosnia and Serbia right before the war, and most who stayed with us sat at night at the edge of the village, trying to figure out how we could actually defend our fields and homes.

We were not an organized army. It was hard to know who was in charge of us. If we simply banded to defend the village, that made sense, but to be part of the army with an unclear chain of command made me uncomfortable. We called ourselves the Croatian army—at the time Croatia wasn't recognized and wasn't a country but a region of chaos—simply because on the other side was the Serbian army.

Pretty soon it became clear that the special police controlled us, and it wasn't always clear who controlled them—whether it was Mr. Marcup, a businessman, or Tudjman's party (Croatian Democratic Union). Often it seemed nobody controlled them because they had a free hand in many ways, especially with the women. Half the Croats in the police group came from other regions—except for a couple locals—and spoke mountain dialects. The other half spoke some kind of nasal English. They came from the States, Canada, Australia, Argentina—hard-core types with tattoos; there was a wild energy about them, like around a band of strays who are suddenly intoxicated with their ability to inspire fear.

I found it disturbing that the special police often searched Serb homes—even the homes of my friends—for guns, and sifted through their papers. This was a standard intimidation strategy, essential to ethnic cleansing; Serbian police did the same in the villages under their control.

As soon as the police got to the village, they usually came to the radio tower and wanted me to make them coffee. They smoked and looked out from the observation tower with powerful binoculars. I got to know the commander, Goran D., with a blond crew cut in the manner of the American marines, and his assistant, Igor M., whom I knew from my high-school days—he used to play soccer for our school, and was a particularly brutal defense player, taking pride in his slide-stop. Igor had a lisp since he had no front teeth, probably lost them in soccer. His back teeth were perfectly healthy and white. While he talked, I was distracted by the lolling and bobbing of his tongue.

"Hey, what do you think?" the commander, Goran, asked me once, after we'd exchanged a couple of jokes and slapped each other on the shoulder. "Are those Serbs of yours trustworthy?"

"Yes, why wouldn't they be?" I was no longer laughing. "I've known them since childhood, they've never cheated me. We slaughter our pigs together, and together we harvest and dance barefoot every fall on our grapes in the barrels to squeeze the juice out and make wine; we even cut down the oaks and cook the planks to curve them for these barrels. We are all just peasants, not nations."

"Oh! You talk slippery, more like a city slick than a peasant. Why do you say Croats, too, like we'd take anything from anybody that wasn't ours?"

"What I mean is, our fellow Serbs wouldn't want any army to come here and burn down their houses."

"Any army," he echoed me sardonically.

Talking to the policemen, you had to be on edge—they drove their points brutally. But mostly they joked obscenely (in their rounds, they collected jokes); strange, now I can't remember anything funny. They offered me brandy—and gave me bottles of Jack Daniels to keep, which I did—although as a rule they didn't drink themselves. I had a sip now and then, knowing that wasn't smart. They even offered me women if I cooperated with them and helped them monitor the local Serbs.

But two weeks after our "cooperation" started, they shouted at me that I hadn't collected any information, that I better shape up, what use was I as a communications director, and so on.

One late afternoon, as I was harvesting rye in the lush green and orange splendor of late summer fields on the edge of deciduous woods, I heard screams. I went over the hill and saw two men handcuffed to two young oaks. Several members of the special police force were punching Jovo and Dragan, and kicking them with their boots.

I laid aside my sickle, and rushed over.

"What are you doing?" I shouted to Goran.

"What do you mean, what are we doing? Isn't it obvious? Just minding our business. Ask what they are doing."

"What?"

"They want to run over there, join their Serbian brothers."

"How do you know?"

"We know."

"For sure?"

"Somebody overheard them in a tavern."

"So it's just a rumor. I don't believe they'd do it. Why don't you let them go?"

"How come you trust Serbs?"

"These guys are my friends."

"Your friends. Well, they aren't friends of the Croatian people."

I insisted that they be freed, but Goran laughed. "I don't have the keys to their handcuffs."

"Who has the keys?"

"The guy with the keys is gone to the grocery store."

"At least you can stop beating them!"

"All right, we'll do that. But let this be clear to you." He leaned his face into mine and pushed his forefinger into my neck, into the V of my larynx, so that I couldn't swallow my saliva. "If they go over to the other side, we'll be back, and we'll continue the beating where we left off—but this time it'll be on you. You understand that? You still vouch for them?"

"Of course I do."

"What's 'of course' about it? Make sure the 'course' doesn't get you. You must know about them, haven't you done your homework?"

And the policemen began to walk off toward a jeep.

"Hey, who'll unlock them?"

"What's wrong?" lisped Igor. "They look good like this."

And the police drove off.

The two friends groaned. Jovan thanked me; Dragan kept moaning, hanging from his handcuffs.

I went home to get a metal saw and brandy to wash their wounds and to soothe their throats, but when I got there, the police were back, and this time they had the keys.

Naturally, after the treatment they had suffered, my two friends ran away. I don't know where they went, but where would they go? Who knows, maybe they just fled abroad.

The police came three days later, and Igor asked me, "So where did those friends of yours go?"

I was surprised that he now could shape all the consonants while he used to loll his tongue to fake most of them.

"How would I know?" I shrugged.

"How wouldn't you know? You were so chummy with them, they'd confide in you, wouldn't they? And if they wouldn't, why did you put your neck on the line?" He grinned widely. He used to cover up his mouth, embarrassed by his missing teeth, but now he had fine porcelain teeth. Such teeth you couldn't get in socialist dentistry before; this was private enterprise, expensive stuff.

"I didn't even know they had disappeared." I didn't want to appear nervous, but I spoke out of breath anyway.

"You guaranteed that they would stay with us."

"No, I said they wouldn't run over to the Serb side. Anyway, I'm not their keeper. I couldn't lock them up. They are free to go wherever they like, why not?"

"Deserters. They didn't stay with us. Where do you expect their loyalties to lie anyhow?"

The cops kept repeating their line, and it would have been a boring conversation if there hadn't been a distinct sensation of threat to it. They told me to walk out with them to the back of the building, gave me a glass of wine. "You never know," said Igor, "this may be your last. No point in leaving without one. Besides, you might enjoy it better if you're a bit tipsy." The commander, Goran, didn't say anything. He used a nail clipper, and in a moment of silence, the clips sounded loud. When he'd done clipping his fingernails, he took off his boots, sat on a thick root, and clipped his toenails and then with his fingers cleaned the dirt between his toes.

The police thugs formed a circle around me, and they took turns hitting me. Fists, boots, gun barrels, clubs. A blow brought me to the ground. I had a sensation of heat flashing through my brain and down my spine. I passed out, and when I came to my senses, it was getting dark, a blue evening. An old man with a sponge of cold water was washing my head. He told me that I'd been out for an hour. "Can you walk?" he asked.

No, I couldn't walk. The man helped me to his tractor and drove me home. My mouth hurt and bled. I was missing most of my front teeth. My right flank was soaked in hot blood, and I shivered although it wasn't cold.

"Why are you helping me?" I asked the man, and recognized him as the old baker. "I hope you didn't ask them to stop beating me?"

"No, just watched from the side."

"Did they see you?"

"Sure."

"Do they know you are helping me?"

"They know everything. What do you want? That I dump you in the field?"

"Might as well."

He drove me to my grandmother's place and gave me a loaf of soft bread, but I couldn't chew it; it would mix with the blood of my gums. For now I wasn't hungry; I was drinking my own blood with each swallow. My tongue got stuck against my palate, and I could hardly unglue it.

My grandmother nursed me for days. She was, as I said, my only relative in the village. So that makes it understandable why I stuck by my friends so stubbornly, though, obviously, it did me no good. Grandmother washed my wounds with brandy and garlic juice and laid slices of onions over them; she gave me a lot of goat milk to drink. The more time passed, the more I hurt. As soon as I made a step, there'd be a painful jolt in my head. I wondered whether I had internal bleeding. I knew I couldn't take any aspirin, because it would increase the bleeding. I couldn't breathe in hard; my side scorched, where the bayonet wound, or a knife wound, was healing without stitches. It needed stitches, and my brain a CAT scan for the concussion. I'd read you could die from blows to the head even a week after you got them, and I thought maybe I would die soon. How would I go to the hospital now? If I went into the town, I'd pass checkpoints. How could I tell them that the Croatian police beat me? I could lie, but the police probably knew about me.

I had fevers; my wounds were probably infected. But I was at peace. Nothing to be done. I could die, for why live? Death would be easy in the moments when I was passing out anyhow.

My grandmother called up my uncle Ivan. The phones still worked. He drove over from the town of K., packed me in the trunk of his Opel, and drove me to Zagreb. During the ride, each stone on the road jolted my brain.

On my Yugoslav passport I went to Hungary by train. The border was still controlled by Yugoslav police and the Federal Army. A tired cop asked where I was going. I said, "To the hospital."

"Don't you have hospitals in Zagreb?"

"I couldn't go to one in Zagreb. Their military police beat me."

"Would the hospital people know that? Anyway, why should I care? Keep going."

Clearly I couldn't be used as a soldier by any army anymore. Who'd want to keep me?

I tracked down my mother in Mannheim, Germany, and she said she'd let me stay with her for several months, or, as she put it, "until you get your feet on the ground" (or cement). Divorced, she lived with a parakeet, who kept squeaking at the most ungodly hours. The cage was right above my bed next to the window so the bird could enjoy sunlight—and it was sunny about ten minutes a week, from what I could tell. For the cage floor, she used newspapers, mostly the porous kind, like *Die Zeit.* So at night, crap would melt holes in the paper, and this mush of cellulose, lead, piss, and crap dripped on me. I moved the cage to the other end of the room, but my mother put it right back above me. So I bought the thickest glossy magazine I could find, *Der Spiegel,* not to read but to fortify the cage. When I opened the cage to place the magazine inside, the colorful shooter flew out. Only now, as the bird kept flying, did I notice that a window was open, just a crack, but the bird flew right out. My mother was furious, and she wept, and then threw me out. So much for family.

Luckily, I had already made friends with a student of theology in Heidelberg, where I hoped I could study radio communications technology. Hans let me stay with him for several weeks.

I applied for asylum status in Bonn. The judge, who listened to half of my story, turned me down and said, "We've recognized Croatia as an independent country. One of the conditions for the recognition was that human rights be fully respected. The Croatian foreign minister vouches that all refugees will be safe upon return. You as an ethnic Croat have nothing to fear."

"To begin with," I said in German, "the local commander of the special police force became a member of the parliament. His assistant, Igor, became the chief of the police in the town that's the county seat for my village. The only way for me to live in Croatia is to get the papers in that police station that controls my county. How would he react when he saw I was back? I'd rather not find out. He probably thought they had left me dead in the field. I know there is a legal system there that looks good on paper, and if I knew people of influence and had enough money, I could sue everybody who beat me, and he knows that. This chief of police would want to eliminate me."

The clean-shaven judge with golden glasses nodded and said that whatever I was saying was psychological and personal, not political. "If everybody sought revenge or the means to prevent revenge, then most of the region, up to twenty million people, could seek asylum, probably in Germany. Wouldn't that be absurd? Since you aren't a political enemy of the ruling party—and the ruling party even allowed opposition to participate in elections— and you made the point that you were apolitical, belonging to no party, I deem that it would be safe for you to return to Croatia." He gave me one week to leave Germany for Croatia. When I asked for my passport, he said they would mail it to Zagreb and would issue me exit papers that would allow me to travel only to Croatia.

Naturally, I didn't go to Croatia. I tried to get asylum papers at the U.S. Embassy in Bonn. When the officer found out that Germany had declined my application, she discouraged me from applying, saying that the Germans were much better informed about the situation in the Balkans than the Americans.

Hans wondered how he could help me. He suggested that he could find me a novice position in the Benedictine monastery in Ziegelhausen, just north of Heidelberg. "You'd love it there," he said. "You could walk on the Philosophenweg in the woods every day, brew beer with them, and I don't think that they would even need to report you to the state. Anyway, their giving you a shelter would make you immune, I'm sure."

Monasteries never appealed to me. Besides, I believed in America. When all else fails, go to America—hasn't that been the European formula for the last three centuries?

As we talked, I stared at Hans. With his closely cut black hair, a wide nose, and a big jaw, he resembled me.

"Why don't you lend me your passport!" Before I was even aware that I'd formed the thought, I'd shouted it. "Get a visa at the U.S. Consulate, and lend me your passport."

"What do you mean, lend?"

"I'll mail it back to you from the States once I get there."

In a week, he gave me his passport with a tourist visa stamp that was valid for one year.

In the States, with the help of the passport, I got a driver's license, and the license is everything, your citizenship, practically, or so it seemed. It didn't bother me that I didn't have a green card. There were many illegal aliens in the country, and now and then there was an amnesty program.

But pretty soon it began to bother me that since I had an ac-cent, I had to identify myself, by nationality, when I worked as a porter at a Hilton. If I said I was an American, people raised their eyebrows.

"This is a nation of immigrants," I said, "isn't it?"

"Sure, in a way," they'd say, "but where do you really come from?"

So I'd have to say I came from Germany, and sometimes, when Germans cheered up at that thought and switched to German, I had to decline to speak in German—they would have read me—and a couple of times I claimed I was a Romanian German, a *Volksdeutscher*. I found that uncomfortable, especially when a German journalist visited me to make a report on how *Volksdeutscher* lived in the States. I declined the interview. Lying itself wouldn't bother me so much, but somehow the sensation that I could never introduce myself did. I felt my old land—I don't mean Croatia, but my region and village—to be part of me, and never to mention it hurt.

I began to introduce myself by my real name and real region. I legally changed my name from the assumed German one to the Croatian one, although that seemed odd: If you have a foreign-sounding name, you change it to something like George Johnson, not something even more foreign. On my state tax return—I wanted to become an honest American—I filled out the name-change forms.

A very simple thing, however, happened. After a year, when the visa on the German passport expired, the INS officials showed up at my address, at my uncle's. They tracked me down through my employers.

The officers, when I opened the door, asked, "Are you Hans K. . . ."

I said that I wasn't the German, but while I talked to them, for some reason, I had a strong German accent.

They showed me Hans's photo from the visa application, the duplicate, and said, "Sure looks like you." I said that was just a co-incidence, which of course it was, but they shackled me. I asked them to release me so I could show them my papers—new driver's license, income forms, and the tax returns, where they read that I had changed my name. I'd forgotten it was all there. I told them then the whole story—they were even touched—and when I asked to be allowed to appeal to the courts, they agreed, and let me go free so I could pursue the asylum application, and gave me three months to do so, and they gave me extensions, so a year later the deportation trial took place.

There's one system of justice—with jury—for the citizens, and another for the asylum seekers, without jury. For the latter, a judge and a lawyer suffice.

The judge listened to the INS official demanding that I be deported and to my lawyer—a Jewish woman of Polish origin who had just graduated from the University of Chicago Law School and who volunteered to protect me—that I be allowed to stay. I trusted my lawyer's sharp mind. I was attracted to her, but the asylum was more urgent, and I was as timid as a schoolboy around her. She told me that if I married an American, I'd easily become a legal resident, but uncertain of how to introduce myself, I hadn't talked enough to any women to develop a relationship.

I was the only witness for myself. The judge asked me many questions, which worked more as an interruption to my story than any kind of clarification. Whenever I managed to start explaining what had actually happened, what kind of secret police Croatia had, he'd ask me something technical and irrelevant, like the name of a river.

During the testimony, the judge nodded off while my lawyer questioned me about the threats that awaited me at home (the Croatian army's offensive that drove Serbs out of the region paved the way for ruthless police rule in the provinces). When it was His Honor's turn again, he woke up and said, "Now, in your testimony, you said that your grandmother had to leave your village before the Croatian forces attacked, peacefully, and in your written statement in the application for asylum you claimed that your grandmother was kicked and knocked down and forcefully taken out? Can you explain the discrepancy?"

"Yes, I can. My English wasn't good enough when I submitted

the application first, and my uncle, who was writing this, misunderstood me, and we never got to correct this."

"Why would the Croatian army drive her, as a Croat, out?"

"It was a blitz attack. They first drove everybody out—they had no time to check IDs and all that—so they could bomb the hell out of the place without worrying about the civilians."

"Why wouldn't you want to return to your village?" asked the judge.

"I would, Your Honor, but the village doesn't exist. It was razed to the ground from what I have heard."

"What army did that?"

"It's hard to tell. After I left, Serbs bombed and took the village, and the village changed hands several times. The war activity destroyed it."

"So where would you live if you went back?"

"So I'd have to live in Zagreb at first, and to my mind, that's the same thing as living in Chicago—I could just as well live in Chicago or Los Angeles."

"Well, why not go to Zagreb?"

"One of the policemen is now a big shot in Zagreb." I even added that the village mayor would be after me because he'd found out that I'd had an affair with his wife.

At that, the judge threw up his arms. "There's no such thing as asylum for protection from jealous husbands. Moreover, to the question of whether you were a habitual fornicator, you answered negatively on the application form. So what can we believe of you?"

"It wasn't a habit. And, I haven't had sex in two years."

The judge glossed over my final reason for the asylum application; namely, that since the war in the former Yugoslavia would probably keep going on for a thousand years—if you believed the American newspapers, you'd have to believe that—I could not live there with my post-traumatic stress syndrome.

He replied: "This country has invested enormous resources to make sure that the peace in the Balkans would take hold, and therefore I see no reason why the country should put even further resources in taking care of refugees who would apparently be safe in their native regions."

The judge asked for the proceedings to be adjourned. When he came back, he asked me: "If your application is denied here, what other country would you consider moving to in order to apply for an asylum?"

My lawyer asked for clarification: "To apply to stay here or in that country?"

I thought for several minutes—I was dazed. What, will they deport me? Are there cops around? I looked over my shoulder. Cops, no matter what nationality, terrified me.

The judge asked again, and my lawyer urged me to answer.

"Australia," I said. I knew nothing of Australia, except that it was something like Texas stuck in the middle of the ocean.

The judge then read the verdict, off the top of his head, from what I could tell—something like this:

"Since the claimant was not wounded severely enough to seek hospitalization, there is no ground to suspect that his life would be threatened in Croatia. If the group of men from the police force had wanted to kill him, they could have done so in the war. Now in peace, the likelihood that they would have motivation to kill him is low, according to my estimate.

"The claimant has one month to leave this country voluntarily for Croatia at his expense or to Australia if the Australian government agrees to accept him. If he doesn't leave in thirty days, he will be deported to Australia within ninety days or to some other country that agrees to accept him, and if none does, he will be deported to Croatia. I will give him five years before he may reapply for asylum in this country."

And that was that. My scars, my passing out, my bayonet wound, the teeth knocked out, that didn't qualify as a credible threat and something that should have gotten medical attention.

I know that many people who had never been threatened or

were threatened much less than I had been—Croats from Serbia and Serbs from Croatia—got asylum.

I marveled that the judge, who probably lived in a wealthy suburb—played golf and retold stories from the court to entertain people at cocktail parties—that he should judge who was safe and who wasn't in the Balkans. Anything that deviated from the formula—divisions along the ethnic lines—didn't work for him and for the German judges.

So what do I do? Go retell my story in Australia? Why would it work there? They'd say the Germans and the Americans know better, and if they think you'd be safe, why should we think otherwise? Could I end up like that man without papers who lives in a Parisian airport? No country, no papers, only a story about no country and no papers. That's why I am writing this down, so I can have more papers (an uninterrupted story) to simply hand over to whoever wants to judge my applications.

I thought all this would sound more dramatic. If you say something that is not true often enough, you convince yourself that it is true; and if you repeat something that is true often enough, you begin to doubt it. So here I am, a confirmed un-amnestiable illegal alien. Still, I admired the fact that after the judgment, I was free to walk away from the court. I had thought I would be handcuffed and deported on the spot. That they left it up to me to come back to be deported—that almost convinces me that I would indeed like to stay here.

I am not saying that I'm not going to Australia or Finland (Finland, Endland?). If I leave the States, I want at least my story, such as it is, to stay. I think many Americans might want to know that there's no jury for foreigners, asylum applicants, here. And they should have the opportunity to know that the Balkan problems can't be reduced to a chemical formula of adrenal hatred among different ethnic groups. Am I asking to give a geography lesson? Should I include a map here, or somewhere, of my old land? Better not. For me, that land is disappearing into unreliable memories, and I can't say that I regret that.

The End

Although Daniel Markovich got exile status in the States on the grounds of religious persecution in Yugoslavia, after several years of living in Cleveland he no longer went to church, and many years later he quit reading the Bible. This is how it happened, from the beginning to the end.

He came to the States in 1968 when Soviets invaded Czecho-slovakia; he had believed that the next stop on the Soviet world tour would be Yugoslavia. While Czechs were streaming into the States, he couldn't claim the Soviet threat in Yugoslavia as grounds for being a refugee.

But his claims of religious persecution were not false.

Daniel had wanted to be a geography teacher in Daruvar, Northern Croatia. In the interview, he answered the question, "Do you believe in God?" affirmatively. The frog-eyed principal, a boar hunter—there were still some boars alive at the time in the Papuk and Psunj Mountains—said, "Of course, you can't teach if you're intoxicated with the opiate of the masses. How can you teach the principles of the dialectical materialism if your head is filled with ghosts?"

"I understand the principles perfectly well."

"But you don't believe them."

"God and dialectical materialism are not at odds with each other."

"How about evolution?"

"According to the Bible, God created man last, and according to the theory of evolution, man is one of the last mammals to evolve. The two are in harmony."

"Where is God? Show him to me. See, you can't. You're superstitious."

"I can't show you a neutron either, and you take the scientists' word for granted, don't you? I often do. As for the opiate of the masses," Daniel said, "what is the bottle of *slivovitz* doing on your table?"

The school principal threw him out, and no matter where Daniel applied for a teaching position, he didn't get it—and he suspected that it had to do with his being a Croat as much as with his never denying his belief in God. For a couple of years before getting to the States, he worked for a living as a house painter and mason. He grew to be big-fisted and muscular; and with his broad-chested frame, dark red beard and long red hair, from a distance he looked like a big torch. He got married, to a student of accounting, Mira, a pale freckled blonde with large dark brown eyes.

They immigrated to the States, in Cleveland, Ohio, and Mira gave birth to a daughter and then to a son. At first Daniel spent a lot of time preaching in Croatian in a Protestant church whose congregation was Croatian and Serbian, and instead of learning English, he studied Greek, because he needed to understand Christ in the original New Testament language more than he needed to understand Walter Cronkite, although he listened to Cronkite too, vaguely understanding him.

Soon, however, the church in Cleveland had grown large enough to employ a full-time minister, who'd just immigrated from Serbia. Daniel didn't like being the second fiddle to an in-experienced youngster, who was getting overpaid for doing what should be the labor of love. The services were now conducted in Serbian. Daniel went to church no more than once a month.

Daniel worked as a mason and house painter. Americans, of course, had no use for geography, so his chances of landing a job in that field were even slimmer in Ohio than in Yugoslavia. Daniel was not happy with his physical labor. *All nature travails,* he quoted, to console himself, and considered it unavoidable to suffer. Even Saint Paul worked—made and repaired fishing equipment—for a living; labor was a genuinely apostolic thing to do. Daniel chiseled stones and fitted them together into garden walls on several estates in Shaker Heights—those were good and well-paying jobs except that little glassy stone shards had hit and damaged his right eye. He stripped old lead paint on many houses and painted with new lead-based paint. The noxious fumes gave him dizzying headaches. He joked that labor was the opiate of the masses. By the time Sunday came, he'd be bleary-eyed, like someone who had been drinking brandy all week long. After a couple of years of working like this, he went to church once every two months. In the evenings he fell asleep with the Greek New Testament in his hands or sliding out of his hands onto the floor, where one day his dalmatian, whom he'd forgotten to feed, ate it—chewed the whole Gospel, and the Book of Revelations, and the Psalms to boot. From now on, he called his dog Saint Dalmatian. Daniel got another Greek New Testament, and continued his practice of dozing off with abstruse verses made even more abstruse and sanctimonious by the ancient tongue.

Daniel didn't like Cleveland winters with icy winds blowing from Lake Erie, so he moved with his family south, to Cincinnati, where there weren't many Croats, and even fewer Croatian Baptists, but that no longer mattered to him. He carried the Gospel in his heart, a portable cathedral, with two atriums and two dark Holy of Holies that were constantly washed in his own blood.

"Let's go to Florida if you want heat," suggested Mira.

"That would be too steamy. Besides, a hurricane might lift our house and drop it in the ocean. Or one of those rockets, if it failed in its takeoff, might fall on our house and burn it to the ground. NASA is the new Tower of Babel, I tell you. God will mix them all up, if Americans and the Chinese start working together: Not only will they lose the common languages, they'll also lose the common math that helps them blast the rockets."

"You are crazy," Mira said. "That's one likable thing about you."

"Why go anywhere else? It's hot enough in Cincinnati," Daniel said. "With you around." Mira, although she was forty, still had outstanding breasts and supple thighs, large and resilient, and when children weren't around, Daniel stroked her, and they frequently made love, wherever they happened to be when lust took hold of them.

They bought a cheap house in Northside, painted the bricks all red, as was the fashion in Cincinnati.

Even after a dozen years of being in the States, Daniel hadn't learned English; he was still improving his Greek. He worked too much, and grew ill. He got scorching pains from his kidneys down the urethra, and when he could no longer take it, he went to the hospital. He had a painful intervention, the old-fashioned way. But what pained him even more, once he recovered, was the bill for $5,000.

He had no insurance, neither did Mira, who worked as a checkout cashier in Woolworth's. Daniel paid the bill because he wanted to be a law-abiding citizen and good Christian. But now he needed to work even more, to the point of his biological limits. Why did God's punishment of Adam—*In the sweat of thy face shalt thou eat bread*—affect him so much, while many other people never seemed to work; they drank bourbon while making transactions?

He no longer had time for Greek, let alone English, and only rarely did he read the New Testament in Croatian. That pained him, but he thought that he shouldn't be selfish and work toward his own sainthood; God should understand that he needed to give

his son and his daughter a chance to prosper. And once they were
off to college, he'd study the Bible more assiduously than ever
before.

Marina, already sixteen, was an "A" student, but lately she had
been restless; she got a driver's license and wanted to go out and
have pizza with her friends all the time. She worried him. He'd
sometimes take a look at her; she was a full-figured woman, who
wore tight skirts. Looking at her womanly body, he felt uncomfortable, as though it was sinful to notice his daughter, and to
resolve his discomfort, he shouted at her that she should wear
longer skirts, and threatened to beat her if she walked out like
that, nearly naked.

"Dad, if you beat me, I'll have you arrested for child abuse."

"You are no longer a child. You paint your lips scarlet like a
harlot."

"Dad, what do you know about harlots?" she asked, pouting
her full red lips. "They don't exist in this country, do they?"

He didn't answer but looked at her sadly. She was brazen, and
he resented that. What a country, where you have no means to
discipline your child, but where without discipline a girl could
perish, be gobbled up by frolicking and drug-crazed mobs.

When she turned seventeen, she eloped with a law student
who attended the same church as the rest of the family. Mira
blamed it on Daniel's strictness. "If you'd been more lenient, they
could have dated for a while, she could have brought him home,
we could have gotten to know him. You should be happy anyway.
I know him from the church; she made a catch, I'd say."

"How can we be a family if we run away from each other? Is
that the American way?" To his mind, they were all, except him,
Americans now. They spoke English among themselves, and his
kids, from what he could tell, had no accent in English.

Mira said to him (in Croatian, the English equivalent of this):
"Don't worry, later she'll be in touch with us—when you calm
down."

"Yeah, when he impregnates and abandons her."

"Why do you never see the bright side? He's a good Christian."

"Do good Christians elope?"

"You should know. Jacob with Rachel and Leah."

"Oh, in that case . . . Jacob actually waited awhile first—for fourteen years. These kids waited for fourteen minutes at the most." But, he was glad. Things might be easier now. At least he wouldn't have to save for her education.

Tony was a "B" student, not brilliant but steady. He helped with painting houses, and maybe he'd be an "A" student, thought Daniel, if those fumes hadn't gotten to him as well. So he owed it to his son, to send him away to college.

Daniel and Tony watched TV evangelists; Daniel liked the idea that you could worship at home, together with a million people at the same time. One Sunday morning they watched Schuyler interview a former Miss America, who had failed to win the competition in her state, and then prayed for a year, believing that God would help her, and God blessed her so that she not only won her state competition, but the nationals as well. "If you want something, believe that God will give it to you. If you want to be Miss America, pray and believe, and you'll be Miss America." That's what Miss America said, and Schuyler agreed with her and repeated it. Daniel laughed. "No matter what I believed, I could never become Miss America. I'd be lucky if I became an American. What nonsense. One more false prophet. Switch off the TV, son."

Years passed. Now and then the Markoviches got cards from their married daughter, who lived in Seattle. On Sundays, overworked Daniel needed to sleep; church was in his bed, where he celebrated Sabbath, the seventh day, in perfect rest, supine and sometimes prostrate, as if in prayer, and he couldn't keep his bloodshot eyes open. By now he'd lost most of his hair, but in compensation, grew a red beard.

Mira and Tony, now a senior at U.C., attended services at a

neighborhood Baptist church. One morning, Mira said to Daniel, "Come, let's go to church, at least your English will improve."

"For that I can watch TV," he said. "Or better yet, read the word of God."

"Your soul will improve."

"If work doesn't, I don't know what will improve it. I need rest, wife, not stiff benches. My back hurts."

"Go see a chiropractor."

"But that's a witch doctor, isn't it? How can you recommend one and go to church? They are too expensive anyway. To pay to see one, I'd have to work one more day and hurt myself."

"And how do you think you'll pass the citizenship test if you can't even understand the questions?"

"Good question. Let me rest."

He fell asleep on their orange sofa and snored even before the sun set.

In the morning, he woke up Tony to go out and work. "Got to pay for school," he said. With nostalgia, he thought of the old days in Yugoslavia, where higher education was free.

They drove to Hyde Park in their Toyota pickup with ladders on top. On the way they stopped for coffee at Dairy Queen. Tony picked up a newspaper, and as they drove on, he said, "Dad, look at this, there's a war in Croatia."

"Nonsense."

"Why, look at this, in Dalj near the Danube Bridge, Yugoslav forces killed seventy-two Croatian policemen."

"Really? What else does it say?" He spilled hot coffee over his white shirt. "But that's not war," he said. "Just several dozen people killed."

"And to you that's normal?" Tony asked.

"Not normal, just not war."

"What is war then?'

"Big armies attacking each other, not just incidents."

But while he painted he was worried and absentminded. His wrists hurt, swollen with arthritis. His brush strokes often went over window sills, and he had to wipe the paint. A kid's room that was supposed to be half red, half blue, he painted all blue in quick rolls, with the blue paint dripping from the ceiling onto his paper cap and brows. He'd made a cap out of the *New York Times*.

During the citizenship test, Daniel could understand almost no questions.

"Maybe we should wait," said the officer. "You must be able to speak English to participate in our democracy. How will you know what you're voting for if you can't understand the language? Out of five questions, you got only one right, that Bush is the president."

"I know. I learn," Daniel said. "Ask more."

The officer, a middle-aged black woman, said, "All right. Who is the governor of Ohio?"

"Voinovich!" Daniel exclaimed. He knew—there were so few people from Yugoslavia in politics, and here was one. Although Voinovich was a Serb, Daniel was proud of him—it made it easier in a way to be a "vich" in Ohio. "And Kucinich was the mayor of Cleveland," he said.

"We don't have to worry about Cleveland right now," the officer said and scrutinized him. "All right, you pass. Welcome to the United States of America!"

"Thank you, thank you!" he said.

As he pulled out of the parking lot on Court Street, he said to Tony and Mira: "Can you believe it, the Serb governor's name saved me from flunking the citizenship test. You never know where help will come from."

"It's amazing," said Tony.

"I was so worried that you wouldn't make it," Mira said. "We are all Americans now, can you believe it? Isn't it great?"

"Sure thing," said Tony. "Except, who's going to believe Dad? He speaks English so badly."

"At least they'll believe you," said Daniel. "Especially when they draft you. You had to say you'd bear arms for this country, didn't you?"

Daniel was proud of being an American, and as a true American, he watched the six o'clock news every night after work, and later CNN. Although he still spoke with a heavy accent and without much grammar, he understood English. And when one hot morning he got the news that his hometown, Pakrac, in Croatia was attacked by Serb irregulars backed by the Yugoslav Federal Army, he did not go to work. He tried to call his old uncle who lived on the eastern side of the Pakra river—he couldn't get through. He couldn't get through to any members of his family in Croatia. He grew anxious, and read the Bible but found little comfort.

Daniel bought a shortwave radio and listened to the news every night. He got Croatian radio, BBC, *Deutsche Welle*. There was a report of the Pakrac hospital being bombed, and another of Vukovar being surrounded by 20,000 troops, and people massacred. Gradually, he managed to hear from most of his relatives, but he still feared for their lives. But even more he feared for their souls; most of them were atheists.

Vukovar fell three months later, and Daniel's life went on as usual; after work he watched CNN and listened to the pulsing shortwaves on the radio until he fell asleep.

A couple of years later the war in Croatia was at a standstill and the war in Bosnia reached a high pitch; some of Daniel's relatives from the vicinity of Banja Luka disappeared. One day as he worked and worried, painting wooden siding in a Hyde Park house among many large trees, he saw a blonde woman in a tennis skirt nimbly stretching on the floor. He gazed at her strong muscular and smoothly feminine thighs and her freckled cleavage as she bent to touch her Nikes with her fingers. Daniel's ladder shook and scraped on the wood siding.

"Oh, goodness, you'll fall if you don't watch out," she said.

"That's the problem. I watch."

"Let me hold your ladder," she said.

He was leaning over the tall window, his knees at her eye level. She grabbed the ladder.

"Not necessary," he said. "It's firm."

"Is it?" she said and touched his crotch. Like a youngster, he got an instant erection. "Oh, that's a compliment," she said. "My husband doesn't react like that to me. Thank you, my friend." She spoke up into his crotch, and it wasn't clear to him whether she was talking to him, or to a part of him. She sounded delighted at any rate. She unzipped his jeans, and held his penis in her hands. With a brush laden with dripping white paint, which sprinkled over her hedges along the house, and another hand holding on to the bucket of paint, he couldn't defend himself, unless he said something, and he couldn't think right away what he could say that wouldn't be rude. And by the time he could think to say something, like "You are beautiful but I am a married Christian and therefore this is not the right thing to do," he felt tremors of lust and a delicious comfort in yielding to what was happening with such dexterity; her gently sliding nails made his lower abdomen twitch.

Daniel moved, bending lower a little bit, and he put the brush on the can of paint, and fastened the can along the ladder; the hairs on his forearm got stuck in a screw. Probably thinking that he wanted to jump into the room, she said, "Oh no, this is a fine arrangement. You keep doing your thing, I'll do mine if you don't mind."

When he came, he was flushed, with sweat drenching his shirt. "This is fun," she said. "Why don't you come here tomorrow, and we'll play some more through the window?"

"But job done today."

"I know. We could do a bigger one tomorrow."

After this Daniel felt a mixture of shame and guilt. What's the big deal, he thought. It happens. It's not like I have done anything.

I just stood there; she did it. What choice did I have? But that reminded him of Adam's excuse in the Garden of Eden. She did it. Why be selfish and worry about himself; he had to worry about his relatives in the Balkans. So what if he wasn't a saint?

That evening he went to a gathering of Croatian immigrants at a winery, Vinoklet, in the suburbs of Cincinnati. The sun was setting colorfully over the vineyards, and Daniel had the impression that he was in his native region. A Croatian engineer who ran the winery had nearly replicated his native landscape here—rolling hills with rows of vines, greenish fish ponds, and scattered groves of apple trees. At the entrance to the winery, a sign read, "Warning: consumption of our wines in moderate amounts creates an aura of well being that may lead to pregnancy."

Passionate emigrés gave speeches about the importance of writing letters to the White House, to the state senator, to alert them that there was a large Croatian population that wanted something done to stop the war in Bosnia with a fair settlement for the Croatian minority. "You can all give twenty dollars apiece to hire someone who will send the messages to the White House by e-mail if you don't have the time for it."

Daniel gave, and then drank the wines, "Tears of Joy" and "Sunset Blush." He chatted with a man who had lost his arm in World War II; he enjoyed speaking Croatian and feeling like he was not a foreigner. "I was just a lad then," the man said. "I was harvesting in a little wheatfield when Chetniks came, surrounded us, and took us to Knin, where they hacked us with knives. I woke up in a mound of bodies, and crawled out. A nurse helped me, and I was between life and death for months, and for ten years my wound kept festering, until I finally recovered, probably thanks to wine. I love wine."

"Probably God saved you. Not wine."

"Maybe the Virgin saved me."

"Which one?" Daniel asked.

"As far as I can tell, you don't mind being saved by wine either, my friend, do you?" The man laughed loudly, with a smell of garlic and wine coming out of him.

True, Daniel was drunk, as he hadn't been in years. He realized that although he liked the man he didn't like arguing with Catholics, and if campaigning for Croatia meant simply campaigning for Catholics, he wasn't enthusiastic. But he had to do something to help his relatives. He had another glass of red wine.

And next morning, he had a headache. He listened to the news about a great earthquake somewhere in China, a flood in northern Europe, further starvation in Somalia, and more massacres in Rwanda.

The accumulation of so much trouble at once made him feel uneasy, especially since he felt guilty that he had drunk so much the night before and even worse, that he had enjoyed a woman's playing with him, and that at night, he had awakened, wishing she were holding him again. And so, penitently, he read from the Bible, in Croatian, the equivalent of this English translation (Matthew 24:3,6-7):

> *And as he sat upon the mount of Olives, the disciples came*
> *unto him privately, saying, Tell us, when shall these things be?*
> *and what shall be the sign of thy coming, and of the end of the*
> *world? (3)*
> *[And Jesus answered] . . . And ye shall hear of wars and*
> *rumors of wars: see that ye be not troubled: for all these things*
> *must come to pass, but the end is not yet. (6)*
> *For nation shall rise against nation, and kingdom against king-*
> *dom: and there shall be famines, and pestilences, and earth-*
> *quakes, in divers places. (7)*

Daniel panicked. The end of the world was coming. He did not know how fast—maybe there was a year to live. And he was not ready.

He told his wife—who was doing crossword puzzles, proud

that she had such a good command of English—that the end of the world was at hand.

"Of course it is," she said.

"But why do we take on mortgage then, why do we save for retirement?"

"That's different—so that you wouldn't pay taxes, silly."

"So you believe the end is near?"

"Depends on how you look at it. Nobody knows when exactly, and people have waited for generations."

"Yes, but now there are more wars and earthquakes than ever after Christ."

"How do we know that?"

"Don't tell me you're a skeptic, you go to church."

"Yes, as a matter of fact, I am going there right now. I don't want to worry about the end of the world; that'll take care of itself."

He admired his wife's attitude, and her straight posture as she walked out, and he stayed troubled. She no longer worked as a department-store cashier, but as a real-estate agent.

The following morning, Daniel went to Mira's Baptist church, and knocked on the minister's door. A chubby minister with a tight shirt buttoned on top—he literally had a red neck—opened the door. They had met before, because for religious holidays Daniel still visited the church.

"When do you think Christ comes to this planet?" Daniel asked.

"He's here now, with us," said the minister and yawned.

"No, I mean serious. He gonna come soon, you think?"

The minister looked at him with his eyes wide, and then walked over to his coffee machine, which was percolating. "You want a cup of coffee?"

"We have time for that?" Daniel asked.

"Why not?"

"What if Christ came?"

"Where two or more gather in my name, I will be there, or something like that. That's what Christ said. So if we gather in his name, he'll be with us, he is with us. He came. Anyway, this coffee is going to feel like an earthquake, like the world's ending. You like it strong, don't you? Milk and sugar?"

"No, thank you."

The minister poured three spoonfuls of sugar into his black coffee and slurped, his eyes closed. "All right, now I'm ready for the second coming of Christ." He walked over to his desk and turned on his computer. Windows '95 came on. "You play chess?" the minister said. "You must, considering you come from Yugoslavia."

"Croatia," Daniel said. "Yes, I play."

"Here, I got a program that's almost as good as Deep Blue. You want to check it out?"

Daniel stared in disbelief. Clearly the minister didn't worry about the second coming of Christ. It was ten in the morning, and he was only waking up. Cushy job, being a minister. "No time for games. Not now," Daniel said and walked out.

Later, when his hangover wore off and his guilt about the hangover vanished, and the impression the Biblical verses made on him diminished, Daniel went back to work. There he met a blond Romanian with a black mustache. He knew the guy from before; he too was a Baptist and a construction worker. They talked in a mixture of languages. "Hey, it gets old working like a dog for a living, *nicht wahr?*" asked the Romanian, Nikolai.

"Yes, *konyeshna,*" said Daniel.

"Let us organize business, together, and find young blood to do *rabota* for us."

"Sounds good, but how to *zdyelat?*"

"I tell you over a glass of wine."

While they were still planning the joint venture, Nikolai visited Daniel, and as the two of them sat and discussed real estate, Mira served them orange juice and hot dogs. Daniel stealthily gave hot dogs to Saint Dalmatian, who, Daniel believed, was still filled with Greek letters. Mira sat down in the armchair and joined in on the discussions, speaking clearly without mixing any of the other languages, and for the first time in a long while Daniel noticed that she was stylish. He wondered why they made love only once a week. Now he could notice her through someone else's eyes and imagine what impression she was making. Her dress was short, and she sat comfortably, crossing her legs, so that her thighs—in thin black stockings that shaded the curves—were as visible as if she were an actress visiting David Letterman's show. Her tight cashmere white sweater made her breasts slope with milky and hazy fullness. Scarlet lipstick luridly accented and exposed her allure, as though her fresh blood had surfaced and spoken, ready to be licked.

Daniel commented, "You could sit up straight, so you wouldn't display yourself."

Nikolai sat stiff, his eyes focused on a cup of rose-hip tea steaming on the wooden table in front of him.

"You're making your visitor uncomfortable," she said.

"Sorry about that," Daniel said to Nikolai, and then to his wife, "At least you look comfortable."

"Why don't you invite me into the partnership? I'm a licensed real-estate agent," she said.

And then, all evening long, while Mira worked after-hours, Daniel daydreamed of sleeping with the Hyde Park woman. I shouldn't think like this, he thought. Christ will be here soon. But that thought now, as he was possessed by lust, drove him to a different conclusion. The end of the world will come, and I will not know what it is like to sleep with another woman, other than my wife. Who knows what I am missing, maybe a true ecstasy. I'll probably go to hell anyway, for I have lusted in my heart, and I have quit reading the Bible, and I have drunk, so what's the difference? At least let me go out in a spasm of ecstasy.

In the morning, around eleven, he called the woman from

Hyde Park. Yes, he was welcome to visit, after she came back from her art lesson in the afternoon.

Daniel went to Walgreen's to buy aspirin. He bought a *Cincinnati Enquirer* and read, in the store, about the heat wave that had gripped the continent, beating all records. When he stepped out of the store at one o'clock, the temperature was above 107 degrees, humidity nearly 100 percent. Daniel could barely breathe, and the air stung his nose and bronchi. He coughed. His eyes watered. He drove downtown over to the Rhine, an old German neighborhood that was now a ghetto, with gentrified pockets, where white folk could go to their breweries, restaurants, music clubs, and cafés. He drove past Kaldi's café; on the other side of the street was a Baptist church, named John 3:16. He knew the verse, of course, what Baptist didn't? People sat on shaded steps, sweating, drinking water and beer. A window pane cracked all by itself, and Daniel thought it did so from sheer heat. Down here with all the asphalt and cement, the temperature was unbearable. He stopped to have iced tea at Kaldi's. As he drank it, he thought he noticed that the waitress—who crossed her legs in a masculine fashion, ankle over knee—wore no underwear. Maybe her underwear was black, so he couldn't tell there was any. He strained to see, hoping she wore none. Maybe that's how she fought heat; maybe she liked to shock people, tease them. Why should he notice, he wondered. Why? Because he was possessed; lust pulled him by the nose and fixed his gaze in search of flesh everywhere.

He drove toward Hyde Park. He stepped out of the car on the edge of Eden Park and watched the thick brown layer of smoke choking the city around the Ohio River, and the river itself foamed, as though it were a cauldron of water boiling over. He couldn't see clearly across the river, into Covington, Kentucky, for the thick brown smog. High up, the clouds were pink and orange. He'd never seen colorful clouds in the middle of the day before. When he walked back to the car, his soles sank into the glossy black asphalt. One of his shoes stayed in the asphalt. He pulled it up with his hands, and as he bent over, the heat from the road scorched him.

Daniel thought that what he saw was not natural. God hadn't created the world to be so dirty—and then it occurred to him: God was choking the world. It was the end of the world. It was happening already. Maybe it would be over in several days. He panicked, suddenly certain that the temperature would continue to rise, and rise. God said he wouldn't flood the earth again. God even said, *I will not again curse the ground any more for man's sake* (Genesis 8:21). Yes, it says, "the ground," and doesn't say anything about the air. So He could do it with air. He probably wouldn't burn the earth either. But He could just suffocate the earth in its own stench, sending the heat through the ozone holes. This is it, Christ is coming, and I am choking in the lust of my own eyes.

He rushed home—drove as fast as he could—to tell his wife to get ready for the end of the world.

But at home, his wife was gone. Green beans were simmering on the stove, so she must be somewhere near. Yet he couldn't find her anywhere. He couldn't even find his Saint Dalmatian.

He recalled the verses (Matthew 25:40-41):

Then shall two be in the field; the one shall be taken, and the other left.
Two women shall be grinding at the mill; the one shall be taken, and the other left.

This was it; his pious wife was ascended to heaven, as were no doubt the other few pious people, and the rest of them, including Daniel, were left to suffer the seals of God's wrath.

He called his son, but got through only to the son's message machine.

He went to see a Baptist minister, and the minister was home. That did not surprise him. *The first shall be last, the last shall be first.* Many ministers had fallen, like Swaggart and Bakker. "Have you looked outside?" Daniel said. "The end of the world is here. Have you seen how the air simmers? We are all choking."

"That's a Cincinnati summer for you, my brother."

"You don't believe in it?"

"In what? The summer? Well, you just hide away from it."

Daniel figured out that the minister didn't believe much. *There shall be many false prophets.* He thought about it—there were false prophets everywhere. Faithless priests. Davidians. Deepak Chopras. Self-help gurus. Diet gurus (religious practices, fasts, without a God). Everybody offering happiness, with false gods, selves. Worship of the ego; wasn't that the root of all evil in the garden? Man and woman imagined that they could be like God, self-sufficient and all-knowing. Now again, men want to be all-knowing, and have the illusion that they are; you just finger computers a bit, and they give you the information you need; computers are nearly omniscient, and of course, many computer operators have the conceit that they themselves are omniscient. Daniel had had a conversation, with a doctor whose house he painted, about what Moses would have done if he'd had a computer with CD-rom programming; the Ten Commandments would have been written on CD-rom. Maybe they would have been different; instead of, Thou shalt not covet thy neighbor's ass, a commandment might have turned out to be, Thou shalt not spill coffee or any other liquids on the screen while surfing the net. He shuddered, afraid that his thought was sacrilegious, and then wondered whether Moses climbed Mt. Sinai with a hammer and a chisel to lend to God so the commandments could be engraved into the stone tables, or did God keep such tools, or did God simply blast grooves in the stone with his fiery breath?

He went home alone. Intentionally he left the windows open, to feel the heat. He didn't want to use air-conditioning; he had concluded that air-conditioning was a part of man's arrogance against God—to create a mini-climate, avoid God's winds. No, he'd bear those winds. He wouldn't contribute to the destruction of the world; for it was not God himself who was directly destroying humankind. Humankind was destroying itself through its greed and pleasure-seeking.

Usually, they kept the windows not only closed but locked because there was crime in the neighborhood. But what harm could a crime do to him now?

Maybe it was not too late for him to be ascended. He had noticed the end, while most hadn't. He prayed. And after his last "Amen," and he said many of them, he looked up. The moon was scarlet red, and there were three rings around it. He'd seen one, never more, on cold nights, when the moon was full, but now, the moon wasn't even full; it gave off little light, and around it, there was a blue ring, and a red ring, and a hazy white ring. Daniel remembered, *And there shall be signs in the sun, and in the moon, and in the stars* . . . (Luke 21:25); and, . . . *the sun shall be darkened, and the moon shall not give her light* . . . (Mark 13:24).

He didn't sleep. In the morning he turned on CNN, expecting to see reports about the coming of Christ. Would they try to interview Christ before he got to his business of resurrecting the dead and ascending those who'd been truly forgiven into heavens? Who would do that? Christiana Amanpour?

Instead, there was a report about how Srebrenica was overrun, and how thousands of Muslim men and boys were rounded up and bussed away into the fields where, according to "unconfirmed reports," mass executions were taking place.

So there it was. *Now the brother shall betray the brother to death, and the father the son; and children shall rise up against their parents, and shall cause them to be put to death* (Mark 13:12). These were basically the same ethnic group, in Eastern Bosnia, Serbs and Croats of Muslim religious tradition who lost track of being Serbs and Croats, and Serbs of Orthodox tradition, who perhaps lost track of religious tradition, but not of being Serbs. Brother against brother—in the name of God, just to add sacrilege to the massacre, which already was sacrilege.

Daniel decided to go watch the end of the world from Eden Park. There he sat and waited.

On the horizon showed up dark clouds and lightning. He wondered whether God's host was coming. Then a terrible hailstorm came, hail the size of a cliché, a golf ball, although of course, once he could catch it, it was the size of a peanut.

The storm was soon over. Other than a few indents on the roof of his pickup, there was no other damage. The air was cool now, cool and clear, as though the world was washed clean. Daniel felt a moment of sadness. He wondered whether God had changed his mind. What had happened? Like Jonah, who would have liked to see the destruction. . . .

He drove home. At least his wife then would be back. Who knows where she'd gone that long.

The machine blinked. He played the message. "Hi, here's Nikolai. Just calling so you wouldn't *sorgen*. Mira and I . . . we decided to live together. She says you haven't treated her *harasho,* and I try my best to help her. Here *Schatz,* you tell him too, so he knows." There was weeping, and Mira said: "We couldn't go on like that any more. You never paid any attention to me. We'll be in touch about splitting up our property."

Daniel shrieked with laughter. And he thought she'd been ascended to heaven! Cold air streamed through the window. The end of the world. Shit, how could he have been that stupid. And then he was incensed. She had seduced Nikolai right in front of him. She even chided Daniel for noticing it.

He called his daughter, Marina. Marina believed that her Mom was kidnapped, and advised him to call the police. He didn't believe his daughter.

He drove off to a pawn shop to buy a gun. Yes, he'll find those scoundrels. Whom should he shoot? Just him? Well, he didn't even know him that well. Her? Obviously, he didn't know her that well either. You could live with someone all your life and never learn. It wasn't worth the bother, shooting somebody, going to courts, being pictured in the newspapers as a demented maniac. Ridiculous.

He walked into a phone booth and dialed the tennis player's number in Hyde Park to play Windows '95 with her. No answer. Surely, she was not ascended, he thought, and the thought entertained him. As he laughed, he felt a terrible relief.

He no longer believed in the end of the world and in the prophets, not even the prophets of the global warming effect. He knew his reasoning was not quite right now, as it hadn't been right before, but he was sure that the granite faith of his transatlantic youth was gone. The faith had through years attenuated into a delicate crystalline structure that broke down the light— broke it down into the aura of transcendent, otherworldly, seeking and relishing extreme spectacles of collapse; and this fragile aesthetic faith crumbled in the heat, into a heap of glass dust that could no longer be resurrected into crystal, and that would be lost in the sand of the entropied world as a spittle in the ocean.

A Free Fall

やみ

On a putridly sultry summer day my naked mother-to-be, longing for refreshment, jumped out of a plane. In her womb, during
the free fall, I must have had a sensation of weightlessness akin to
what I would later feel at the beginning of elevator rides down.
When the parachute opened, I must have had the sensation I
would later have during sudden decelerations of a downward elevator, my whole weight pressing against the floor, except there
was no floor in my mother: I fell through. She noticed. While
balancing her jolted parachute, she gathered enough motherly
affection—when is a mother more a mother than while giving
birth?—to intervene; she grabbed my left foot, which remained
in her hand. So now it was my turn to fall quite freely though I
didn't want to. I fell into a huge heap of freshly cut hay.

My crying brought three peasants to the heap of hay. If I had
smiled all the way through, I don't think I would now be here,
discussing methods of birth. I don't know what direction the
peasants came from, whether the East, like the three Magi, or the
West, like syphilis, or . . . I imagine my mother had flung away my
foot to concentrate on the parachute. Neither the mother nor the
foot was found to be reattached to me.

Since my earliest walking attempts, I have never started the day on my own left foot—but I don't mean that I am a lucky man. I step on an artificial left foot.

I don't have to change socks on my left foot more than once a month. My natural foot—well, how could I claim that my artificial foot, made of such splendid oak, is less natural than my incoherent flesh and bones?—is quite a pest. Nails grow out of it with incredible zest. I cut them with nail clippers large enough for a horse, and ten days later they are again piercing through my sock. The large toenail widens the hole, and the sock tactically gives in a little and widens, creating a noose around the large toe. The strangled toe *tingles* with the *loss* of sensation. I turn the pierced sock inside out and put it back on, so that the hole would be over my little toe. The hole slides toward the large toe and chokes it again.

Visiting acquaintances, I take off my shoe when the noose itches me, and everybody runs away. To entice my conversationalists to come back, I have to put the shoe back on—quite tiresome. My sock accumulates sweat and layers of dying skin, which dissolves in vapors that precipitate when the shoe walls are cold. Millions of bacteria feast on the resulting glue. The sock organizes the cultures into a league of nations, to launch an expansionistic attack on my toes. The condition is commonly called "athlete's foot." There's nothing athletic about my foot. On the brink of defeat, I wash my foot, peel its skin wherever it's loose, buy a dozen socks, which, smelling of ink and store scents promise deodorized times.

My oak foot, on the other leg, accepts any sock with dignified indifference, and wears it without offending it or being offended by it. Another great plus for the oak foot is that you can't sprain its ankle, having none. I am far more attached to my detachable foot than to my biological foot.

If an offensive dog is in front of me, I lunge Oaky at it with abandon. I do not mind falling on the ground as long as my foot lands on the dog.

A dog once followed me into an alley, and bit into the only tailored suit I had ever had. Next time I saw the dog, I ripped into his ribs with such crushing enthusiasm that he flew and ran, that is, some twenty yards, whereupon he collapsed on the gravel and moaned so miserably that tears rolled down my cheeks onto my hands and onto my foot.

I could have in my youth exploited the pity my foot aroused; I could have begged. In my town many Gypsies used to, and probably still do, make a career of lameness. I think many more other people do it too, but as soon as they do it, everybody calls them Gypsies. These poor people sometimes maim their children in infancy, to give them a profession. A maimed beggar can make a lot more money than an able-bodied beggar. In my town you often see a mother on a brown blanket—her eyes glowing in the cold, her breath, little gusts of steam and mist—holding a one-legged child with its mouth open, shining from saliva.

Many women find me a touching sight when I limp across the street and cars drive at me so that I have to run although I cannot—I jump, make curious motions like a drowning swimmer, which don't accelerate my progress nor decelerate the cars'. Sometimes I fall and my foot rolls away; I catch pained glimpses among the pedestrians though not among the drivers. I smile on the edge of the pavement, like a swimmer on the shore of a tempestuous sea—though I am not sure the saved swimmers smile (they probably vomit). Women help me onto the shore. Somebody rescues my foot among honking boats; I attach it with a click and nonchalantly walk off. People on the pavement make way for me, and I lift my hat as a sign of grace.

By now you may think that my life is a grim affair. No, it isn't. I can laugh at one and the same joke many times. When I hear it for the first time, I laugh if I understand it, naturally enough, and also if I don't because I still don't get it while everybody else seems to—that somehow strikes me as hilariously independent. When, hearing the joke again, I am finally getting it, I laugh because I feel I am already forgetting it. In defense of my intellectual faculties, I should say that our jokes sometimes take hours to tell, and our country itself is a joke over seventy years long. That I should ever remember a joke, Stalin forbid! To be able to laugh at a joke only once would be sad.

My doctor tells me that my slipped lumbar disc presses against my left sciatic nerve—and if I had the left foot, I'd suffer a lot of pain. He asks me whether I feel anything where the foot should be, akin to loss of sensation. I could object (though I don't) that since I have no foot to have sensations in or from, I could not lose the sensations—you can't lose what you don't have. But that's a subtlety. I should do sit-ups and leg lift-ups to strengthen my torso. It's beyond my strength or will to do such things. My will is willing to will something that is beyond it, but it realizes the full danger of willing what is not beyond it: It would result in work. My doctor tells me that I should have a lot of pelvic-thrusting sex. I object that I could gain pleasure only from work-unrelated activities. A woman is atop me and does all the work—that's pleasure. But to sweat, puff, strain all my muscles for fun? Preposterous.

Why do I think about myself all the time? I don't. I even write poems. Here's one: Eat Heat Beneath my Wreath. It has a nice expanding rhythm, doesn't it? It's a long poem actually . . . there's more to it than the title. I am scientifically minded too. The observations, I admit, start or end with me, but they are coldly scientific, nearly objective. If one drinks water right before urinating, one will urinate more than if one doesn't, although the new water hasn't had enough time to reach the bladder. My theory: There is a body information system monitoring the quantity of the water in the body, including in the bladder. The more liquid there is in the body, the more dispensable the liquid is. If one drinks water before urinating, the monitoring system allows for release of the bladder liquid quite liberally; otherwise, not so. The finding is surprising because I should think the liquids in the bladder quite useless. But, perhaps, in case of dehydration, the bladder liquids can be recycled. I would like to organize a grand experiment on this theme, to employ a statistically significant population. I do realize that one bladder, even if mine, is statistically insignificant to draw any conclusions.

Since I don't like to walk far from my bed at night, I urinate in milk bottles at bedside; I've filled a whole larder with a decade of bottles, which I will donate to science.

My foot is old enough to be an antique. Oak feet are no longer made. I could sell it any time for several thousand dollars to a roving American or a speculative German. I doubt it. Although a replacement, my foot is irreplaceable. Not all replacements are like that. I used to grit my teeth until many of them eroded and others fell out. I wanted to replace them with wooden crowns. My dentist wouldn't hear it, not even ebony was hard enough for him. So I went through plastic, porcelain—all with steel or silver posts; I was never prosperous enough to make it to gold. I stole a golden watch at a supermarket, but the dentist wouldn't melt it because he suspected I'd ripped someone off for the watch, as if he hadn't ripped off all those who opened their mouths in his office. All I have in the way of teeth is one bone tooth, a real one, and I wish I didn't have it because it cuts into my gums.

The tooth reminds me of my son's dog. The beast follows me. The son follows the dog, so indirectly he follows me though he is indifferent to me. I still find it touching that he ends up following me. I am farsighted, so I can see my son, in sharp detail, following behind me forty paces or thirty crutch swings; and I can't see the dog at my heels, so it looks as though my son trails me. If the son followed me closely, he'd dissolve into a pinkish cloud, like vapors at sunset, and I wouldn't even know he was by me. When he happens to be right next to me and I feel lonely, I ask him to go away, five yards or so, so I would be more aware of his presence. The three of us take walks at the foothills of a mountain, and one day we'll go mountain climbing because I am irresistibly drawn to the sky.

I talk now about this fragment of my body, now about that one, provided I miss it. I usually remember how I lost a piece of my body. My hair fell out more gradually than grass grows. Forgetting that causality is a philosophically untenable concept, I took dandruff to be the cause of the recession of my hairline, and I washed my hair in gasoline several times. The dandruff disappeared; and whatever hair had remained on my skull made rapid exodus. I refrain from claiming that gasoline caused my hair to fall, but I do point out the sequence of events. I used to be unhappy about my baldness because I hadn't understood the dialectics of beauty. If you are genuinely ugly, like I am, then you are so strikingly unique that you must be genuinely beautiful. Most beautiful people look alike, but each ugly person is ugly in his own way. A strikingly crippled person takes your breath away—evokes visceral sympathy and awe—more than a famous and wholesome actress with perfect porcelain and platinum teeth could. The ghosts of missing arms, ears, eyes, legs, start dancing behind your eyes, dipped in deep colors of your brain, and for a second or two, you are a reincarnation of Goya, piously creating *ex nihilo* in the red of your blood. And there's truthful creative beauty for you.

Penis I still have. I sometimes dream that it has fallen off. I pick it up from the gravel among beer caps, ants, cigarette stubs, spittle, and put it in my sport's jacket among aluminum coins and cloves of garlic. I double-check for holes in the pocket for I wouldn't like to lose that ejaculatory patent. Not that it would make a tremendous difference if I did, but it comes in handy sometimes, as personal sewage system, by which I can tidily (and ebbily) direct the flow of my urine without defiling the floor tiles or window sills. Besides, I can use it for socializing—contracting and communicating diseases as proofs of there having been intimacy.

Balls too I still have. At least I have one ball. The other developed an ever-growing cyst, and a doctor told me I had an option of a complicated treatment or a simple operation. When I learned that after the simple option—amputation of the testis—I could stay at the hospital for a whole week, prostrate, fed, nursed, I thought, What is a mere ball compared to being nourished by nurses? But in the hospital the bromides in my diet made me so sleepy and listless that I didn't pinch nurses. It was the best and dreamiest period of my life nevertheless; I ate right and I dreamed right. I only wish I could remember more of it—I don't mean of my ball—but of my floating state of mind at the hospital, with the buena vista of two rivers, shimmering with cloud-refracted sunsets, confluencing beneath fifteenth-century ruins of a fort against the Turks. The fort hadn't worked, the Turks had swept over southern Europe. The dreams were cool like the white sheets of my bed. The resolute sheets had their own will that rubbed off on you a contagious health. My sheets at home are always soft and spineless because of my sweat and saliva in them (I sleep with my mouth open). I am not repulsed enough by my sweat to wash the sheets. The sweat comes from me, having been in me, having been a part of me. I didn't shun it when it was me, why should I shun it now that it has left me? If I should get rid of my sweat, why not my blood, my liver? Where do you draw the line in self-hatred? I should throw away my body in a ditch, which I temporarily do when I get drunk and frank about what I think about being (in) my body.

Since I lost one ball, the other one hangs lower, swinging freely, playful and proud and lonely, fanning my thigh. This is an improvement: My balls used to push against the skin between my thighs and my crotch, sweating, itching, provoking me to scratch until I got sore and daydreamed of cutting the balls off. For a long time I didn't have the balls to do it. But the summer is here again, and with the global-warming effect, I just might cut off the solo ball if it's true that People's Hospital is getting air-conditioning.

Sometimes I go to the barber's, and when the barber reminds me I have no hair, I feel terrible; I cannot cut anything to feel rejuvenated—like I could start anew. The nails just don't do the trick for me. Too bad I hadn't grown up with at least a dozen balls, to cut one a year. Not that removing a ball is a spectacular change; on the contrary, as I am in the habit of hiding that part of my body, it would be an aspectacular change (nonspectacular?).

Since I was born in an unprofessional fashion, my umbilical cord sticks out an inch and a half. If it were longer and harder, I could use it as a penis. Some women like it as is. Most people have just a black hole there, an anti-umbilicus, sunk in the fat. But that too has an erotic potential. I slept once—I wonder why not more often—with a woman whose navel cut deep into her pillowy abdomen. We had a double coitus, one of commonplace description, and above it, my cord in her navel. It drove her into ecstasy and did almost the same thing for me. Then she lay over and between two beds, and her belly drooped to meet me on the floor. And while my penis was taking a sauna in her navel, my cord strained to reach her vulva. That was such a good feeling! I cannot remember it. I suppose it was good.

Chronologically, I am a middle-aged man, barely, yet why be greedy and think that I have much more to live? I've lived my life to its emptiest. Is there life after death? Either there is or there isn't. What if there isn't? Nothing. And if there is? I imagine I would get my teeth back so I could bite. What kind of heaven would it be if I didn't have any of my natural knives on me? My hair would be restored to me: God or his apprentices would merely look at my skull and say, Let there be hair, and plenty of hair would spring from my skull at once, tearing through my scalp. My ball would be repaired to me. My penis would be taken away from me for there would be no sex in heaven, at least not via such a primitive and unreliable artifact. The thalamus and hypothalamus would be stimulated directly, without straining the penis or clitoris, to bring electrical shocks into the erogenous centers of the brain. There would be a direct way of storming the centers, perhaps a permanent short circuit.

I cannot imagine that we would have no attachments to our past—the way we now dip steamboats into rivers on our national holidays. During festivals, we would take our old penises out of the refrigerators and put them on—but I've forgotten there would be no need of refrigerators, because there would be no corruption. One of my ears would be given back to me. My eyesight would improve so I could see my son from a foot away. My umbilical cord would be leveled with my abdomen, or perhaps, the whole cord would be restored and connected with a big belly in the middle of heaven, a big Uterus, from which nectar would flow into my self without the mediation of chewing, licking, and gulping. Billions of people would be hooked via their umbilici to the Heavenly Uterus, murmuring Gregorian chants.

My Oaky would be taken away, and I would get another foot of flesh and bone, exposed to socks for strangulation. (That reminds me, I better crutch out to get the new dozen.) This about completes what I now have to say about my life, from sperm to worm.

Real Estate

☙☙

I've lived in Osijek, Croatia, nearly all my life. I've visited nude beaches and smoked since I was twelve, drunk red wine and made love to a German tourist woman among the coastal rocks at thirteen, and just as my freedom was to be curtailed, my father, who worked as a railway man, was killed by a gas-tank-coach explosion and my mother lost her mind. She stayed home on a pension and talked to herself twelve hours a day, not noticing me but cooking and setting the table for three each night. That was fine—I ate my dish and my imaginary father's dish too, and I grew fast. I read a lot, studied, excelled, since there was not much else to do, and during the summers, I did as I pleased. I had a happy boyhood, I imagine, as far as boyhoods go.

But not a happy youth. I think it all had to do with Serbs. What's there to think? I know it had to do with them. To give you an example: I was the best basketball player on our high-school team, the highest scorer two years in a row. A scout for Cibona, Zagreb—where Drazen Petrovic played—came to our high-school championship game. Just as I was jumping for a dunk—I was already over six feet and I could tip the ball over the rim if not slam it—Boro, a Serb player on our team, shoved me from behind. My head narrowly missed the metal post, and I crashed down on my shoulder. I was dizzy and had to sit down. In ten minutes when I recovered my senses, and the coach didn't invite me in to play, I grew furious. The bald scout with a goatee who smoked a cigar wouldn't get a chance to see how talented I was. I ran onto the floor straight at Boro and slammed him in the chest. Though I cut his breath, he tried to hit me back. I hit him in the neck, and he staggered. I jumped on him from behind, brought him down to the floor with a thud. We hit sideways. I tried to strangle him, but someone kicked me in the kidneys. Still, half a dozen people could barely separate us. When I got up with white spots crackling in my field of vision, I noticed no scout. Even if he was somewhere in the hall—there was no chance in hell, and even less in heaven, that he'd be interested in me. A player who fights with the opponents may be good—each team should have one or two piranhas like that to intimidate the other team—but the player who fights his own teammates, who needs that? I could have ended up in the NBA, and now I'd be rich with no worry but how to save my back and knees. I'd even be thin and healthy.

Anyhow, at the end of high school, I fell in love with a Serbian woman, Slavitza. That's not unusual. If two nations have problems with each other, it's the men who do; the men wage wars, women don't, with some exceptions. In fact, though I've always loved women, I could never get along with Croatian women. If Croatian women had been more pleasant, maybe Croatian men wouldn't be so grumpy and we could get along even with Serbs. I went out with her to the park, and we embraced and bit each other's necks lustily, but she wouldn't sleep with me right away, and I didn't press—I wanted to prove that I had class.

She was a year younger than me. I went to law school in Zagreb while she was finishing up high school. I always had a strong sense of justice, that is injustice, resentment. Law is a system of prohibitions and punishments, akin to revenge—it's civilized re-

venge, more thorough than brute physical revenge. I liked imagining that law was a complex spider web, that I would sit in the
middle spinning silky and shiny lines, and obnoxious people like
mosquitos would in their unconscious flights get stuck in the web
and hang around, flailing helplessly, entangling themselves deeper
with each move, and I would observe them dispassionately and
perhaps release them after they disgusted me with their panic. But
the main reason for my choosing law school stemmed from being
tired of poverty; I hoped to become a gentleman who went every
morning before work to read the dailies in the best café in town.
I lived in an overcrowded student dorm, with loud music and
mobs of testosterone-crazed hicks.

I came home a couple of weekends a month. Slavitza and I did
a lot of petting, and we used the American term for it, and joked
that if we continued like that, we'd become Americans. She was
marvelously attractive—smooth fuzzy skin, pert breasts, a long
neck, delicate bones that from her dimpled chin went straight, like
the sides of a triangle. Her wavy black hair shone, with ephemeral
tones of blue and crimson. Her cheekbones seemed to pull her
eyes into a slant that gave an Oriental impression of tacit knowl-
edge. I couldn't tire of stroking her. A bit of abstinence is good
while you're courting; it helps you sink into love.

But, one weekend when I took a walk with her on the banks
of the River Drava, she was gloomy. I'm not particularly intuitive,
so I still went ahead with my proposition that we get married.

"You know, if you'd asked me just a month ago, I'd do it. But
now I feel I can't."

"How is that?" I asked.

"I don't know. Just the spark is gone."

Later I found out that she had gone out with Boro, and done
some petting with him, except that he pushed and forced himself
upon her. I know it was a rape, even though we didn't call such
things rape. I remember how with other kids, when we talked
about how we liked women, several said they liked resistance, so
they'd feel more manly in their conquest, pinning the woman

down, fighting her wiggles. Basically, they were describing a rape, date-rape, which the Western legal system defined, but we in the Balkans would never get to that stage. She didn't let me touch her. She said men physically disgusted her. I didn't see her for a while; I was busy studying. A year later she married him—I still don't know whether out of fear or love.

I married a couple of years later, a Hungarian girl I was seeing on the sly while with Slavitza. Perhaps I should have mentioned that before—subtle love is easy when you have carnal love elsewhere. Gretta had bad grammar (had no command of the gender of nouns since her native language had no gender nouns), which made her speech charming, and she had a sensationally curvaceous and lanky body. She became a bank teller and then a regular banker.

Still, in the streets, I grew excited whenever I saw Slavitza; I couldn't breathe well. We pretended that we didn't recognize each other, but I could tell that she was out of breath too. I hoped that one day I would still sleep with her, finish the unfinished business, keep an adulterous affair, which actually could never be really adulterous, since she should have been mine, I thought.

Soon after Gretta and I got married, Boro and Slavitza moved to Belgrade. My resentment grew, not just toward him, but toward all Serbs. It was obviously a generalization, and as a lawyer, I was aware that my induction was faulty, but I went ahead anyway—because I had more bad experiences with Serbs.

At Saponia, Osijek, in my first job as a lawyer for a soap factory, I did my work honestly, eight hours a day, six days a week, yet in ten years I didn't get a promotion. Whenever there was anything complicated to do, the director brought it to me, but when the questions of promotion came, he promoted Serbs—peasants from the Bosnian mountains with bogus degrees. They could hardly put a sentence together on the page—they mixed Serbian and Croatian diction. I understood that it was a deliberate campaign to irritate Croats—using Serbian expressions just to show us that we were a part of Greater Serbia. I don't even know why they bothered to fight a war later on—if things had stayed as they were, and they had just made a few concessions to Croats, Slovenes, and Muslims, Yugoslavia would have stayed together as a great Serb playground, a huge drunken party. I don't mean the communist party, although of course you had to be a member to get anywhere.

I was unscrupulous enough that I joined the party, even gave speeches in worker's self-management meetings. I knew there was no harm in saying all that verbiage, filled with acronyms and thoughtless ready-made phrases, since meetings were just a *pro forma* thing, where nobody except a couple of secret agents listened. But not even that got me anywhere, except to understand better what was going on. Or what wasn't going on—hardly anybody worked. No wonder the system collapsed, wages fell, discontent grew. Everybody wanted to blame somebody—it had to be somebody's fault, people imagined—and who could you blame? Not yourself, not somebody like you, your ethnic group, but someone a bit removed—Croats blamed Serbs, Serbs blamed Croats and everybody else, including the Pope, Muslims, Germans. To their minds there was a great international conspiracy to keep the Serbs down—which of course in the end became true as a self-fulfilling prophecy. Croats thought that there was an international conspiracy to keep them down, although of course most people had not even heard of Croats before the war.

At the Saponia factory, even though this was in Croatia, Serbs, who were about half the work force, openly ridiculed Croats. They could afford to—most of the police were Serbian. When a Serb clerk called me Shokatz, a name for lowland Croats, not necessarily a pejorative one—but the tone in which he said it was pejorative, or at least I imagined it to be—I punched him and broke his nose. I lost the job, and I appealed in the courts. What kind of lawyer would I be if I didn't? But the judge was a Serb. He ordered that a breathalyzer test be conducted on me. I'd had only half a dozen beers before the proceedings. The judge ordered that I be sent to a psychiatric ward for evaluation. Many Croats ended up in asylums; the Serbs imitated the Soviet psychiatry, getting rid of their potential opposition in this way.

What a shock I experienced when the psychiatrist who came in to check on me turned out to be my childhood "friend," Boro.

"Oh, how wonderful to see you after all those years," he exclaimed, and stretched his hand to shake with me, his creased cheeks glistening despite hair growing even on the skin over his cheekbones—blue hair with black dots at the roots.

When he saw that my hand was not coming, he said, "Oh, you do have problems. Passive aggressive."

"Don't give me that bull," I said. "When did you get an MD?" I was sure that his was a bogus degree too.

"Novi Sad," he said.

"How come you're in Osijek?"

"Job opportunities. No jobs in Novi Sad. Besides, this is my home."

I didn't say anything, I had a cousin who was a physician and couldn't get a job anywhere for years.

"How time flies," he said. "I see your hair's receding as well. Graying too."

He was bald on top, but kept long hair on the sides, and a beard. He had no gray whatever—scoundrels and people without conscience hardly ever do.

"We had such wonderful times in high school, how we played basketball," he spoke, with his eyes glazed. "What happy days!"

"Easy for you to say."

"We did, and for a while we were great friends. I don't now what happened that we didn't keep it up. But no matter, here we are, and what a break for you, let me tell you."

"How's that?"

"They want to lock you up."

"Who is they?"

"You're lucky your old buddy is here. I mean, we'll still send you to a detox clinic, but only briefly, for a week or so; otherwise, they'd keep you in the asylum and drug you up for years, until they managed to drive you clinically insane."

"I'm not an alcoholic."

"I know. We all drink. That's our wonderful culture. And now, and this is just a formality, sit down and take this test, MMPI."

"That's ridiculous. I won't."

"At this point you have to. Otherwise, they'll lock you up as an enemy of the people, for subverting the system of medicine. There are cops outside this door."

"As if I hadn't noticed."

"Hey, be a sport. Grouchiness won't get you anywhere."

So I took the test. According to it, I had self-destructive, possibly suicidal, traits. "See, I told you," said Boro, as though he'd had a brilliant insight. "What do you say about that?"

"Who doesn't have suicidal traits around here? If I'm not mistaken, the Pannonian Plains of Hungary and Croatia have the highest suicide rates in the world, higher than the Nordic countries, even though we don't have the perpetual night—that is, in a manner of speaking, we don't. I'm sure if you took the test honestly, you'd find suicidal traits. Isn't that the national psyche of the Serbs, celebrating your major defeats in history, the Kosovo Battle for example?"

"All right, don't rave now. Be careful what you say. Honesty is suicidal. In times like these, learn how to be tactful and hypocritical."

"There's nothing to learn. We've all been doing that for decades under an ideology that only idiots believed."

"Listen, I like you. Just remember, you never know where you need friends. If things don't go well for us, remember me."

"For us, whom?"

"Don't pretend. You know, I know. We don't need to say anything."

Before I could react, he gave me a bear hug, there were tears on his cheeks—there was also brandy on his breath—and he looked into my eyes soulfully.

What an idiot, I thought. But I said nothing.

Just as he said, I was out in a week, and I even got my job back, though I wished I hadn't. Serb lawyers constantly insulted the Croats, calling us fascists, cowards, losers. Serbs held loud rallies outside the factory gates. Even Boro spoke at one of them, about how history called upon Serbs to improve it—how Serbs always won in war and lost in peace, and that therefore Serbs should not fear war. I listened from the shade of a kiosk, scandalized at the lack of reasoning. Even if you were a pacifist—and particularly if you were a pacifist—after listening to Serb rallies and reading Milosevic speeches, you had to abhor Serbdom.

I thought I would rejoice when the war started, a storm of relief after a long humid summer. But I didn't. Croatia had hardly any weapons. Many Serbs left the town—not that they were threatened at that stage, but to make bombing the town easier. Serb planes dropped bombs on the factory when I was taking a day off, and burnt down most of it.

I'll admit one thing—I could be brave when it came to fist fights. That's not hard to admit. I'll admit another thing: I was scared when the town was bombed. Some people in the basement of my tenement building could take it well; they were used to the worst case scenarios, but I turned green. I had to go to the bathroom five times an hour. We used buckets, covered them with short planks of wood.

The basement was a maze of woodshacks; to every apartment belonged a little cubicle made of rough fir 1-by-2s, separated from each other by two inches. People sat in these shacks and in the corridors. Our shack was nearly full with a broken washing machine, a pair of rusty bicycles, my old textbooks, my wife's boxes of old clothes from the times when she was lean, and piles of chopped beech logs. So we sat in the corridors on blankets and pillows. The high windows were boarded up; there was no electricity, and we used a flashlight and a few petroleum lamps— strange that the whole thing didn't blow up from the leaking gas. We crouched in the orange-reddish dark, with people's shadows lurching across the walls and planks of wood with each slight movement.

My wife fell asleep; she could sleep anywhere, any time—not even fear could prevent her from sleeping. She was in her bodice. The air raid had come in the middle of the night and her skirt in the closet had been too far to pick up in a rush. She now stretched loosely, sleeping with her lips parted. One of her breasts was exposed; through age, her breasts had grown large, succulent and wobbly, and it was hard to contain them. I had covered her legs, but she kicked the blanket off, and I gave up on covering her, even though with each shift, the rim of her bodice slid further up. I was dozing off, too, but I noticed a shadow of a long pointed head with large ears leaping over the ceiling and sliding off onto the sandy wall in sudden jerks. I looked down. Behind the planks of wood a young man's eyes shone like a wild dog's in the moonlight. His head was moving rhythmically, as though he was listening to rock, but he had no earphones. He is masturbating at my wife, I thought. Now, how could you tolerate that? Of course, many men don't care, and I don't know why I should have, except that I took it as a matter of pride, manipulated by silly cultural rules of manliness. So I strode over in my underwear, and jumped on him. He slipped out of my grip—his hair was oily and his head egg-shaped, thinner than his neck. As he slipped away, I elbowed him in the jaw and then pushed him down over an empty barrel that boomed. He rolled over it and fell, with a yelp. Several men gripped me from behind and held me by the elbows, while many people gathered, yelling, sighing, scandalized at my behavior. They hated me, I could feel that. Only now did I notice that the youth's tight jeans were on, zipped, that it was impossible that he had jerked off. The young man looked at me with fear and hate. It flashed through my head—he too is a Croat. They all are.

We sat down again. I closed my eyes, and tried to doze off. When I opened them, I saw the same shiny eyes, even shinier than before, maybe from tears of pain; his head was bobbing again. I wondered what was going on; I tiptoed to him, barefoot, over the sandy concrete cement. His hands were limp on his side. One of his legs was shaking, up and down, as if in a trance. I guess it's some kind of disorder, some neural loop closes, and there it goes. Anyway, I'd attacked a poor nervous wreck. That shows you how easy it is to draw conclusions. I felt ashamed, a sensation I am rarely capable of.

Still, his jerky leg drove me crazy, and I thought of dogs again. If you scratch a dog at a certain spot, his leg will go berserk, as though it had a brain of its own. I saw this neural autonomy in spider legs too. You kill a spider, squash its body, and a long leg will keep bending and unbending. I know this all sounds awfully misanthropic, but it's not. I like spiders.

There was no such thing as deodorant around, and if there was it would have added a chemical insipidness to it all. Hair sprays that women and men sprinkled over themselves—dead flower extracts mixed with alcohol derivatives—scratched my eyes and aggravated my bleeding nose. Add to this smokers, with their aura of nicotine; alcoholics, with their boozy and vomity smells; then people with bad teeth and unidentified lung diseases who breathed out swarms of bacilli; and the smell of moist basement, with city liquids of fear and shame seeping through the walls. As my sense of sight deteriorated, while I tried to read *Beyond the Good and Evil* in the dim light, my only sense that seemed to improve was smell. I stank too; I could blow into my fist, and catch my foul breath. We were all rotting together. I had had it with tenement living. In what other country would you be living in an apartment complex after being a lawyer for ten years? I decided I would become rich, no matter what it took. I'd have ten houses—all in different landscapes, so I could choose where to be, rather than to be stooping in a shitty basement. Wealth can keep the rot of the masses at bay.

I used to think that if you gathered a group of people that were only Croats and Hungarians, and no Serbs around, it would be a pleasant group, with civil, playful, and intelligent conversation. But now all these jerky dull people around me were Croats.

Maybe I drew another wrong, hasty conclusion, to detest my own people, large groups of them, and what larger group is there than a nation? I knew right then that nations were not for me. Most people are unpleasant. I am unpleasant too, no doubt—another reason to stay away.

If I didn't like Croats, I certainly hated Serbs—the drunken bands shoving missiles into their cannons and firing mortars randomly in high trajectories. Mortars burst, sharding window panes and digging scars on the pavements that looked like flowers, with a stem head where the mortar fell, and petals springing and spreading out of it. More precisely, the scars looked like fossils of big flowers from the times of cavemen; and these were again the times of cavemen. The bands lived in holes in the ground, trenches, bunkers. But now I could understand the bandits. Some of them may have been as misanthropic as I was; they could shoot like this at anybody, knowing perfectly well that they were shooting at detestable misery. Many Serbs had stayed in Osijek; the Serbs bombing us were bombing them. Could I shoot like that at Serbian towns despite their being some Croats? I envied the gunners. It would have been delightful to be outside Belgrade sending missiles into trajectories.

Now I think differently. Why destroy houses, when you could buy them and sell them and have people stay in them rather than in the streets where they would clog up the traffic? Why kill people, when some of them one day may make enough money to buy a house from you?

Anyhow, after Vukovar fell, there were close to fifty thousand Serb soldiers surrounding Osijek. People panicked. Hatred for Serbs became a communal fervor, fever, even against those who had decided to stay with us and who may have disagreed with the Belgrade aggression. The prevailing Croat opinion was that every Serb loved the Serb conquests, that the Serbs with us were hypocrites and only seemed to condemn the aggression. Croats harassed many Serbs in the city. And at the same time first Croatian victories came, in Western Slavonia; economic sanctions hit

Serbia; there was talk about the U.N. interceding to end Serb expansion.

So Serbs ran, north to Hungary, to cross into Vojvodina and Serbia. Croat refugees and Croat police moved into the abandoned houses.

Strangely, the house that I wanted for myself belonged to Boro Milenkovic, the spychiatrist. I see I misspelled his profession, one of those revealing slips. Anyway, I won't switch sp into ps; it would be now a post scriptum (or pre scriptum) to an ychiatrist, eye-chiatrist, someone who sees the obvious. He and his wife stayed in the town, boarded up the windows, probably not only to protect it from the Serbs but from potential Croat fire as well. The house was pockmarked from mortars like any other, but it was still an old magnificent Austrio-Hungarian piece of provincial architecture with a frieze of naked angel babies below the roof where doves nested and shat white. One day as I walked past the house I saw a woman with a brown shawl wrapped around her head walk out of there. By the gait and the swing of a lean waist and sloping hips, I knew that was Slavitza. I wanted to talk to her, persuade her to go to a hotel with me, to surrender herself to me and my lust, so we could revise our youth, rewrite our love history, perhaps cure ourselves of fear and greed, but she slipped into a bakery before I could catch up with her.

I walked past their house several times in the evening, and there was a pale trembling light coming between the boards in one room. I rang the bell. It was one of those old-fashioned bells that you can pull from the outside with a handle and jingle. I heard a stirring in the house, a cup on a ceramic saucer, a squeak of an old wooden floor, and a cat mewed, but the door did not open. I rang the bell the following day, and the day after, and I wrote a note that they had nothing to fear and that I would call them precisely at 3:00 in the afternoon with some good news for them. I didn't want to call them at night, a scary time. Boro answered, "Who's this?"

"Your childhood friend," I said. "With some sound advice."

"I don't need advice. I'm leaving."

"Then you really need advice. What's happening with your house?"

"Who knows? I hope one day . . ."

"Listen, how much do you want for it? I'll buy it from you."

"Are you crazy. One day I hope to come back."

"Don't be naive. Osijek will never be Serbia, and you know what fascists Croats are—I heard you in your rally speeches. They'll never let you come back. They'll remember your inciting the masses against us; you'll be a war criminal."

He swore under his breath; I could hear that, but he didn't hang up.

"So, how much do you ask?" I said.

"Half a million German marks. It's worth more."

"You're nuts. I mean, there's no insurance policy here that works anymore. The house could be a bombed out shell tomorrow. It could burn—more likely than not. You'd be selling a bird in the bush. Ten thousand marks is all."

"No way. This is mine. My family lived here for generations. I'd rather burn it myself than sell it for such an insulting sum."

"What's insulting about it? For that you could buy an apartment in Novi Sad. You'd be set, among your own lovely, friendly people. If you love them so much, why don't you just go?"

"I grew up here; this is my soil."

"That's silly sentimentality. I thought as a psychiatrist you would be above that. All right, I'll give you thirty thousand. That's a great deal, like selling dead souls, since it's not certain that your house exists."

He hung up.

My education in history of law helped me. The war would of course be over. People who possessed houses, no matter where they were now, even if in Serbia, would still have the legal right to them once the war was over; Croatia wanted to belong to the Western democracies. You can't just jump into a house and claim it's yours. You need the deeds, the papers. Boro could run away, and maybe he believed someone could usurp his house; many Croats believed they could do that. But I knew better. I certainly needed the deed, and even a hundred thousand marks wouldn't be too bad. But why pay that much?

A little bit of chess playing could help. At night, I played a prank, a harmless one, that could however yield results. I lined up a string of big fire crackers along the wall of his house, and lit it. They were powerful blasts; it would be hard to tell that they were not mortar a bit farther away, and he certainly wouldn't open the window to judge the distance, intensity, etc. I also called up, on a phone that I made crackle with static, through a piece of cloth, after I ate scratchy honey. I spoke in a low distorted voice. "If you don't get out of here, we're going to nail you to the floor and burn down your house. You have seventy-two hours to vacate."

"I'm tired of this crap. Will you stop calling, for heaven's sake?"

I hung up because I was laughing. So there were other people trying to intimidate him. Good deal. That was the technique of intimidation Serbs used all over in Banja Luka and Knin. I was glad to see that Croats were learning too—they were slow learners, but they learned. Serbs became like the Turks, who dominated them for centuries, and Croats have finally become like Serbs, who have dominated us for almost a century.

Boro called me the following day. "Let's meet for a shot of *slivovitz* and talk. How about my place?"

Now the idea made me cringe. I would be in his territory. He could have guns. He could lock me up, burn me with the house.

"How about my place?" I said.

"No, I can't even walk down the street anymore. I feel uncomfortable, somebody might shoot me."

"Well, that's true. All right, I'll be over in half an hour."

He needed me, just as he predicted that he might. He hadn't had this in mind, but now even this could help him. So I was safe. I just wouldn't bring my money along; otherwise, something might fall on me from the door. It was easy to imagine traps.

Sure enough, as soon as I opened the door, he said, "Have you brought the money along?"

"No, but if we agree on the sum, the money will be here soon." His wife brought us a bottle of yellow brandy and sat down with us, pale and exhausted, and her pallor only intensified her appearance of exquisite fragility. She looked more suffering and passionate than I had ever seen her before; age added to this effect. "I will help you. I am your old friend," I said. It felt good to ridicule his game. "We had good times playing basketball, no need to have a bad time playing real estate."

"You bet. We were so talented we should have made it to the first league."

"Oh yeah? I know I would have made it if you hadn't knocked me over when I was going for the rim. After that, we were in a brawl, and it was all over. What came over you to be so mean?"

"Is that how you saw it? Man, you are crazy. One of their players tripped me, another pushed me, and I flew straight at you and bumped into your back, smashing my nose against your monkey bone."

"Why didn't you tell me that before?"

"Who could tell you anything? You sulked, avoided company."

Could I believe him? Maybe it wasn't his fault. But taking Slavitza from me certainly was. I leaned over the table as though we were playing chess, and with my knee, I touched her leg. Her leg at first withdrew and then came back, lightly. My knee grew warm. Color came into her cheeks.

"How much do you want?" I asked.

"Two hundred thousand," he said.

"We went through that. Don't be unrealistic. Twenty."

He drank brandy, and offered it to me. I declined.

"Let me consult with my wife in private." They left for the bedroom. That made me uncomfortable. Of course, they had guns under the pillows. But soon they came out, and he said, "We agreed, fifty is our absolute bottom line."

"Now can I talk with you in private?" I asked him.

"Sure."

So he and I went into the bedroom. I said, "I'll give you forty, and that's a great deal, if you let me sleep with your wife."

"What?" He clenched his fists.

"Don't play that game," I said, and held his fist. "You know she was mine before she was yours. You stole her."

"You do have a lot of misconceptions about the past. You stole Gretta from me."

"Come on."

"I thought you knew that?"

"You're nuts."

"If you want to swap wives, I'm game. That would be a new start."

"No, I'm not up for swaps."

"Not even for a night?"

"So if it won't hurt your feelings that I'm sleeping with your wife, why not simply do it this way: I sleep with her, and you get 41,000 marks, for a house that will be ashes in a week anyway, most likely."

"But my wife won't be ashes."

"Eventually, we all will be. So what's the point?"

"If that's the case, let me sleep with Gretta, I'll go over there right now, and you can spend the night here."

"You are a pervert," I said. We both started laughing like crazy. "Isn't life ridiculous?" he said. "Did you ever imagine we'd be having conversations like these, when you were a kid?"

That day I wouldn't have minded swapping wives. It would have been fun, or at least, it would have tested everybody's feelings. War was boring. If for not other reason, then for excitement. That's partly why I wanted the house—it was a game.

There was a knock on the door. "What are you guys doing in there?" She looked worried.

"You want to join us?" I said.

"So what price did you agree on?"

"Forty thousand," I said.

"Well, we'd rather let it burn than sell it that cheap," she said.

"OK, do as you please," I stood up. "You know my number. Will you ask her?" I addressed Boro.

"Sure, if you ask yours."

"Yours, what?" asked Slavitza.

"You'll find out," I said.

At home Gretta was in a bad mood. She was haggard, unable to sleep—my snoring bothered her. I snore whenever I am anxious— I guess this chess game with Boro did make me anxious. It wasn't in my nature to be a bully. At any rate, right then I didn't feel attracted to her. I was tired of her, tired of my life. Perhaps just to irritate her, I said, "I talked to Boro. He wouldn't sell the house for thirty, but would for thirty-five if you agreed to a swap."

"What kind of swap?"

"Wives, for a night."

"And you'd consider that? You'd sleep with that bitch of his?"

"Why not?"

"Many reasons, not least of all diseases."

"We could get condoms somewhere."

"I doubt it. Anyway. What an insult, to me."

"He always lusted after you, he told me."

"So? What difference should it make to me?"

"Isn't that a compliment, at your age, even coming from him?"

She whacked me over the eye with a hot teapot. I could have hit her back. We never had that problem—wife beating. I scrupulously avoided that Balkan past-time, and for that reason felt even more entitled to a bit of extramarital activity. So much for that idea.

Boro called. We agreed to meet at my place. Gretta was gone, shopping. He had a black eye too. "So I needn't ask what answer you got to the swapping suggestion, do I?" I said.

"Geez, we are both victims now." He laughed.

"That's true. This is my first war wound," I said.

But we didn't joke much. We sat at the kitchen table, and he

still wanted forty thousand. I offered to give him thirty five, plus a
rental truck and driver to get his furniture to Szeged in Hungary,
where he could pick it up once settled in Serbia. I knew a guy
who'd do that for five hundred marks. He pulled out the deeds,
and I the money. I counted it out, 35,000. I kept the money on
my side of the table, and said, "All right, let's sign the papers, and
the heap is yours."

It all worked beautifully. The bums were out of there. I must
say it felt good to help them get away. (The fact that Slavitza refused to spend a night with me was insulting, and I'm sure finally
purged her from my mind.) Why shoot them, and fill them with
resentment, so they'd want to come back for revenge? Screw
them, get the better of them in a deal, and make sure they're out,
preferably down and out. Maybe they wouldn't have left if I
hadn't made it easier. In a way, this was an act of ethnic cleansing
par excellence. Guns wouldn't keep Serbs away; they'd come back
because Serbia's economy should be among the worst in Europe;
they'd come back even to Croatia once the guns had cooled. But,
if their property was signed away, all in a proper legal manner,
they wouldn't be able to return easily.

This new house ownership filled me with self-confidence. I
walked taller. I saw nobody in the streets any more; I was near-
sighted, so I couldn't recognize them anyway, but now I didn't
even think of bothering. Once the U.N. was entrenched, and the
war moved to Bosnia, it became clear that the house would survive. With the huge influx of refugees, the house's value shot up.
I sold it for 200,000 marks, and now I had enough capital to buy
up many houses in contested regions, and to open an office in
Szeged, Hungary, a neutral territory where Serbs and Croats
could meet and transact.

Soon I found it less cumbersome not to buy houses, but to
work as a real-estate agent, a matchmaker. I took a good commis-
sion, 20 percent, sometimes more if both sides were in a rush. At
first the idea of ethnic cleansing entertained me, but later I didn't

care. Business is business. All business is ethnic cleansing in some way.

I dealt with war criminals too. Since they couldn't go to Croatia to sell their property and sign their papers, I set up an office in Hungary, in a basement next to a bar, where a lively prostitution business took place. I figured out that as an incentive, I could work with the prostitutes; I provided not only the booze, but a good lay, after which the sellers and the buyers would feel a little more lenient.

My business has branched out. I help persecuted Croats move out of Serbia, and sell their houses cheaply to Serb refugees from Krajina. I help Serbs ethnically cleanse themselves of their Croats— but it's not ethnic cleansing. I help keep people out of harm's way. I'm sure I have saved many lives this way. I may have missed the NBA, but I'm not much worse off. I don't blame Serbs any more. Why should I? Their awkward aggressions created this unique business climate. Heraclites says, War is the father of all. And it is. There's a new Croatia. And there's a new me. Rich, generous, no longer hateful, but self-actualized, unprejudiced, practical, happy. I'm even a father now; for years Gretta and I tried to have children, and finally it has worked. I'm not nostalgic about anything. Am I congratulating myself? Yes. People sometimes write their obituaries, their painful confessions. I don't have anything to confess. I have risen from lonely misery of parentlessness to a lordly aloofness. I don't need anybody anymore. I don't make friends. I don't make enemies. I've reached the epicurean ataraxia. Nothing excites me, not even the young Hungarian whores. I often fish in transparent green streams, and when a fish bites, I pull it out and toss it back in; I gaze at the pebbles at the bottom, and sniff the clean smell of sun-struck pines.

The Enemy

❦❦

Treat your friends as though one day they'll be your enemies,
and your enemies as though one day they'll be your friends.
— *Turkish Proverb*

I haven't lived well because I didn't know until recently who the
enemy was. I thought the enemy was outside, somewhere far removed from me—the communists, the Serbs, the Muslims. I didn't
know that the true enemy was much closer at hand.

Once the war started in Croatia, and then in Bosnia and
Herzegovina, it was obvious Serbs and Muslims were my enemies. I was drafted into the Croatian army and sent to Mostar.
Croats were a minority in Bosnia and Herzegovina,—17 percent
of the population—and we were underarmed. It was easy to believe we were threatened, because we were. I didn't have to think
much; I only had to fear. And since I knew who the enemy was,
I felt determined, even happy. Forget about good friends. To prosper, all you need is a good enemy. Friends help you relax; they tell
you it's all right to be self-indulgent; they invite you out, drink
with you, help you while the time away, so that after twenty years
of friendship you are a fat, good-for-nothing bum. Having a good

enemy, on the other hand, stimulates you, strengthens you; you compete, sharpen your skills, your mind, your body.

Before long, however, I realized that I had an oversimplified notion of who my enemies and friends were. I was underpaid, underfed, and underarmed by my friends, the Croatian command, while the officers drove BMWs and drank the best whisky and wine. In fact, they sold gasoline to the Serbs—never mind that it enabled the Serb tanks to encircle us. (Our officers probably figured that if they didn't sell to the Serbs, the Greeks and Albanians would.) The Serb officers, in return, rented us their tanks. We'd pay them 500 deutsche marks a day to fire on them, but we did them no harm; they were well bunkered and entrenched—at least, the bosses who rented out the tanks were. In a way, it was more of a playful camaraderie than it was a real enmity. (It reminded me of the games we played as kids: We'd collect bagfuls of stones and hide out in old German bunkers. A couple of kids would stay in the bunker, and we'd throw stones at them, and they at us, until someone got hit in the head and was bleeding, and then we'd all panic.)

During the day, we could freely visit the Serb side; we'd radio them and ask, "What's on the menu today?" and they'd say, "Today we have a shipment of fifty VCRs. What have you got?"

"Oh, we've got twenty kilometers of fishing line and a hundred boxes of chewing tobacco."

And then our low-ranking officers would go over there, or theirs would come to our side, and they'd barter. Sometimes even regular soldiers crossed the lines to trade.

One day I shouted over the radio, "What's cooking today?" and the other side replied, "A traveling brothel. Twenty deutsche marks a shot. Everybody welcome."

I went to the brothel. Later, I found out it was a rape camp, though at the time I couldn't tell. That the women all looked depressed was nothing unusual in my experience. Before the war, I had visited Germany, and the attitude in brothels there was the same, beneath perfunctory friendliness. (Of course, German prostitutes are really slaves—women enticed from Russia, Poland, the Czech Republic, and so on, to work as waitresses. Once they get to Germany, they are detained, beaten, and forced to pay a certain sum of money to buy their freedom, an amount they could never make waiting tables. So most German brothels are no better than rape camps.)

The atmosphere in the Serb brothel, which was set up in the cellar of an old burned-out house, pained me so that, though I was with a pretty girl, I had no lust, and all I did was squeeze her breasts nostalgically, like a weaned toddler remembering his mother's milk; and after a while she probably gave me a blow job, I'm not sure. We talked for a long time, but I was so drunk I don't remember what we said. Or maybe I do, but what difference does it make? I'm not making excuses for myself. All I want to say is that I did something despicable. The details don't matter, or perhaps only exacerbate the meanness of the act.

I am perfectly aware that I'm not entertaining anybody by the way I'm telling this: To entertain, one must make scenes, create the illusion that the events are really happening, like on a stage. Well, forget the stage; I have stage fright. Forget entertainment; I don't laugh at jokes. The only jokes we could laugh at in the Balkans were ethnic jokes. The jokes caused the war, I swear. I don't mean that jokes should be illegal, that there should be a jihad against them—quite the contrary. Maybe the war started because we ran out of jokes. We couldn't keep going. After we told ten thousand anti-Muslim, anti-Serb, and anti-Croat jokes (but mostly anti-Muslim), we wanted guns.

I know my story is not beautiful. But I don't think anymore that anything is really ugly or beautiful. If you see something beautiful in enough detail, it appears ugly. Take a woman's smooth, healthy skin: Seen through a magnifying glass, it appears greasy, perforated with holes, with hairs sticking out; the detail destroys the beauty. But detail can also destroy ugliness. Under a microscope, a drop of spittle becomes a troupe of rainbow-colored creatures dancing around in silent cosmic harmony. (Of course, most

of them are angling to gobble each other up—some harmony.)
The absence of detail creates a forgiving haze around an image,
making it beyond beauty and ugliness. The absence of detail veils
my experience enough for me to deal with it. Not that I need to
deal with it. Remembering my experience in Bosnia and Croatia
doesn't do any good, or harm. It's irrelevant. War is not the problem. Viruses and bacteria are the problem.

   You see, I'm sick.

In 1993 I visited the States as a tourist and stayed on illegally. I
lived in Astoria, in Queens. I probably became ill after I got here.
For a while, I ate from the Dumpsters behind bakeries. Or maybe
I got sick during the war. That's the only reason, other than force
of habit, that I keep thinking about the war. Did I get the bacillus
in the rape camp for twenty deutsche marks? Or in the trenches,
where I got athlete's foot? No, not trench foot; athlete's foot.
Maybe it was because I wore sneakers. We didn't have enough
boots to go around. My living conditions in Astoria were certainly unhygienic. I shared an apartment with a Serb, an Albanian
Muslim, and a Pole—not that their nationality had anything to do
with the poor hygiene, but our being illegal aliens did.

   We played cards and chess, and the air was saturated with
smoke. If I breathed in deep enough, the smoke gave me a nice
scratch in the back of my throat. Something in my lungs begged
to be scratched and scraped, so I inhaled as deeply as I could.

   The Albanian, Omar, worked in a pizza parlor and got me a
job there. It had maps of Italy all over the walls, but most of the
people working there were Albanians; in fact, most pizza parlors
in New York are run by Albanians.

   The Serb, Drago, gambled in Atlantic City and played chess
and backgammon in the New York City parks for money. He was
the only one of us officially diagnosed as sick, with hepatitis B or
C, I forget which. At any rate, he was gaunt and all yellow in
the face; even his eyes were yellow. He didn't want to go to the
hospital—he was afraid he'd be deported back to Belgrade. When

192 | Salvation and Other Disasters

he became so sick we had to carry him, he married an American friend's girlfriend; she did it to save his life. Only then, marriage certificate in hand, did he dare go to the hospital. The doctors said his drinking had weakened his liver, but when he came back from the hospital, still sick and taking all sorts of medicine, he kept drinking and smoking.

Adam, the Pole, made the most money—he'd landed a lucrative job as a gravedigger in Brooklyn—and he bought the beer and wine. (We spent only a few hours a day sober.) Adam was thin, moody, and a chain smoker. The cigarettes might be the reason why he was so thin—or maybe old bacteria leaked out of graves and invaded him.

My roommates and I shared everything. For transportation, we had a beat-up Audi. Adam took care of the parking. He'd stolen a fire hydrant somewhere, and whenever we went out in our car, he planted it by the curb, reserving our spot. When we came back, we simply put the hydrant in the trunk. Parking would have been impossible otherwise.

I contributed in my own way. None of us liked to do laundry, and for two months we just got dirtier and dirtier, until I came up with a solution. (Going down to the Laundromat would have been too obvious.) My mother lived in Rijeka, Croatia, and I had friends who were Croatian sailors, so once a month I'd collect all our laundry, pack it up in a crate, and ship it to her across the Atlantic. She'd wash the laundry and ship it back, and we'd all be clean again. The whole exchange took three weeks. She was happy to help, and enjoyed keeping in touch, even if only through my filth. I'd lived at home well into my thirties, and she was used to my ugly ways.

My roommates and I did what our Eastern European totalitarian systems failed to do: develop a workable communist system.

One day, Drago and I went to a coffee shop in Greenwich Village and sat in a courtyard near a fountain, chatting and laughing. At the table next to us sat two women, one a luminous blonde, the other a gloomy brunette with a thin nose, a wrinkled brow, and dark blue eyes. The brunette sighed. I asked how come she wasn't more cheerful on such a splendid evening.

"It's a long story," she said.

"I like long stories," I said.

"But you won't believe this one—it's like a dime novel, something that could never happen in real life."

"Go ahead, tell him," said the blonde. "I think it's funny, and if we all laugh, maybe you'll lighten up, too."

"OK," said the brunette. "By the way, I'm Natasha and this is Jane."

"And this is Drago, and I'm Igor," I said.

"Why are you talking to us?" Natasha asked. "Are you trying to pick us up?"

"No," I said. "I was just curious what made you sigh. I'm not trying anything."

"I wouldn't mind if you were," Natasha said. "I could use an ego boost right now."

"All right, we'll try," said Drago.

"That doesn't mean you'll succeed," Natasha said.

"You know, it's great how openly men and women talk here," I said. "Where I come from, in Croatia, that doesn't happen, and it probably doesn't happen either in Serbia, where Drago comes from."

"Serbians don't need to talk," Drago said proudly. "We just do it." He exhaled a stinging cloud of pipe smoke.

"What a paradise that must be," Jane said sarcastically. "Hey, wait a minute. What are you two doing together? Aren't you supposed to be killing each other?"

"We were failures as soldiers," I said. "Anyway, maybe we are killing each other. Like now, he blows so much raw smoke at me that it amounts to chemical warfare."

"Warfare is my second nature," Drago said.

"What's your first?" asked Jane.

"You'll have to kiss me to find out," he said.

They leaned over and kissed, long and deep. I hoped he was over his hepatitis. Natasha and I were too embarrassed to look at each other.

"You're interrupting Natasha's story," I said.

"Sorry. We'll behave," Jane said.

"I'm in a bad mood," Natasha continued, "because my fiancé stood me up."

"What's the big deal?" I said. "Drago's dates stand him up all the time, and he doesn't mind. He doesn't even notice."

"It would be no big deal," Natasha continued, "except that he stood me up at our wedding. He was too drunk to show up. The guests had already arrived with their gifts, the band was there, the wedding cake—everything was ready. I was so embarrassed, I could have died. And that was just this morning, so how do you expect me to be cheerful?"

"Better to discover at the last minute than after the wedding, right?" I said. "You should be glad you found out in time."

"But for me it was a double disaster," she said. "I work at a detox clinic, and he was one of my greatest successes. I thought I'd cured his need to drink. So I failed in my professional life and my personal life. I was a wreck—I *am* a wreck."

"Good riddance," I said.

"But he was a rich guy," Jane said. "She would have been set. Famous family, too: du Pont."

"Never heard of them," I said. I had, but I felt like being provocative.

"Oh, you've heard of them," said Drago. "Without them, the First World War would have been dull. They made most of the gunpowder—for both sides—so everyone could keep blasting each other. We have a lot to thank them for. Real noble family."

"Screw them," I said. "You shouldn't bother with noble families. They grow spoiled and degenerate. You should marry someone from peasant stock, like me."

"Is that a proposition?" Natasha asked.

I looked her in the eye and said, "It sure is."

"Don't act so surprised," Drago told her. "He needs a green card."

"Oh, in that case," Natasha said, "since you cast it in such a romantic light, by all means—forget it!"

"You said yourself the cake is baked, the band is hired—it would be easy," I said.

"You take the phrase 'a marriage of convenience' literally, don't you?"

But she didn't turn down a date with me for the following day. We went to her apartment, drank wine, made love in the traditional way: missionary. Afterward, she said, "You've blown it. If I marry you now, it will be for real."

Still in post-orgasmic lethargy (at least, I was; I'd come too quickly to give her an orgasm—although I probably depressed her enough to give her lethargy), we descended the tilted staircase, slipping a bit on the threadbare red carpet.

On the way out, she checked her mail, and on one envelope was written, in elegant calligraphy: *Princess Natasha Romanova*.

"'Princess'?" I said. "How tacky. Who's your cheesy friend?"

"It's not tacky if it happens to be true."

"You're a Russian princess? How can you be?"

"Somebody's got to," she said.

"Must be a tough job."

"As a matter of fact, it is. Most of my family was killed by Lenin and his cronies."

I was astonished, although, when I thought about it, I realized there must be hundreds of Russian princesses—a veritable horde of them. Still, I was impressed.

"I suppose you want me to be impressed or something," I said. "So you're rich; so what?"

"No, I'm totally broke."

"Can't you ask for your inheritance—part of the Kremlin, let's say—now that Russia is a democracy?"

"Can we talk about this later? I've got to go to work."

She rushed off to her substance-abuse job. What karma, I

thought—not just for her, but for her old drunken nation: a Russian princess working in a detox program.

We continued to see each other, our sex improved, and I still needed the green card. "Why don't you apply for exile status," she asked, "so we can see each other just because we want to, not because you also need something from me?"

"They wouldn't believe me. If I were from Bosnia, no problem, or maybe if I were a Serb from Croatia—but a Croat from the Croatian coast, where it's safe? Forget it. It might have worked in early '92, if at all."

This was during the Dayton Peace Accord negotiations. For me, that was the worst side effect of the peace plan—no more exile status. You might say the war was undertaken so the world, which had previously ignored the Balkans and shut us out, would not only pay attention to us but invite us in as exiles. It was a collective green-card scheme. I'm joking, of course. The war was real as such things go, but the benefit for many people who wanted to emigrate was that now they could. Unfortunately, I jumped on the wagon too late.

But Natasha was a compassionate social worker, so it didn't take too long to convince her that I was a miserable wretch who'd die if I went back to Croatia, and that, in order to save me, she should marry me. Maybe she liked me—or maybe even loved me—only because I was miserable. I am not being cynical; I mean that as a compliment.

I thought I was getting married just for the green card, and Natasha would go on being my girlfriend. But the wedding was such a big to-do, with so many preposterous, haughty, drunk Russians—bumpy-kneed ballet dancers, clean-shaven writers (I'd thought all Russian writers had beards), well-fed musicians—that Natasha and I had stage fright; our lips trembled as we kissed. I think we were scared that, after such a big ceremony, we could no longer pretend it wasn't real. All those gifts and kisses and tears just for a green card? Come on. Suddenly I knew we were actually married, stuck with each other.

I had an aversion to being stuck, and one possible, if only temporary, solution was another woman. So during the reception, I flirted with a catering girl as she poured me a single-malt Scotch. She blushed, and I asked for her phone number, knowing perfectly well I'd never call her, but feeling like a member of the upper class nonetheless. I was having an attack of lust, pure and simple, for this girl with her taut, shiny skin; small, tight, upright breasts; and smooth, sturdy legs. Even before she could write down her number, I ran to the bathroom and jerked off, imagining her clinging to me.

As a result, I couldn't make love on my wedding night. I pretended I was too drunk. Actually, I *was* too drunk, and while pretending to pass out, I really did pass out.

The following morning, when I made love to Natasha, I was again both pretending to be doing it and doing it. Our lovemaking was self-conscious, official, as if marriage had alienated us rather than brought us together. It didn't feel like a big adventure—but in fact it was. Bigger than we suspected.

Natasha wanted to get pregnant right away. I was scared of being a father; I couldn't take care of myself, let alone someone else. Besides, why not take care of the people who are already in the world? (Of course, I didn't want to take care of them either.) But my wife said she was going to have a baby no matter what. Sex took on a biblical character for her: Procreate and multiply. But her attitude didn't worry me. I'd read articles about the decline in sperm counts and was quite sure mine was too low. And anyway, I lacked a certain biological self-confidence.

Natasha got pregnant only two months into our marriage. With that accomplished, she refused to have sex.

At the same time, I lost my appetite and began to grow thinner and thinner. Walking upstairs to our apartment left me out of breath and wheezing. I'm no complainer—if you can believe that after reading this—but I could tell something was wrong. Although I mistrusted medicine, I mistrusted my body even more.

One evening, my wife said, "What's wrong with you? Just look at yourself; you look like a concentration-camp victim."

"Maybe I have a hyperactive thyroid or something."

"Whatever it is, you'd better go find out. Are you sure it's not AIDS?"

"I'm not sure of anything, but I don't know how I could have gotten it."

"You haven't visited any prostitutes, or—"

"Come on," I said.

"I need to know, for the baby."

"How about for me?"

"For you, too, but if you don't want to find out for yourself, you have to find out for our child."

I went to see a doctor, who asked where I was from. I told him, and he asked whether I'd been in the war. When I answered yes, his bearded, salmon-colored face lit up. "Post-traumatic stress syndrome," he said. "You need a psychiatrist."

"Give me a break," I said. "That's an American thing. We don't get that, just like we don't get allergies; they're a totally American privilege."

"You've got it, all right. I can tell by the way you talk. You need to see an expert."

So I went, but when I couldn't climb the stairs at the expert's office and my vision turned green and all kinds of noises started coming from my lungs, I thought, *This is no fucking psychological problem.*

I went to a new doctor, who, without talking much, sent me to a lab for X rays, and then showed me that there were spots and lesions on my lungs. "Whatever it is," he said, stroking his huge bald skull, "it's not good."

Terrified, I asked, "Is it cancer?"

"Doesn't look like any cancer I'm familiar with, but you never know. At this stage nothing can be ruled out. We'll have to see how your other organs are doing. Your heart rate is kind of high, but that's probably because you aren't getting enough oxygen. You're gradually losing your lung functions. I wonder whether it could be AIDS."

I wondered why he didn't keep such thoughts to himself; I was panicked enough as it was.

"What's your sexual history?" he asked.

"Nothing to boast of: An affair here and there—a quickie, usually. All heterosexual, no professionals."

"Dentists?"

"I haven't made love to any."

"No, have you been to one recently?"

"Yes, when my molar broke. At first I didn't want to go, because I couldn't pay the bill, so I pulled it out myself with a pair of pliers. But a fragment stayed in and bothered me, so I had to go after all. In taking out the fragment, he pulled another tooth by accident. His fingers were cold and slimy, and he didn't wear gloves."

"Hmm," the doctor said. "You'll have to be tested."

I went to a lab, where they drew blood and sent me home. I spent my nights in terror, thinking that must be it; the dentist's office hadn't been clean. I'd chosen it because my roommates had said it was cheap.

My wife was panicked, too, and was now having morning sickness. We were both miserable. It was worse than the Balkans. There, at least you could hide in a basement, in a trench, and have hope. Here, if I had the virus, there was no place to hide, no hope. But how could I have come down with AIDS so quickly? Or could I have gotten it in Bosnia or Croatia? Probably not. A health worker in Croatia had told me there was only one good thing about the war: it had stopped tourism, and thus curbed the spread of AIDS, which was brought in by German tourists. So in one small way, the war might have improved the health of my people.

The test result came in several days later: no HIV. This threw the doctor off. He thought it couldn't be TB, because TB usually occurred with weakened immune systems. In new X rays, my lungs looked even more scarred than before.

"Maybe you have sarcoidosis," he said optimistically.

That didn't sound good to me; in general, *sarco-* wasn't a good prefix—sarcoma, sarcophagus—but he explained that it wasn't deadly, in most cases. At any rate, I'd have to have exploratory surgery.

The hospital where he sent me was a diagnostic center, and was full of terrified, thin, anxious people standing around in hushed carpeted corridors. Now here was a real war between life and death, with death gaining the upper hand; yet nobody acknowledged it. In Bosnia, you had Chetniks waving flags with skulls and crossbones, loud explosions—the whole fanfare of death—and in the end almost everybody survived the attacks. I bet even in Bosnia more people died of disease than of bullets (let alone in world history—billions have perished from diseases, and only millions from wars). Even on the battlefield, if you find someone dead you don't look for a bullet hole. He may have died of a heart attack, or from a contagious disease, or stomach cancer—we ate so badly.

I looked out the window of my hospital room. I couldn't smoke anymore—a cigarette could kill me—and I didn't know how to handle my nervousness, what to do with my fingers, my lips. I saw hearses departing several times a day.

The exploratory surgery turned out worse than expected. During the operation, one of my lungs collapsed. They had to cut away the top third because it was shot through with cavities and scars. When I came to, I saw only white ceiling and white walls. Nobody was around. My eyes hurt, my body hurt, my chest burned, and I had a terrible headache. I wasn't religious, but I thought I was in hell, a hell of white nothingness and scorching pain. I had fever, hallucinations; I was lost in Antarctica, abandoned by my sleigh dogs, tossed in a snowy ditch.

A pulmonary specialist came to see me, dressed in green and wearing a mask over his face—not just a little one, either. He said, "You'll be all right. We found out what it is: TB."

"And that's good?"

"Considering the possibilities, yes."

"So I can go home now?"

"No. We have to test your wife to make sure she doesn't have it. Your form of TB is highly contagious. We'll keep you here as long as reasonably possible."

"How long is that?"

"Three to four weeks."

That was a year ago. I'm out of the hospital, but I haven't improved. My TB strain skillfully evades large doses of antibiotics. Maybe the doctors have slowed the progress of my disease; I don't know. They tell me some parts of my lungs have repaired themselves, while others have deteriorated. I've taken all sorts of drugs. Some seem to help, for a while. Who knows? If I hadn't taken them, I might be dead by now. Sometimes the bacillus develops a tolerance to a drug, which means the drug no longer sees the bacillus as an enemy: instead of attacking and killing it, the drug hangs around amicably. Their friendship kills me.

I live with Drago in Astoria again. When he found out about my TB, he said, "What can that do to me? If you Croats haven't killed me, a little bacterium won't either."

"Don't be so sure," I said.

"No, really. I had childhood TB and nearly died, so I'm immune. I can't get it again."

And so my supposed enemy is now my only friend. We play chess and cards. My wife can't see me because my TB is contagious, even through the air. She doesn't want to risk it.

She's had the baby. I'd like to say *we* have a baby, but I haven't even seen my child, except in pictures. She's a beautiful girl, Victoria, another princess. Sometimes I feel vain—I have fathered a princess. Does that make me a king? Probably not, and it doesn't matter. Meanwhile, my wife has been taking her heritage more and more seriously, reading about bones uncovered in the Urals that might be the remains of her murdered ancestors; genetic and radioactive tests are being used to ascertain their identities. Meanwhile, she's suing the Russian government to get back her family's gold, artworks, and summer palaces. I hope it works for her, although to me it all sounds preposterous and outlandish.

Even if I don't recover, Natasha will continue to be my wife, I guess. She sympathizes with me, and cries when we talk on the phone. I long for a simple family life. Strange how I didn't appreciate it when I had it (if I ever did). I wanted something extraordinary. I didn't know that the most extraordinary thing is to have an ordinary life: health and family and any job that doesn't destroy your health or take you away from your family. Everybody seems to know this. I wonder why I have realized it only now.

I should be ashamed to state such platitudes if I hadn't arrived at them the hard way. Life is like a complex math puzzle with a very simple solution—say, 1 or 0. Of course, when you come down to it, what is 0? What is 1 but a complicated philosophical concept that can't be explained without redundancy, without resorting to itself? In the long run, the simple things are the most puzzling, the simple life the most unattainable.

When in a certain mood, I spend hours remembering each encounter that might have led to my infection. I suspect even my wife. After all, it's an old Russian disease, consumption. Other times I live almost pleasantly, gathering enough energy to take subway rides, look at pretty, overworked women, go to a coffee shop. I know I shouldn't do this because I often sneeze—some susceptible person might catch my bacilli. But then, if not from me, they'll catch it from someone else; these bacilli must float all over the city.

I once thought that simply being in America would make me happy, but now I know better. The American poet W. S. DiPiero once said, "America is grief parading as opulence." I'd say America is disease parading as health. Everywhere you look, you see joggers, white teeth, youth, smiles, but when you talk to people, you hear only about cancer, heart failure, and AIDS. My parents cling to an image of America as pure happiness. I haven't let them know that I'm sick—I can't. I don't even send my mother laundry anymore. (I wonder whether the disease came over on the ship, rats nesting in my clean clothes.) I hope I'll outlive them, so that they'll never have to learn how miserably I have ended up. I send them old pictures of me, and new ones of my wife and child. I tell them I am not in the latter because I took them.

I don't mean this as a lament—I'm having a lot of fun right now. I'm strong enough to sit up, for a change, and am semi-conscious enough to rave. How beautiful that I can still do this. (Although I renounced the concept of beauty before, I'm coming back to it.) I am in a good mood, I won't deny it. I'm having a strong cup of coffee at the moment, and I don't feel absolutely exhausted and pained. I'm scribbling down these words, creating an illusion of memory, pleasantly fleeting and ephemeral. Just now I'm feeling wonderfully alive and alert, not wheezing, or spitting, or shivering; just waiting. But for what? Health? Death? Anyhow, I'm passing the time. I play chess with Drago, who continues to live unhealthily. He still has hepatitis, and cirrhosis. I don't know why, but we Eastern and Central Europeans don't know how to live. Soon, we'll all be wiped out. I've read that the average lifespan for a Russian male is fifty-three. Although Drago and I are not from Russia, I suspect ours must be similar. If America is disease parading as health, then Eastern Europe is disease parading as disease.

Well, I'm forty-three. I've lived. I should be glad to have made it this far. At least I've discovered who the enemy is: It's nearly invisible, like purified evil, a form of antimatter that annihilates body and spirit. This story, this disease, has an open ending, thanks to the new dark ages of medicine, in which once again we know hardly anything. I wish I knew how long I can postpone the ultimate ending. But maybe I don't want to find out; maybe it's better for me to live in this hazy daydream of uncertainty. Yes, it is pleasant, this haziness. It makes me dizzy, makes me want to sleep.

—

JOSIP NOVAKOVICH is a fiction writer and essayist. Born in Croatia, he is currently an assistant professor of English at the University of Cincinnati. His published work includes *Yolk, Apricots from Chernobyl,* and *Fiction Writer's Workshop,* and many of his stories, essays, and poetry have appeared in *DoubleTake,* the *Threepenny Review, Ploughshares,* the *New York Times Magazine,* among others, and in three *Pushcart Prize* anthologies and *Best American Poetry 1997.* He is the winner of a 1997 Whiting Writers' Award, an Ingram Merrill Award, the Richard Margolis Prize for Socially Important Writing, and a NEA Fellowship for Fiction Writing. Novakovich has a B.A. from Vassar College, a Masters in Divinity from Yale University, and a Masters in English/Creative Writing from the University of Texas. He lives in Blue Creek, Ohio, with his wife and two children.

This book was designed by Ann Elliot Artz.
It is set in Bembo type by Stanton Publication Services, Inc.,
and manufactured by Edwards Bros., Ann Arbor,
on acid-free paper.